A.H. CUNNINGHAM

Recycling programs for this product may not exist in your area.

ISBN-13: 978-1-335-04162-3

Out of Office

Copyright © 2024 by A.H. Cunningham

Harlequin Enterprises ULC
22 Adelaide St. West, 41st Floor
Toronto, Ontario M5H 4E3, Canada
www.Harlequin.com

Printed in U.S.A.

To Mami y Papi and your everlasting love story.

Los adoro, thank you.

AUTHOR'S NOTE

This story depicts a character's journey after
their parents' passing in an uplifting manner.
As always, stories that deal with life after grief and loss
can resurface our own memories, so I hope I have
handled this topic with care and love.

In addition, this story is about a queer person and their
many joys and injustices in our current society.
As always, I dream of a world where we experience
all the joys and leave the injustices behind.

With love,

A.H.

One

Genevieve

Diligence. Ambition. Drive.

The three words were engraved in my psyche. Especially today as I sat in this trailer office with the cheap beige carpets and IKEA furniture, my cell phone ringing for the tenth time. The words were a compass and a constant reminder of my goals in life. The ambition to triumph, never settle, and make my mother proud. Being the only child of a single overachiever came with expectations to shatter my own glass barriers.

Diligence. Ambition. Drive.

The words might as well be my mantra. I'd heard them since I was six years old, the weight of my mother's dream heavy on my shoulders even then.

As I finished the last emails of the day, I attempted to put together the agenda for my return to Florida but couldn't muster the energy. Not with this nervous current running through me. Not with the calls on my cell phone screen hovering over a day that should be celebratory.

My mother had put herself through college, the first of the family, but that wasn't enough...oh no, it also meant that I needed to provide some firsts. Starting with an MBA, to the detriment of my ever-present debt. Youngest General Manager of my company at thirty-two, and my third first loomed close. You'd think I'd be ecstatic, but another first threatened, not allowing me to be great: complete and utter burnout.

My entire life had become a never-ending stream of deadlines, where the goalpost continued to be moved upward, never to be reached.

Even thinking of her mantra tonight tired me. Relaxation never penetrated my mind enough to pause and release me from my daily stressors.

That's why the decision to take two weeks away from my predetermined, meticulous plan was unprecedented. And that's why my phone had been ringing off the hook for the past three hours, and it rang again as if I had summoned it up.

"Genevieve Raymond, what do you mean you're not returning tomorrow?" Mom asked the moment I answered the phone.

A cold pang radiated from my chest, making my palms sweat as I debated my response. At work, they called me the Silent Sniper. I had been known to make more than a few directors cry after my visits, but a simple call from Lissette Raymond and I lost my power of speech.

"Hello, Mother." I attempted to hide my hesitation. Mom would pounce on it.

"Don't *Hello, Mother* me. What is this you texted me? 'I'm

taking a vacation.' A vacation isn't in your timeline until you finally get your promotion next year."

"Yes, well, it's company policy to give me two months in the office until my next assignment. So, why not take the benefit?"

The silence on the other side of the phone materialized as an apparition deployed to haunt me. Mom usually used this tactic successfully in her professional life, and apparently now with me.

"Mother...Mom. Silence, unfortunately, doesn't work on me. I'm staying in Panamá. Two weeks of relaxation and exploration. I've decided." A rush of rightness flowed through me and settled my aching chest. Every step of my career had been delicately orchestrated, with mentorship from my mother. There was no decision I'd made without her guidance; after all, why not leverage the most successful person in my orbit? Mom had learned the treacherous path of corporate America for a Black woman and wanted to spare me any missteps. We had started clashing lately because some of Mom's advice remained based on the corporate America she knew, but things had changed since then.

"Well, I guess you've made up your mind, and I have no say in this decision."

Ah. Guilt. A seldom used weapon in Lissette's arsenal but highly effective. The shot was a glancing blow, nothing else.

"Yes," I replied serenely. Mom always forgot I was a grown woman at thirty-seven.

"At least you have your laptop; you have to get ready. You know they'll open the VP of Ops position soon."

"Well, it'll have to wait. I'm not taking the laptop." I tried to ignore the sudden itch on the palms of my hands. I wasn't codependent on my work. I could and would disconnect for two weeks. Heck, the company plugged off my email whenever I took paid time off, and part of the two-month break included unlimited PTO as needed. And I needed it. Lately, my entire body ached, the tension between my shoulders so solid my trapezius could cosplay as a bodybuilder's.

"Now you're just being reckless. Call me back when you are serious." The beep signaling the end of the call served as a poor goodbye. I wouldn't let the roiling guilt of taking time for myself overwhelm me. Mom remained keenly attuned to what it took to grow in any career, and her mentorship of young Black professionals was well-known in our community. It was why Mom pushed me so hard, but two weeks in an affordable B and B wouldn't splinter my dreams or the bank.

I meant to enjoy this interlude.

Shaking off the down brought by my call with Mom, I walked out of the office I'd inhabited for the past four months as I assisted in the pre and grand opening of the new Tropics hotel and casino in Panamá City—the first of the company.

My heels' rhythmic clicks and clacks interrupted the silence in the satellite office across from the new hotel. Soon, the silence evolved into a buzz of chatter and music as I traversed the tunnel that connected the pre-opening offices to the main building.

Tropics Hotels had experienced a rapid expansion in the past two years, including adding new countries. I'd capitalized on that expansion, volunteering the last year to onboard new general managers, open properties, and cover during transitions in the Latin America and Caribbean area. When they opened the VP position for the Caribbean/LATAM region,

I hoped my name would be foremost in everyone's mind. I'd busted my behind to make sure of it.

A glittering chandelier hovered over the open lobby, surrounded by floor-to-ceiling windows, with views of Balboa Bay. The hall dripped with opulence, with bright blue, green, and white murals designed by an upcoming Panamanian designer. The architecture and design of the hotel were exquisite, and *finally* seeing it full of stylishly dressed patrons filled me with warmth.

Panamanian professionals had spearheaded the entire project, one of the key requirements in the company's expansion. The importance of working with locals was one of the other reasons the new region of Latin America and the Caribbean appealed to me. So many companies tended to bring Americans to crucial hotel positions, but Tropics had recruited from each country. I might not be close to my father, but his Panamanian descent had made me eager to be part of the preopening team here. If only I'd explored the country instead of losing all my hours at work. Sigh.

Regret had no place in tonight's festivities. I approached a smiling banquet server who gave me a cold champagne flute.

"How's it going, Manny?" I asked him.

"It's good, Miss Genevieve. I'm so glad you recommended that they open last week and waited until today for the party. It really helped us get ready for all these people!" He gestured around the grand lobby as guests milled about in their cocktail attire.

"That wasn't just me, though. All of you contributed to the decision. I wish I could just go to my bed, but I have to socialize." Working the room had never been my forte; I'd trained myself over the years to push through events like this.

One of the many things I never considered when I plunged into my career was being an introvert in an industry that required constant networking.

"I hear you, Miss Gen, but you'll be alright. You know how to turn it on." Manny winked and melted into the crowd.

"Genevieve! This is a success!" My boss, Anibal Montoya, marched toward me with Anita Johnson, the hotel's general manager. Working alongside Anita these past four months had been a joy; the powerhouse Afro-Panamanian was the best person to lead the team for such an important project.

"Thanks, Anibal," I demurred, uncomfortable with the praise.

"I couldn't have done this without you, my friend." Anita clinked her glass with mine, and a sense of completion washed over me. Anita looked stunning in a white dress that accentuated her beautiful plus-size body.

"What are you talking about? I couldn't have done it without you. From day one, I'd nearly tanked this project between my limited Spanish and American ways." A voice similar to my mother's whispered in my ear: *No one respects a leader who does not see their worth.*

"You don't have to be modest." Anibal's dazzling grin and striking good looks stunned me for a second. It didn't hurt that he looked like a husky linebacker. He still surprised me no matter how long we'd worked together. The man could have been a telenovela actor, the son of a long lineage of Afro-Colombian celebrities, but instead, he'd gone to college for hospitality in Florida and never looked back. He'd been one of my strongest allies and supporters this year.

"She can't help herself. Hopefully, we'll soon hear good news from Corporate in Fort Lauderdale." Anita raised her eyebrow at Anibal, and Anibal's laugh boomed, making some guests turn back to look at us.

"You're not subtle at all, are you? Listen, I'd love to have Gen as my colleague. Right now, I have all these hotels under me as they continue the expansion, and it is becoming a lot of work. The only way it's been possible to keep up is because Ms. Overachiever here is already doing the role, stepping up with the newly opened hotels in the islands and Latin America. Really, I don't know how she does it, but you know it is not up to me." Anibal shook his head, making Anita roll her eyes.

"But who better than you? I get it's the big bosses' decision, but you have worked with her the longest. You need to be vouching for her," Anita pressed, and I was grateful, but I didn't need Anibal feeling forced. I'd done the work, and my name should be the first on the list when that position opened. Anibal's eyes flashed in challenge, and he opened his mouth, ready to respond.

These two... Anita had been clear with Anibal, when he arrived three days ago, that she wasn't impressed by overlords who came once a quarter to dictate the goings-on of her hotel. Since then, they'd been at each other's throats, to the point I worried Anibal would think Anita too direct. However, he'd seemed to relish the encounters and met every opposition with one of his smiles and witty commentary.

"Don't worry, Anita. I know Anibal is gonna look out for me once they open the position. If I get it, I'll be the first one of us. Well, first Black *woman*." I gestured at Anibal, who nodded. "I'm going to miss working with you every day, though. Who's going to get me to close my laptop by six?" I asked, attempting to defuse the situation. Anita's squint turned to me instead. Oh great, I should have kept my mouth closed.

"Six? Wow, Anita, you're a miracle worker. I can't get her to log off before eight." Anibal nodded, impressed.

"That would not fly here. I needed to ensure Gen knew she was in Panamá and we would not accept her workaholic ways. Y'all talk about work-life balance but don't even know what that means," Anita said, siding with Anibal.

How did they go from sniping at each other to ganging up on me? Damn.

"And you still slipped off today to work after I'd given everyone a half day. But I couldn't say much because you're technically over me." Anita gave me her signature glare. She should know better. I'd already grown accustomed to her tough love. Besides, I appreciated Anita's perspective. She embodied the example of someone who valued their personal life as much as their career—a Black leader just like me, who was successful in her own right. Would Anita be equally as successful with her philosophy outside of Panamá? Ugh, here I was, thinking like Mom, judging everything from the lens of overachievement.

At this point, I'd realized my judgment of people's ambition was a bug instead of a feature, one that I worked hard on minimizing. I had no business expecting everyone to see the world through my eyes. Anita's vibe had captivated me from day one, and I wouldn't let the phantom of my mother's expectations color my perception of Anita's drive.

It was time to move on.

"Listen here… I didn't rush to change in my office, to come to be attacked at this event. I could have just stayed, wrapping everything up before my vacation. So, with that, I bid you both adios. I'm going to mingle." I waltzed away from Anibal and Anita as they both chuckled at my departure.

The dissatisfaction I'd been feeling lately with my career gnawed at me in the oddest moments. Two years, I'd been working hard for the next step in my career, and each month closer to the finish line my doubts popped up more and more. I didn't want to give my concerns any space tonight. Tonight was all about celebrating more firsts.

An hour of hugs and kisses followed. Damn, I thought Floridians were touchy-feely, but Panamanians won the affectionate Olympics. After a few glasses of champagne, I was ready to call it a night. I searched for Anibal and Anita, but they were both in the middle of an intense conversation with a few other general managers in the area. All my forced extroversion had dissolved away with the alcohol in my system.

Only my quiet apartment could save me now.

Going down the marble stairs of the grand lobby, I held on to the railing, feeling lightheaded and jittery.

A whole two weeks off. And I'd asserted myself to my mother. I really did kill it today.

Now, if only I'd had someone to celebrate my wins with, that would have made this a great day. The rush of displeasure returned, threatening to wash away the joy of the night. I'd never needed someone, never wanted a life partner. Casual companions were enough to fulfill my physical needs and occasional social needs.

Travel and time off had been rewards for a job well done, and I hadn't reached my next goal, so stopping to indulge seemed counterproductive. The few friends that I had were as career driven as I, and understood what it took to be on this path. Self-care used to feel like self-indulgence until I slowly started taking time to rest, taking a couple of days after a work trip to explore a new city or accepting a few more dates than before.

Lately, a bug of discontent had bitten me, and I didn't know if I wanted to give it voice and space.

The dissatisfaction had been gradual. But the intensity ramped up, starting with talks with Anita sharing her impending nuptials. Then my best friend, Gino, met someone that made him happier than I'd seen him in years, but the actual start had been...

A familiar tall Black man awaited at the bottom of the steps. His brawny body rested against the wall next to the exit, and I flushed hotly at the sight of him. Thank God for my deep mahogany skin that hid any redness. Every time I saw him, he elicited a convulsion of emotions inside.

Not every man could handle my five-seven height and solid bones, but this man right here? He could probably hoist me up on his broad shoulders and carry me away like a bag full of balloons. Just the thought made my heart skip. I may or may not have used that exact image as my finger bank these past few months.

He wore a crisp white shirt opened at the collar, and faded jeans encased his thick thighs, his warm chestnut complexion enticing me to touch.

What would it feel to run my lips right there at his collarbone?

Realizing I had my horny face on, my gaze flicked back to his eyes. His mischievous deep brown eyes flashed with heat, then his every-present mask of politeness returned.

The smile made me shiver, and the dimple on his right cheek had me saying a brief prayer for sanity. The close-cropped hair had been freshly cut since this morning.

Did he do that for me? Nah, I knew better. He was just here to do his job.

"Buenas noches, Ms. Raymond," said Adrián Nicolas. My driver.

Two

Adrián

"Hey, are you coming through tonight?" Julín asked me. Damn, he was my best friend, but he could be annoying with the demands.

"Later, I'm picking up the Tropics' job in ten minutes." I attempted to say that with no inflection. Maybe it would spare me his comments on the matter.

"Ah, I see. So, you couldn't call dispatch and ask them to pick her up, even though her usual pickup is at six, and it's eight right now?" So, no chill. Alright. The suspicion in Julín's voice didn't faze me. Anytime I got remotely attached to someone, it raised Julín's hackles. Let him think what he thought. I'd stopped having this particular conversation with him a while ago.

"Oh, so you're just gonna ignore me? Instead of accepting this woman has you out here, doing transfers, which you said you didn't want to do anymore now that we had enough drivers?"

The goal of reaching ten drivers for our little company had been arduous, two years in the making. Julín and I were now making enough money to pay the bills and our team. We still had time to be with our loved ones, which remained the company's main objective. When we'd decided to do this together, I had been desperate to cut back on long hours and all the sacrifices that had cost me precious time now lost. So, Julín wasn't wrong in calling me out, but his concern was misplaced. I never planned to let my career ambitions dictate my life ever again.

"What's your point?"

"My point? What's my point? I mean, I don't know. I'm just saying you have the hots for her," Julín said, sounding deflated.

"Yeah, well, I haven't hidden my attraction for her, which is why I'm going to pick her up and take her home instead of calling dispatch." Julín was well familiar with my admiration for Ms. Raymond. At first it had all been physical—a beautiful woman, tall, voluptuous, dark brown skin that glowed in the early morning light when I picked her up. Demure smile that transformed into a full leg-disabling grin whenever she was excited about a topic of conversation.

And did I mention her curves?

Have mercy.

Her innate elegance intrigued me because as the days passed, she opened up, and we started talking, I noticed a shyness that I never would have guessed existed. But that shyness dissipated as our conversation grew deeper, from trivial tips for Black people visiting the country, to intense discussions of the diaspora's future, and how we could grow our communities and families to be strong and self-reliant.

Ms. Raymond was the type of woman who didn't mince

words, but had a deep understanding of their weight, so she deployed them with care. That spoke to me, to the person I strived to be. Care of your fellow person placed on the same level of importance as your own feelings was a rare sight.

"Damn, it's not fun if you accept it." Julín sighed. I stifled a laugh; Julín sounded as if I smacked an iced raspao out of his hand.

"I'll come thru for dominos after I drop her off. It won't take me more than thirty, forty minutes," I said and heard Julín's grumble.

"Don't flake," Julín warned.

"Never."

Julín's frustration wasn't unprecedented. It was Friday night, and we didn't need to be working right now. Based on my new philosophy in life, work was only a means for living. When the job became living, adjustments were required. So having to drive at eight at night on a Friday would be a sign for a quick adjustment, but not tonight.

Not this time.

I pulled up the fancy driveway of the new hotel, admiring the final project. Filled with pride, I studied the steel structure's sleek lines with glass encasings forming an arch across the valet entrance. The overall design and structure were sound and gave a feel of opulence with a welcoming warmth that wasn't supposed to work, but it did. With a sense of closure, I acknowledged things past and accomplishments deferred. This building was the last thing I'd designed before leaving a career that no longer served me to live the life I wanted to embrace.

The career that had given me the seed to rebuild my parents' dying little hostel and our humble town. The career that had taken me away from my parents in the last years of their lives, with demands that now seemed insignificant.

Many would think me a fool for leaving a career just at the cusp of success. Many would think me irrational for putting the money I earned into my family's guesthouse, which barely saw any guests, and rarely made any profit.

But I needed my family, friends, food, and a bed to rest my head at night. To be there to lend my hands and strength to my sister, brother-in-law, and their kids, to be there for my cousins and community as we fought to exist every day.

All those boxes were ticked.

Only one tick was missing, but I was a patient man. First, I needed to ensure I was whole before giving my heart to anyone.

When I had ambitions of my own, I'd lost myself, lost my sense of place and community. My reacquaintance with the person I'd become after losing my parents had been a slow, perfidious road, but I began to like who I saw in the mirror once more.

Shaking away thoughts of the past, I hopped out of the Escalade, gesturing to the approaching valet attendant.

"Yo! I'm just picking up a guest. Can I leave it here?"

"Dale, manito!" The driver dapped me up, smoothly taking the five I slid into his palm.

The brand-new hotel smelled of jasmine. The inside was equally stunning, and I loved what the interior designer had done with the beautiful murals depicting the fauna and flora of the country in patterns of blue, green, and white.

Resting along one of the entrance walls, I settled to wait. There hadn't been a day that I'd picked up Genevieve Raymond from work and she'd been on time. In the morning, she'd been ready: usually outside the condo her company had arranged for her, waiting with her cell phone in hand, already working. But when the time to leave for the night arrived, it was as if she couldn't detach herself from the building.

I didn't envy her the position she was in. She'd explained the amount of work it took to open this building, to make it habitable, to train the team, to set the new procedures. Ms. Raymond took her work seriously and I profoundly admired that, but she also thought all of it fell on her. My familiarity with that belief ran deep, and I wish I could help her get rid of it.

I remembered similar occasions in my past, when leaving for the night was a struggle, and I ran my arm over my chest, glad for the sense of calmness that accompanied me.

That calmness dissipated the moment she descended the stairs.

Damn, she was stunning.

My stomach took a swan dive, and my heart raced faster than Julín in his Sunday night drag races. She wore her relaxed hair in a high ponytail, the silky strands bouncing side to side as she descended the steps. Her balance seemed off today. Usually, she emanated elegance and powerful strides, but she clutched the railing, gingerly taking each step as if afraid of falling. Her face, usually impassive, boasted a self-satisfied grin, and my breath hitched at the sight.

Damn, I loved seeing her this playful. But was Ms. Raymond tipsy?

She'd gone from a dreamy smile to a preoccupied scowl when her gaze met mine. It took everything out of me not to smirk.

Her lush lips parted, and the tip of her tongue touched her

top lip adorned in a burgundy color to match the burgundy strapless cocktail dress she wore. She stole my breath; that tongue of hers long and dexterous. What would it be to taste those sweet lips?

Her dress deserved to be studied by scientists because of the mystery of how it could handle her abundant cleavage. The fabric wrapped perfectly over her thick hips and luscious legs, a slit showing some of her thigh. The slight hint of her belly underneath the silky dress made me ache to feel the combination of soft and compact strength of her. Some men would cower at the type of woman who exuded confidence and had a body to match. Tall, thick curves, with a deep brown complexion that still managed to flush dark when embarrassed, as it did now as I met her heated glance with a challenging stare.

Warning bells flashed, and I remembered I was working. My word and name were all I had. Pulling it together, I tempered my attraction.

"Buenas noches, Ms. Raymond."

Her eyes fluttered, then she looked back at me with the same polite smile she'd given me every day of the four months she'd been in the country.

"Hola, Adrián, I've asked you so many times to call me Genevieve. Tonight is our last night. Can't you grant me that gift?" She grinned, her stance fluid. The sound of her husky voice and how she pronounced my name produced images of sweaty nights and entangled legs. For tonight, I decided to lean into my attraction just a little, I had nothing to lose and a lasting memory to gain.

"Okay, Genevieve." Saying her name did odd things to my insides.

Her toothy grin in response confirmed she was tipsy, and if

I wasn't a hundred percent certain, the fact she'd come down with no bag bolstered my assumption.

"Where's your laptop bag?"

She turned around, searching behind her as if it would appear from thin air.

"Damn, I left it in the office. I don't really want to go back to get it. I'm tired," she complained and shifted back and forth on her heels. If she were mine to care for, I'd remove her heels and carry her to the car. But she wasn't mine.

"I can get it for you and drop it off tomorrow morning."

"Oh, I wouldn't ask that of you. Tonight is the last night." She waved her hand haphazardly, the reminder that I wouldn't see Genevieve Raymond again souring my mood.

"I know, but I can do a solid for you." I shrugged, stepping aside so she could lead the way.

The balmy air engulfed us in the humidity of the night. I wished this was a date instead of me taking her to her apartment. Opening the door, I waited until she entered the SUV, her sweet and spicy scent, mixed with the smell of alcohol, lingering around her as I closed the door gently.

The drive to Costa del Este, the condo's location, was a short one at this time of the night. We were uncharacteristically quiet on the ride home—no exchange of anecdotes or recounts of the day. No questions from her about today's local news, or how my day went. No signs of our easy banter. A silence eerily like the first day surrounded us, making my stomach knot in protest.

I'd only known this woman for four months, and the knowledge was superficial at best, but the ache in my chest as we approached our goodbyes didn't sit well. The urge to say something to her, to prolong our time together, ate me up inside, but I wasn't certain what I could say to change this situation. Genevieve had a life in the US, and I had a life here. On top of that, our aims weren't compatible. Genevieve had a long-term career plan that would put me too close to the type of goals I'd eschewed for myself and didn't plan to ever retake. And of course, there was my family. There was always my family.

"I'm going to miss riding with you," she whispered in the quiet car as we arrived at her building. Her sadness punched me in the gut.

"I told you I'll bring the computer for you tomorrow morning, so you don't have to go out before your flight."

"Oh, I'm not flying away yet… I'm leaving tomorrow for Colón for a two-week vacation." Her words ignited a spark of hope.

"Really? Where in Colón?"

"A bed-and-breakfast. Anita, the general manager at the Tropics, recommended it. She knows the owner. It's in Aguaimar?" She said, taking care to enunciate the town.

Aguimar? Home?

My heart skipped a beat at the news, but I held my peace for now. Just because she planned to visit my hometown didn't mean she would want to spend time with me.

"Aguaimar is beautiful. I'm sure you'll be able to relax there," I said instead.

"Really? Oh good," she said in a dreamy voice. "Well, I guess I'll see you when I see you." Soft lips pressed against my cheek, the scent of her so close making my mouth water. She'd crept up, sneaking between the passenger and driver seat, to press the chaste kiss. There was nothing chaste about the way my body reacted to her. Everything told me to whip around and crash my lips with hers.

Then I remembered this was work.

"Do you want me to leave the computer bag downstairs with the receptionist?" I asked, with no hope of my pulse slowing down, giving her an out but hoping for the best.

"No, I want to see you again, give you a proper hug. I'm really going to miss you, Adrián." The husky words crashed into me, disturbing my equilibrium, even though she'd whispered them.

"Okay, I will see you tomorrow." I cleared my throat to get out the words.

"See you tomorrow."

Before she could exit, I jumped out of the car and opened the door for her. The swing of her hips acted as a pendulum on a clock until the glass door closed behind her, dislodging me from my trance.

I had less than twelve hours to figure out how to insinuate myself in Genevieve's plans for her last two weeks in the country. We might not have a long-term future together, but we certainly could explore a short-term one. People like Gen came only a few times in life and I'd learned the hard way not to ever waste those moments.

I couldn't let this opportunity pass me by.

Three

Genevieve

My head swam in a sea of regret. Last night's champagne seemed like a good idea, but I lamented the decision to have more than two glasses during the celebration. Bolstered by my resolve during my conversation with Mom and the banter with Anibal and Anita, I'd forgotten to practice moderation, which at this point should be my middle name. I was that child, the careful one, the one who friends appointed as the designated driver in college. Carefulness was my brand.

A quick shower and a cup of blistering hot coffee remedied some of my aches. Somehow, I'd had the presence to wrap my hair, so I placed it in a ponytail, put on leggings, a tank top, and an off-shoulder T-shirt on top.

Saying a quick thank you to past Gen for my already packed vacation bag, I pulled my cell to see the timing to order a shared drive to the nearest car rental. From there, I'd take the two-hour drive to Aguimar. Like it was 1999, I printed the directions, just in case the signal was spotty on the road to the town, even though everyone assured me that wouldn't be a problem.

As an extra precaution, I also printed copies of my reservation at the hostel Anita had arranged. My vast experience had taught me well—people that took arrangements made for them for granted could easily find out they had incorrect information and nowhere to stay. If I had to explain to one more Vibranium member that I couldn't build a room in a sold-out hotel…the joys of hospitality.

The intercom pulled me from my mental inventory, startling me.

"Hello?"

"Hi, miss, I have a Señor Adrián to see you?" Jose, the security guard, announced.

Was that my heart attempting to escape my chest? And why did everything feel warmer all of a sudden?

Why had Adrián returned? My memories were murky at best, and I didn't remember if we had agreed for him to take me to the rental company? Running through the events of last night, I found the reason within seconds. By the time I remembered my missing laptop bag, a firm knock had reverberated through the apartment.

With my heart in my throat, I marched toward the door, taking a quick inventory of my state. Breath check—yikes, I cupped my hand over my mouth, and the smell of black coffee punched me back. Damn.

"Give me a sec!"

I dashed to the bathroom. For fuck's sake, why did I care so much about my breath, of all things? There was no reason for my jitters; Adrián had been nothing but professional these past four months. What did I think? That we would be

tangling tongues one day removed from our professional relationship? He'd never been so close to me to detect my black
coffee dragon breath.

Where was the poised, put-together Silent Sniper? Just the
thought of Adrián standing behind my door had me conjur-
ing ways to convince him to stay and chat for a while.

I'd been sad to part ways with Anita and the team at the
Tropics, but saying goodbye to Adrián had been my hard-
est task. Adrián, who'd given me space to warm up to him
at my pace, and embraced all my questions about his country
enthusiastically, showing a deep interest in my thoughts that
went beyond politeness. He'd integrated me into his everyday, telling me anecdotes of his drives or the day's news, telling me in his easygoing manner, always finding ways to pull
smiles from me.

We didn't always see eye to eye, though; I loved our heated
debates about how to grow our communities and what was
needed the most. Generational wealth in my eyes, equitable
sharing of resources between families and beyond in his eyes.
When he got into his stride, his voice would deepen and I
was a bit ashamed to say, my mind would travel elsewhere,
wondering how that deep voice would make me feel in the
middle of sweaty sex. Who thought deep existential conversations would be so sexy?

The ghost sensation of the rasp of warm skin kissed my lips,
and a flash of memory of how delicious it had felt to press
my mouth against his cheek resurfaced. Yo…had I really told
him I'd miss him?

Incredible, one conversation with Mom where I held my
own, and suddenly I transformed into a hot girl, doing hot
girl things.

At work, I was self-contained and determined. Outside of work, during those elusive couple of hours per day, I lived in my quiet bubble, surrounded by my assortment of quirky coffee mugs, comfy plush onesies, excessive pillows, and my board games. Twenty-year-old Gen would have been perplexed. All that work and that was all I had to show?

Gino, my best friend, had tasked himself with improving my social life. He obviously didn't care about the known definition of madness. Every week he cajoled me into dinner, a movie, and, when feeling really lucky, to a local bar. Every week I managed ways to finagle myself out of the plans, attempting to convince him to hang out at my condo instead. We had a fifty-fifty track record. But lately, Gino had shown signs of fatigue. It wasn't easy being friends with such an introvert.

A blast of mint filled my mouth, and I swished the mouthwash like I would win a prize for it. Displaying unexpected speed, I hurried across the open living room, dining room, and kitchen, my heart beating so hard, I confused it with the knock on the door. I yanked the door open with a show of force I never showed in the gym, halting when I met a wall of white.

My eyes traveled from the torso, adorned by a white T-shirt valiantly covering all that chest, up to the dimple of my weekly dreams. Adrián stood in his T-shirt and jeans, holding my laptop bag. Adrián in slacks and shirts had been a treat, but Adrián, dressed down, was a whole cheat day.

"Hey, Adrián."

Why did I sound as if I had run from Florida to the door?

"Hey, Ms. Raymond." The quirk of his lips pulled my attention, interrupting my fascination with his dimple.

"I thought I told you to call me by my name?" Alert, alert: *The Return of the Hot Girl.*

"Isn't Ms. Raymond your name?" He had such an expressive eyebrow. And why did that arch make me want to run my finger over it?

"Oh please, you know what I mean. I'm Genevieve, and Tropics no longer employs you to drive me so we can drop all that professionalism of the past four months."

I waved him in and closed my eyes as he swaggered inside the apartment. The smell of his cologne would haunt me until the end of my days. He rested his deliciously burly body against the white marble kitchen island, elbow relaxed on the counter.

"So tell me, Genevieve, how do you look when you drop your professionalism?" he asked while I pressed myself against the closed door.

"I…well…" *Hot Girl, come back! I need you.* I wasn't ready for this pressure, all this time I thought this infatuation one-sided. How had I missed the signs?

Oh yeah, because I was buried in work.

He grinned. Mmm-hmm, so he was amused at witnessing how I fumbled the bag? I rallied, wanting to leave a lasting impression before saying goodbye.

"We won't ever know, will we?" I shrugged and approached him, extending my hand. He studied me, all loose limbs and relaxed pose, and I realized he was trying to set me at ease. His eyes, though, told a different story. His intense gaze burned through my chest, electrifying every atom in my body.

"I wished we'd met in a different setting," he confessed, and I nodded like a marionette under his strings, the beat of my heart accelerating again. Could he hear it?

"Why didn't you say anything?"

"What could I say? If I made a move, you'd probably ask for a different company to pick you up."

If he only knew. I'd been plotting ways to make his dimple show from the first day I met him. It had all been polite conversation, but at least once a day, I got a glimpse of that breathtaking smile and his sexy dimple.

"No, you should have tried." I reached out to take the bag out of his hand.

The touch of his skin jolted me. I searched his gaze and recognized the same sizzling awareness that tingled through my body. Then that damn dimple made an appearance again.

"How about I try now?" His hand ghosted up my arm, then back down, and he squeezed it. *Genevieve, don't moan. Do. Not. Moan.* The gesture should have been innocent, but it felt as if he'd pressed his entire hard, sturdy body against mine. I relaxed my hand, then dropped the laptop bag.

"Oh shit!" The dull thud didn't sound promising.

We both knelt at the same time, his movements faster than mine. I struggled to keep my composure at his nearness and stood up as he straightened out to his full height. Lord, but he was tall. He zipped open the bag, the sound snapping me out of the fog of need that clouded my senses.

Adrián pulled out the laptop, inspecting it from every angle.

"I think it's alright. Try it out," he instructed, and the way he told me what to do should have annoyed me but instead lit a fire in me. I rested the laptop on the counter, and after a few taps, the screen lit up.

"All good." I sighed in relief.

"Sorry, I didn't know you'd drop it."

"Are you really blaming me for…for all this…" I flapped my hands in his direction, peeved he didn't take ownership of his aura. He must have been keeping it all leashed behind his professional persona. The moment he walked into the apartment, I could sense the difference in him. The intense confidence incredibly alluring. If only we'd dropped our masks earlier.

His laughter boomed in the apartment, a full round sound like a timpani in an echo chamber, making me feel tingly inside.

"I'm sorry for flustering you. I just wanted you to know how attracted I was to you before you left, back to the States," he finished with a rueful smile.

The reminder that this searing intensity between us had no future dampened the mood like a wet, cold blanket. Why couldn't Adrián and I have met on one of those boring-ass dates I took out occasionally? With him it wouldn't have been boring; with Adrián, it would have been memorable and sensual, and thought-provoking… I sighed, I was working myself up for something that couldn't be.

Needing a second, I turned my back to him, closed the laptop, and filled my lungs with air before facing him, feeling centered once more. He had retreated to the sofa across the kitchen island, resting himself on the back of the seat—as if that made him less dangerous to my stability.

"If I'm ever here again, I'll make sure to reach out to you. I'll probably have meetings to attend once the Tropics is over the honeymoon phase." The air between us carried a heaviness of unexplored possibilities and unsaid words.

"Hold up. Before you ask me to leave, I wanted to extend an invitation." He unfurled his body, erasing some of the space between us, his eyes eager on mine. No, it couldn't be. Was Adrián about to shoot his shot? Was I about to be propositioned? This must be the start of my Hot Girl to Ho Girl transition because I'd never been more tempted to say yes.

"So, instead of going to whatever hostel you had at Aguimar, I wanted to invite you to my family's cabanas. We have a little ten-cabin property, very humble but comfortable. I'd love to host you."

The twinge in my chest couldn't be disappointment. Adrián was offering me an honorable proposal. Here, I was imagining two weeks of a calisthenics-comparable sex-a-thon.

"Will you be in the city, or will you be in Aguimar?" I held my breath, his answer as crucial as the air around me. He closed the gap between us, his cologne reminding me of my lust-filled dreams. I swayed closer to him.

"Yes, I'll be there. When you told me you still had two weeks here, the first thing that came to mind was how I could be part of them. I know you have a life in the States, but I can't waste another two weeks wondering what it would mean to be in your presence without any walls between us," he whispered. "I'll be respectful. I know two weeks is a short time, but we can at least get to know each other better."

He pushed back, and I pretended to be unaffected. He grinned and shook his head at me.

"Well, I already had a reservation. I mean, Anita went through a lot to get it for me, and I…well, you said two weeks, and then I leave? I don't know if it would be smart to pursue anything." Was the babble the best I could pull off? Ugh. Thank God for clarity. Logic came to the rescue just in time. My head had conjured many ways I wanted to spend the next fourteen days with Adrián. None of the ways involved clothes. But pursuing those wishes didn't make sense.

"Genevieve, this is our chance." His velvet, smooth voice

soothed me. My famed logical brain seemed to have taken the rest of the morning off as I stood weighing the decision. How wild would it be to ditch my plans, and go with the flow? To experience life without a detailed plan?

"Give me until midday to give you an answer."

"Okay, I'll leave now to give you some space, but I'll be waiting," he whispered, the scent of peppermint melding with his cologne. I nodded, feigning calmness, but inside my heart had started a HIIT circuit.

Leaving with Adrián sounded like a dangerous proposal. And I'd just become a thrill seeker.

Four

Genevieve

My actions the past day were out of the norm, but that didn't mean I had completely lost the entire plot. I sat at my laptop, researching everything I could find about Villa Bonita. The hostel was humble, with little cabana-style rooms, each of them connected by a winding path that led to the main building. The main building looked like a modest home, with cement walls painted in pearly white and colorful window shutters and a stucco roof.

Something about the hostel called to me, a sense of peace and relaxation that reached out even through the computer screen. A sense of a vacation not for a reward or a goal achieved, but for self-care, and reconnection with my inner self. A time that required no permission, no negotiation with myself, and certainly not with my mother.

Thoughts swirled as I considered my options.

One: I could politely say no and continue with my arrangements. That option had merit; it required zero emotional requirements to socialize and expend any effort to be charming. But I would miss Adrián's company, and the new energy he showed in my apartment today intrigued me.

Two: I could say yes, keep things friendly, and enjoy his family hostel while ensuring I put all my walls up. That would probably buy me some alone time and again no emotional effort.

Three: I could say yes and go with the flow, enjoy my time with Adrián, let him take me around to explore, and who knows, maybe we got to explore each other in turn. That option required a lot of socializing and probably would leave my "extroversion in case of emergency tank" drained, but… it might also get me some action. And I was in dire need of action. Things had been pitiful in that department for a long while—double digits month count.

Versions of my two weeks swirled like pages in a hardback, each of them vastly different. After pushing away from the dining room table, I paced the living area back and forth, wondering what the right decision would be. My cell phone burned a hole in my hand as I contemplated the smart thing to do.

A very persistent voice in the back of my head reminded me that this time was to relax, replenish, and disconnect. Would spending time with Adrián achieve that? My tank didn't fill when being social; I just didn't work that way. A quiet room, snacks, a book, or a movie were the only ways I could recover from grueling day-to-day meetings, networking, and all the necessary peopling my career required. I could turn it on like the best of them, but it drained all my battery, and solitude was the prefect charger. But another voice insisted my sexual tank needed more than replenishing. It needed a complete redesign, three coats of paint, some sprinkles, and glitter for shits and giggles.

Conflicted, I did the only thing I could think of.

"Hey, gorgeous, how are you?" Gino immediately responded to my video call. My heart instantly lightened at the sight of him.

"Oh please, you say that to all the boys," I teased.

"Nah, I tell the boys other things, but I don't want to scandalize you." Gino's deep chuckle made me homesick. A call with Mom had me wanting to stay in Panamá for ten more weeks, but just the sight of Gino made me want to get the next flight and go and hang out with my bestie. He was the only person allowed in my charging sessions, and his chatter never drained my batteries. I always wondered why until one day I noticed I'd been sitting next to Gino for three hours and we hadn't exchanged a word. I'd asked him why he was so quiet and he said, "Because you needed me to be."

"What's up, Gen? I'm getting ready to go on this date."

"Ohhh, let me see what you wearing! You're really into this new dude, but I haven't approved of him yet. I need to meet him."

Gino dutifully propped his phone and showed me the pink shorts and white linen shirt he had on. Then he turned around slowly to give me the full effect. Not for nothing, but my friend was a really sexy bear with his deep walnut skin, cornrows, thick beard, thick everything, and the brightest grin you'd ever see. And the men who dated him couldn't get enough of his rugged but sweet personality.

"Damn, you gonna kill him with that booty," I joked.

"Girl, here I am wearing my hoochie shorts, and it's not even spring."

"Boy, please, end of February in South Florida might as well be early summer."

"Not that I don't want to stay on the phone and chat with you, but I gotta go soon, so spill."

The urge to roll my eyes tugged at me, but I couldn't clap back. After all, he had known me since we were both in kindergarten. I couldn't bluff my way with Gino.

"My driver invited me to stay at his hostel for two weeks."

"Oh...his hostel? Is this where you get kidnapped in a foreign country and never return to me?" Gino said as the image from his phone tilted, and his full face framed up close and personal.

"Ugh, why did I bother calling you? This isn't a productive use of my time. You can't take things seriously." I held back laughter when he reared the phone back, then zoomed the camera in until all I saw was one eyeball and a perfectly manicured eyebrow.

"I would like you to know that EYE had plans, so YOU are the one wasting MY time, Ms. Funny."

"Damn, it's like that?"

"You know what time it is, Ms. Gen. So, you want me to quarterback this decision for you?"

"Ahh, sure?" I said. Shit, he'd explained this before, but I remained clueless.

"Damn, with the number of times I've taken you to Dolphin games, what have you retained?"

"The tight pants and all the melanin," I whined, and Gino cackled.

"You ain't lying. Listen. You've been talking about this man for weeks, months. I mean, at this point, I feel like if I bump into Mr. Sexy Driver with the smooth sexy-ass grin, with those tight filled pants that—"

"I've lost you now," I complained.

"What do you want? Fast, don't think," Gino urged me.

"I want to go with him. But it's not that simple. I mean, do I just play to the friendship, or do I do…more," I whispered but damn, did it feel right saying it. Gino had a way of holding me to the fire, but never dropping me into the coals, that worked every time. He was a sorcerer, my best friend.

"Girl, what are we, back in high school? Just go with the flow," Gino said, reiterating what I already knew.

"You're right but…but I just feel so…so…"

"Listen, Gen. You've lived your entire adult life following a script, and you have done a fucking amazing job at excelling. You know I'm super proud of you. But at some point, you're gonna have to assess if the script in front of you is what you still want and need. And not let your momma dictate every single step," Gino said, and my pulse hopscotched at his words. Words of denial immediately rushed forward, the same assurances I repeated to myself daily.

I'm happy, I want this. Life like this is enough.

"Nah, don't say anything. I know you're gonna defend Mama Raymond, and we're not going there today. Just think about it. I have to run. He's here. Make sure you text me what you decide, okay?" Gino said, ending the call before I could say goodbye.

I gently closed the laptop screen and went to my room. In there, all the luggage sat awaiting my next move. I'd been prepared to rent a vehicle, but now, with Adrián's offer, it made sense to cancel it. A blast of adrenaline and joy hit me at the decision as I hung up with the rental company.

The next step was easy. Without hesitation, I pressed a few buttons, and Adrián's voice greeted me after two rings.

"Genevieve." The way he said my name… His slight Panamanian accent made it sound like it existed to be pronounced in a mix of Spanglish. A ball of nervous tension formed in my stomach, making it hard to speak, and I shifted on my feet.

"Uh, hey. Hey. Well, hey."

My God. Was that really the best I could do? I needed immediate aid. The hot girl that flirted with Adrián was nowhere to be found, and all that remained was the same old Gen. The overworked, undersexed, and in dire need of attention, Gen. The rush of adrenaline and good warmth feeling I got earlier—I wanted that back.

When was the last time I'd felt so present, so alive?

A warm chuckle filtered through the phone, and I wanted to die of mortification. He was probably going to rescind the invitation after realizing all my confidence stemmed from my work and success.

"I'm nervous too. I've never done something like this before. I get it. Listen, if it's not—"

"No, it's good. I'm going. Choice three, it's choice three." I blurted out, interrupting Adrián.

There was a pause, then a sigh of relief. Giddiness hit me in the chest; better than sleeping in on a Monday morning.

"I don't know what choice three means, but if it gets you to come with me, I approve."

I wouldn't melt; I would *not* melt.

"Okay, so what next?"

"Next is I come pick you up in an hour, and we make our way to Colón."

"Okay…okay, see you soon," I said, and it came out like a whisper.

"See you, Genevieve." Adrián practically purred my name on the phone and I had to hold on to one of the chairs in the dining room to keep straight.

New sex tank, here I come.

Well, this was a rocky start. I had met Adrián downstairs with my luggage and a smile, feeling featherlight and full of excitement.

He'd come out of the car to greet me, gotten my luggage in the trunk, and opened the front passenger door like the gentleman he was. I appreciated the confirmation that his attentiveness went beyond work. As soon as we boarded his old SUV, we were on our way.

"Sorry, I know you're used to the new fleet. This one is mine, a little old but very reliable," he explained. I nodded along with a grin, but words refused to come out.

I'd never been this nervous around a man before, at least not since junior high, but something about Adrián in his casual clothes with full aura trained on me made me forget how to use words.

Somehow in this smaller vehicle, Adrián's presence appeared even grander. More present. Enticing. I trailed over his thick thighs as he maneuvered the pedals. It was easy to admire his large golden-brown hands with the thick veins traversing the backs of his palms.

What could those hands do? And the size of his fingers, the visions they brought. One of those hands, gliding over my thigh, between my legs, to find the evidence of my body's response. One thick, long finger finding me dripping and—suddenly, I felt parched. I wasn't a small woman, not with these wide hips and lush thighs that refused to surrender to the hundred squats on leg day, but Adrián made me feel soft. Precious.

Distraction. I needed distraction from errant thoughts. I focused on Adrián and found him studying me with a hungry gaze that required a few shifts on the front seat. At this rate, I'd need a change of underwear by the time we arrived at the hostel. This was wild.

"So tell me more—"

"Do you want a blanket? I have one in the back if the AC is too cold."

Both of us spoke at the same time, and I stopped talking to let him finish.

"Sorry, what were you going to ask?"

Talking to Adrián used to be easy, but now that our mutual attraction was out in the open, it was as if we had pressed Rewind to those first days. I shook my head, and then if it wasn't enough to use no words, I gave him a thumbs-up with a vapid grin that made me cringe the moment I used it. Adrián pursed his lips in doubt, then returned his focus to the road.

This was a train wreck; where was my poise? My famed calm, my equanimity?

"So since when—"

"What do you want to listen to?" Adrián asked again, trying to start up conversation. He ran his right hand slowly down his thigh, and he might as well have touched me instead. This was the most sexually tense, awkward exchange I'd ever had. Finally, words emerged from my lips, but they were not enough to spark up the usual easy banter that had been the norm in our rides.

"Whatever you like," I said, then wanted to ask for that

blanket so I could crawl under it and close my eyes for the rest of the trip. The blanket would also help with the way my nipples had decided to broadcast all my dirty thoughts.

Adrián fiddled with the console and soon soft salsa music filled the car, substituting some of the awkward silence that reigned before. The charged silence was better, but the awkwardness stuck around the entire ride to Colón. Adrián attempted to start conversation, and I managed to miss every single attempt.

Soon we settled into an awkward silence. I played with my phone, stealing glances at his thighs and hands, which were working so diligently to drive us safely.

When the SUV wheels hit the dirt road that signaled to Aguimar, my shoulders sagged in relief. The two hours had been torturous, and I wondered if I'd imagined the chemistry of just this morning.

Adrián maneuvered his car into a little town with cute houses, driving past a large town square with a round open structure in the middle of a roundabout and on the opposite side of the round structure, a fonda called La Buenona.

I had the pleasure of eating food in a fonda, which I had equated to the Panamanian version of a dive, and wondered how far this one was from the hostel. As if the drive hadn't been torture enough, my stomach grumbled loudly over the music in the car.

"No worries, my sister probably has some food ready," Adrián said, holding back his amusement.

If the gravel under us could just jump up and bury me, maybe I could get out of this car with some dignity. I smiled at Adrián, but it probably looked more like a grimace.

Honestly, this day couldn't get any more awkward.

Five

Adrián

Dios mío.

The car ride had been a disaster, riddled with awkwardness. During the past four months Gen and I had become friendly she had exuded confidence and poise. But this ride…it made me wonder if I'd made a mistake inviting her, putting her in a position she wasn't comfortable with, and making her retreat to her shyness. I wanted her to relax and be at ease, not worried about any awkwardness between us. She deserved rest. I followed Gen with the luggage as she stood rooted close to the entrance. She was as lovely as ever, fiddling with the straps of her laptop bag and her cell phone in hand, as she stared at Villa Bonita and the surrounding areas in amazement.

Pride washed over me at our little property, unpretentious but beautiful. Ten little cabanas were scattered around green palm trees and abundant rich vegetation, primary colors decorating the walls and windows, the scheme of each cabana unique, with small individual touches I had personally designed.

"This is beautiful," Genevieve said in awe, then turned around and regaled me with a dazzling smile. A full-body tingle wracked my body at that grin. The gesture reassured me—that was the smile she'd given me many mornings and afternoons.

"I'm glad you like it," I said.

"Like it? Nah, that's not enough. I love the way the winding pathways lead to the main building, and if I'm not mistaken all of the units face the beach, right? And the middle structure, it looks deceptively small, but it's obviously the main artery incorporating all the colors from the rooms. It's lovely." The force of her happiness was intoxicating, and I stepped closer, drawn to her. The moment I stood close, she grew bashful, eyes dropping to the ground then back up with apprehension.

"Are you okay? Listen, I know this was a last-minute decision, but the reason it made sense to me is because we already had a connection. If it helps, just remember our rides," I said, desperate to set her at ease. She'd made a big leap agreeing to spend her last two weeks with me and the last thing I wanted to do was make her uncomfortable.

Genevieve sighed, her ponytail shaking; her shoulders rose, and like magic, the determination and poise seemed to materialize in her again.

"Of course, listen, I know the trip here was—"

Whatever Genevieve was going to say was cut short by a cacophony of noise. The ground shook as if a stampede of wild animals was about to descend on us. Gen whirled on the spot as my five niblings, followed by my very frazzled sister, ran out of the main casita.

"Muchacho! Thank God you're here!" Claudia stalked straight to me, enveloping me in her agua de maravilla–scented hug. The way Claudia talked to me, people would think she was a hundred years older instead of her forty-five to my thirty-six. Somehow even though I towered over Claudia's much shorter though abundant frame, Claudia managed to bring me down with a strong arm, my entire body bending to her formidable will.

"What's up, Claudi, why is everyone running around like un mamonio is following you?" I asked, keeping an eye on Genevieve, who had donned a polite smile as my nephews and nieces surrounded her with curiosity.

"Hi, señora, you're so pretty." The youngest of the bunch, Yiya, said to Genevieve.

"Well, not prettier than you. Miss?" Genevieve reciprocated.

"Yiya! Nice to meet you! I'm five and this is my sister Mirna, she is ten, but she is really shy and those two, yes you are right they look the same, they are twins, Tuti and Milton. Mami says they're the most annoying fifteen-year-olds she's ever met, and that right there, the one that looks really old is Chichi. He should be married, Mami says but Papa says twenty-five is too young." Yamilah strung all that information without taking as much as a breath. Genevieve nodded excitedly, following the convoluted information, and Claudia turned around with a hand on her hip, ready to chastise her daughter. I needed to step in before my family showed their entire behind before Genevieve even put her luggage in her room.

"Gracias, Yiya, that was very helpful. Now Ms. Genevieve knows the entire family and will remember everyone's names."

Damn. My family could be a lot at the best of times, and Genevieve already seemed to be skittish even though she was smiling serenely. I wanted to ensure she knew she wasn't expected to know everyone's name nor get involved with whatever was happening in Villa Bonita today, outside of settling in and relaxing. Before I could say anything, she winked at me and turned to Yiya.

"Thanks, Yiya, that's a beautiful name, and Mirna, no worries, when I was your age, I was very shy too! While I'm here, if you just want to hang out in silence, I love doing that. Tuti, Milton, how are you gentlemen? I can't wait for y'all to show me around the property. Chichi, very nice to meet you, and don't worry, you have plenty time to get married, if that's what you want to do. Claudia, how can we help? Because you have an air of 'I need assistance ASAP.'"

All of the children, Chichi, and even Claudia froze, Claudia with a slight frown. All the air stopped circulating around me in anticipation; with Claudia things could go either way. Claudia nodded once as it if to say, "you will do," and I let go of the breath I was holding. It wasn't as if I wanted her approval of Gen. It wasn't as if it was a big deal having my big sister like the first woman I brought to the family in a very long time.

I had no reason to be worried about Claudia liking Genevieve. Genevieve wouldn't be here for long; this was just an impulsive move to keep Genevieve close to me for a few more days before the inevitable goodbye came for the two of us. Claudi liking her or not was inconsequential. So why did I feel much better now that Genevieve had clearly won over my family in less than ten minutes?

"Okay, Genevieve, you can help too. We have a big bus arriving in less than an hour. We need to make sure all the room linens are fresh and clean!" Claudia clapped her hands and started barking orders like a general.

A tingle of dread crept up my back, and I missed half of what Claudia ordered.

"What do you mean a big bus?" I asked, my commanding voice stopping all the chatter.

"We sold out the hostel for two weeks to a group of Americans coming to stay for an excursion. Didn't you see the email I sent you last week?"

"I…" Shit, she was right. I rubbed the back of my neck. She had told me about the excursion coming, and somehow in the excitement of inviting Genevieve, I had forgotten that salient fact. We rarely were able to sell all the rooms at the same time. If anything, we could have weeks with no one staying, so I had my other transportation venture. I needed to keep my family fed, so I hadn't ever thought it would be an issue to host Genevieve.

"I what?" Claudia's eyes narrowed, and the kids scattered, knowing their mother was about to explode.

"Well, Genevieve was coming to stay for two weeks. Maybe the guests coming are friends or family that can…"

"No. No. I'm not telling those people we're overbooked. So that means that you can figure out what to do about your guest whom you brought to us with no reservation. Sorry, Genevieve, usually I'm super nice and welcoming, but we rarely sell out, and it's just me, the kids, and my husband. Adrián comes whenever he can, so I'm stressed-out, girl." Before I could say anything else, Claudia walked away, leaving me with a flabbergasted Genevieve.

"I… Usually I'm very meticulous about checking these things ahead in the booking system, but I…" I floundered, feeling like this was a doomed venture. I'd been so sure this would work out, but since picking up Gen things had started to unravel.

"It's okay. I can call the B and B where I had my original reservation. I just canceled today." Genevieve smiled kindly, and I could tell from our drives together that this was her fixer mode. She scrolled through her phone, walking away from me, closer to the shade, and I stood there watching her move.

Something in Genevieve called to me from the day I first picked her up at the apartment. A sense of kinship, a whisper in my ear telling me that beyond her beautiful outer appearance existed something in her that awakened dormant insights in me.

To think that what I had envisioned for our two weeks together was crumbling in front of my eyes felt like a dream forgotten. Like waking up in the morning and trying to remember what exactly you'd experienced in dreamland the night before. Holding on to that amazing feeling as it seeped away, awash in the reality of everyday.

Gen nodded along on the phone, gesticulating as she probably explained her predicament. Her hand gestures slowed down more and more until she stood still, receiving the information coming from the other side. She slowly turned around, grimaced. Damn, the news couldn't be good. Instead of her having to come to me, I ate up the distance between us in a few strides.

"What happened?"

"They are sold out too. Apparently, they were oversold, but my cancellation evened them out. They were trying to figure out what to do, and it was going to be a first come, first served situation. Apparently, that American group has taken over the town."

"Shit, I'm so sorry, Genevieve, I didn't think this through. I wanted you to relax and enjoy my family's property, and instead..."

"It's okay. I get it. I... I guess I'll need a ride back to the city. I can always just change my flight and..."

A thunderous voice inside of me howled in frustration at hearing Genevieve's plan to leave. Without thinking, I reached out, holding her hand, and the same frisson of awareness I felt in the morning assaulted me again.

The feel of her skin was smooth as I ran my thumb up and down the side of her hand, the gesture appearing to soothe her, but honestly, it was all for me. I inhaled her delicious scent of something flowery and spicy and stepped closer to her.

I focused on Genevieve's large brown eyes, as they shifted from disappointment to languid relaxation. My hand moved without thought to her waist, and she gasped as the touch deepened the otherworldly sensations I felt when around her. This. This was the connection I wanted to explore when I invited her, but somehow, things had unraveled and...

"Adrián, go get that girl's luggage and put it in your room!" Claudia hollered from the side path that led to the back of the main casita. Genevieve stiffened in my arms, and I immediately felt the shift in our connection. I turned around to face Claudia who had a basket of linen propped on her hip. I stroked my beard, hoping it kept me from saying something like "mind your own business, old bat."

"Genevieve's a guest. I wouldn't put her in such uncomf—"
Again, Claudia interrupted with a loud scoff.

"Ay por favor. Look at the two of you. I give you two days

max. Genevieve stay in his room. It's one of the largest cabanas and is not part of the inventory. Y'all can figure it out." Claudia rolled her eyes and stomped away as Chichi called her.

"Listen, you don't have to worry, I asked you for two weeks, but I'd never presume…"

"How big is the cabana?" Genevieve's question took a minute to penetrate fully. When it did, my body flashed hot and cold. Images of the two of us in one of my most cherished spaces raised my temperature, but I played it cool. I always did. Keeping my cool helped when kids at school had learned early how to hurt me because they considered my bisexuality a thing to condemn. And it had helped when my cool then translated into being considered unflappable in business and in relationships.

"Big enough for company."

"My company?" she replied, that shyness peeking through, but she held her gaze with that determination I had seen in her before.

"Genevieve, I'd love to host you for two weeks in my cabana if you want to stay here."

"Okay, I'll stay."

My chest tightened at Genevieve's easy capitulation; it was like she'd wanted this solution all along. Emboldened by her choice, I stepped closer to her again, this time keeping my arms to myself.

"Good, I'll make sure you have the time of your life."

Six

Genevieve

"Good, I'll make sure you have the time of your life."

Those words resonated in my brain a couple of hours after Adrián spoke them to me, with his deep rumbly voice, so close I could have gotten on my tiptoes and stolen a kiss. How would his plump lips taste? Probably as delicious as he looked in the current board shorts and white tank top as he carried some additional rollaway beds with Chichi to one of the guest rooms. I could spy him through the window next to the front desk in the casita, which was deceptively more extensive than expected.

The front desk was adjacent to a little living area with beautiful, colorful decor. The walls sported clay plates and houses hand painted in watercolors with Panamanian folkloric motifs. There was a second expansive room with additional wooden furniture and what Claudia explained in between tasks was the only TV in the hostel. That opened to a large outdoor area and a gorgeous crystalline pool surrounded by palm trees, wicker loungers, and patio furniture.

The group of Americans ended up being a Black "grown and sexy" excursion for singles and married couples. I learned more about the group as I helped Claudia with the check-in, taking credit cards and swiping them for incidentals.

One of the guests, a single woman of forty who recently divorced, accompanied by her two best friends, explained this was a package they'd bought through a magazine for Black travelers and adventurers.

"So what's this excursion about? How do you know all these people?" I asked them.

"You haven't heard of *Black Travel Chronicles*?" The woman flashed her phone to me showing an aesthetically pleasing IG page with photos of paradise or Black people traveling in each post.

I immediately struck up a conversation with them, finding out that *Black Travel Chronicles* was an up-and-coming paper and digital publisher that showcased destinations, hotels, restaurants, and cities that were friendly for Black travelers—not only that, but they highlighted rich cultural experiences for Black millennials and Gen Xers.

"I love the concept! I don't travel for leisure often, but when I do, I'm always looking for information on the city's Black history, neighborhoods, and Black-owned businesses to give my money to!" I said, excited to have found this website and social media accounts. This was a game changer for me when I traveled next. Wow, thinking of my next vacation felt like a step too far, but...why not? There wasn't anything wrong with plotting my next adventure.

"Yeah, girl, we found their social media page a few years

ago and have loved their articles and posts ever since. When they advertised this excursion, I knew I had to jump on it," Telisha, the guest, said as I finished her check-in process.

This little hostel being exposed by the magazine was fantastic. I'm not certain how it had happened, because Adrián and his sister seemed to be surprised by the business, but this was at the heart of the conversations Adrián and I had often shared—how could we invest in us? The possibilities of *Black Travel Chronicles* and Black-owned hospitality lingered on while I continued checking people in.

Thank God Claudia and Adrián had the same system we had in the Tropics; it allowed me to jump in and help Claudia. Once we finished with the line, Claudia sagged with relief.

"Well, now I can go to the Buenona and help out Mario before the excursion descends on the fonda for dinner."

"Oh, you know the owner of the Buenona? I'm looking forward to trying out the food there."

"Waooo, girl, you really just came here with my brother knowing nothing about him? The Buenona is the family's as well. You really must be dickmatized if he got you to come, and you two barely know each other. I mean I wouldn't, but hey, I get it, he's a handsome man. He could really have been taking you to your death, and you just went willing." Claudia's whole body language exuded "couldn't be me" energy.

Damn. She wasn't wrong. I floundered for what to say, shocked at Claudia's assessment. I prided myself on my methodical and meticulous evaluations. Still, for some reason, I'd blindly hopped into Adrián's car and traveled two hours to a remote town in a country where I had very few people that knew me. All on a whim. But of all the people I had connected with in Panamá, Adrián was the one I connected the most. And subconsciously, I recognized I could trust him, and I decided to trust my gut. I did it all the time with work, why not in my personal life as well?

"Tropics vetted Adrián before I even arrived in Panamá. They take security real serious. It just takes a call…" I shrugged and finalized inputting all the information for the day's check-ins. My instinct was to go through the process again to ensure everything was done correctly, but I didn't want to go into overdrive work mode.

"Well, damn. You told me." Claudia winked. "I forgot that Adrián was your driver before anything else. Well, enjoy your stay with us. I really appreciate your help today. You should relax for the rest of the two weeks…oh and—" Claudia's face transformed into a menacing scowl. "You better not break my brother's heart. He's gone through a lot these past years. If you hurt him, you'll have to deal with me."

Everything in me froze; I kept my face impassive. This morning I had been planning to relax and explore Aguimar on my own; hours later, here I was, being threatened by Adrián's sister, like the villain in a rom-com. But this was real life, and Claudia needed to chill. I had only the best intentions about my stay here and if those intentions came with a side of dick, then I was all for it. But I wasn't one to lead people on. I believed in being clear and concise with any expectations.

"Listen, Claudia, I might be quiet, but don't mistake my silence for anything else but that. I came here for vacation and your brother was kind enough to invite me, I didn't ask him. I'll be gone in two weeks, so no need to worry about me hurting your brother, okay? His heart is not in danger here."

Mine on the other hand…

Claudia let me finish, unperturbed…then she burst into

cackles. She threw her hands up, and shrugged, then beamed at me.

"You really believe that, don't you? Oh God, this is gonna be fun."

Armed with Claudia's instruction to find the family quarters, I took the one path that did not connect to the guest rooms. It was easy to find once I realized it was made of pebbles and gravel compared to the smooth cement paths for the rest of the cabanas.

Claudia's words nagged me, same as the mosquitos buzzing around. No heartbreaking would happen at the end of these two weeks because my heart would not be involved in any of the activities with Adrián—only relaxation and friendship. Her words had gotten close to my nightly dreams about Adrián, and my fantasies of meeting him in Florida instead of in Panamá, and what that would have meant for the two of us. But it was a fantasy, nothing more.

Back to choice two.

A light sweat gathered on my back, thanks to the relentless heat. Not even the slight breeze alleviated the torture. I really hoped Adrián had AC. I'd learned that the ventilation system in many houses in Panamá consisted of an abundance of screened windows and ceiling and standing fans.

With the typical humid heat of the country, how were people productive at all? If it was me, I'd be languishing under four fans and still need a large pitcher of cold lemonade to relax. No wonder Anita had warned me to be strategic about my blowouts. Already my hair felt coilier than the morning.

The vegetation around this path grew thicker, wilder than the manicured trails around the guest quarters. The greenery

here had a different quality to it. The trees and plants seemed
to bide their time to reclaim the man-made lanes. My lungs
filled with clean air and the scent of damp earth as I hoisted
my backpack more securely on my back. Adrián had offered
to put it away when he took my luggage, but I'd waved him
away, focused on the work needed to check in the big group.
That had been a mistake.

The path took a sharp right turn into a large clearing
adorned by abundant bright pink bougainvillea along the perimeter. Seeing so many beautiful flowers filled me with a
sense of rightness. On the opposite side of the clearing stood
two cabanas. One was an actual full home, with a cute porch
that had the typical Panamanian low cement wall framing the
gated entrance, leading to the main door of the flat house.
Based on Claudia's explanation, this was her home. A few
yards away from that stood a cabana similar to the ones for
guests but larger. Outside, a small open porch boasted a rock-
ing chair, a hammock, and a few planters.

My home for the next two weeks.

A cold, then hot trickle traveled through me as I approached
the door. Adrián would be behind that door. We'd be together
behind these closed quarters as our connection pulled and
tugged, propelling me to make these hasty decisions. When
we were together, in the quiet of Adrián's vehicle, chatting
on the way to the Tropics or back home...those moments had
become the foundation for each choice, cemented on an un-
deniable attraction and an unmistakable chemistry. I'd traded
my sensible brain for this hot girl summer mentality that made
me say yes to anything Adrián offered. And I wasn't even trying to change that.

I knocked, attempting to chase away my nerves.

"Come in." Adrián's deep voice came from within.

Without hesitation, I walked in, trying to prove to myself that the Hot Girl from the morning still lived inside. The whole day had been as if a doppelgänger had taken over my thoughts and behaviors. My shy, reserved nature, which I'd learned to disguise around people, had come to full life around Adrián.

"Welcome," Adrián said with a sexy smirk, and my lips twitched to mirror his. He leaned against a frosted-glass divider, all relaxed and coiled strength. I looked away before I ended up drooling or something worse, pouncing on him.

The room had a small living area with two wicker chairs and a wicker sofa with comfortable cushions. Windows stood open all around the house, with the necessary screens to keep mosquitos out.

On the opposite side, I spotted a small kitchenette, and right next to it, a working station. A frosted wall stood in the middle as a partial divider between the living area and the bedroom, with open spaces on both sides of the border.

Being in his space appealed to me. It smelled like him, leather and wood, and had assorted knickknacks everywhere. Several different models of tiny homes, vehicles, and even an airplane covered any available flat space, bringing Adrián's personality to the forefront.

"So, this is your little cabana. It's cute."

"Cute, damn. I wasn't going for cute. More like manly, comfortable, sexy."

I chuckled at his aggrieved tone and studied all the little details that made this place uniquely Adrián's. The books stacked on the coffee table in the living area were novels from the look of it. The kitchenette had a bowl full of different fruits.

He probably picked them as he navigated around during the day and brought them here. The TV in the living area had a streaming box, but there was a DVD player and a collection of action movies right underneath.

"It's all those things, as well." I grinned and closed the door behind me.

Immediately I took off my shoes, not wanting to track dirt in his space.

"Did you just clean up?" The fresh scent of house cleaner permeated the room.

"I did, but for the record, the space was already in order. But an extra cleaning don't kill nobody. And I changed the sheets on my bed, you're all good there. Let me show you."

"Oh, that is beautiful," I exclaimed, walking behind him to the sleeping section of his cabana. Adrián's huge bed faced the beachfront. A plushy three-seat oversized sofa sat on one side of the wall. Here, everything was minimalistic. The opposite wall had the door leading to the bathroom. A potent ceiling fan whistled low, no AC, making my hair fly a little.

My heart soared as I focused on the greenery and lush bougainvillea right outside the sliding door. The crash of the waves lured me, and I wandered closer to the glass, afraid to touch it lest I woke up in my bed in South Florida, ready for work yet again. The beautiful Caribbean Sea glittered magnificently in the late afternoon light, and I closed my eyes, giving silent thanks for the day's blessings.

"Oh... Adrián, this is breathtaking. Thanks, thank you for inviting me," I said, facing Adrián, who stood as if a lightning bolt had struck him, frozen. "Are you alright?" I asked.

"Yeah. I'm equally grateful to have you here. Are you good with us sleeping so close to each other?"

I flushed, studying the large king-size bed. The sheets were freshly tucked, and there was an abundance of pillows I planned to enjoy. Unbidden, the memory of Adrián's hand on my waist earlier made me shiver. If that slight touch turned me into molten molasses, what would sleeping next to him do to me?

"Yeah, sure, sharing a bed is…fine. I mean we're adults, and we can— It's okay. No problem." At that precise second, my arms, in a show of unnecessary independence, disregarded any of my mental orders. My arms transformed into one of those inflatable long-armed dancing balloons outside of car dealerships. Smooth.

"Ahm. I'm not sleeping on the bed. I'm sleeping there." Adrián choked, then pointed to the large sofa, which I now noticed also had a sheet draped over a folded single sheet and two pillows.

"No, you're not. That's no…that's not the plan." Heat rose to my cheeks at what my words implied.

"Oh, so I'm going to find out the plan? Does this involve choice number three? Please tell me more." Adrián sauntered toward me, standing much too close for the comfort of my heart and the state of my underwear.

Being around Adrián was like visiting an amusement park. Exhilarating but tummy-ache-inducing. He tucked his bottom lip behind his teeth, and I wanted to kiss him until I could suck the bottom lip into my own mouth.

Madness. That was what this was. How could he elicit so many emotions in me in less than twenty-four hours?

"No, I meant, I don't want you to have to give up your bed. That is not what I intended when I decided to stay. I don't want to put you out of your way." There, that sounded like the thirty-seven-year-old composed woman I actually was. *Girl, about damn time you showed up.*

"Mmm-hmm. I still want to know what choice three entailed. But I'm going to let that slide. Want to go have dinner at the fonda? Then we can come back and haggle about who sleeps where."

Seven

Adrián

"No need to change, the fonda is a chill place," I explained as Genevieve put down her things, then picked up a small cross bag and followed me out of the cabana. I had not been ready for the powerful impact Genevieve detonated within me when she first walked into my bedroom.

Since we met she'd always been moving fast, either planning her day, checking emails and taking calls during the mornings, or animated in discussion with me on any topic we could think of on the way back. She carried herself well, but a thread of tension lay underneath…after all, I recognized that rigidity.

That tension that crept into every second of the day when I was teetering on the ledge of burnout. For me tragedy brought me back from that ledge, but for Genevieve it seemed nothing would. That tragedy closed my chapter for my workaholic ways. The wound of losing myself and my loved ones had cicatrized, but the phantom pain still visited me at the mere touch of it. Maybe these two weeks could restore her. Maybe

I could help her with that. Be her shelter while she replenished and filled her cup again, but was there a way for me to do that without being lured into the same old tendencies she exhibited now? It was heady to meet someone so passionate about her career and how she wanted to leave a mark in the world with her work. I remember that intoxicating feeling.

Standing in my bedroom, I witnessed her slightly softening. Arms loose, shoulders down, back languid and straight. It had been a few seconds if anything, but there was an instant where she was fully present, and it rocked me. I felt the energy and the power just as strong.

The early evening gold and purple hues had crept up as she'd settled her things in my cabana. Mosquitos flew around us, and the night creatures' symphony started its crescendo as we navigated the path back to the main casita and toward the road.

"We can take the car if you want, but the walk is not far. A mile, if anything."

"That's okay, I can do that." Genevieve smiled, and my breath caught at how gorgeous she was under the fading evening light. She wore the same leggings and T-shirt from the morning, the shoulder of her dark brown skin begging for a kiss—Gen swatted that shoulder with her right hand, pulling me out of my horny, addled thoughts.

"Oh damn, did you get it?"

She pulled back to find the dead mosquito that dared mess with her.

"I did, but not gonna lie I'm losing the battle here." She grimaced as she swatted yet another mosquito. Damn. Mosquitos loved new blood.

"Sorry, I should have thought of that, they don't mess with

me much because I'm old blood. They're tired of my ass." The distraction worked; the tinkle of her laugh poured gently over me, warming me inside and out.

"I doubt that..." she murmured, then smirked.

The laughter unlocked something loose in Genevieve, and we continued the banter all the way to La Buenona. This was what we had from our rides—this easy flow of ideas, jokes, and anecdotes. By the time we reached the fonda, the night was fully settled, and the heat transformed from relentless to slightly bearable.

"So, what's the story with the name of the fonda?" Genevieve asked as we stepped up the large cement step that brought us up into the opened structure of the restaurant. The familiar mismatched chairs and tables pulled from different households of my family filled the large cement expanse with colorful plastic tablecloths. Just as I suspected, the fonda brimmed with the new tourists visiting the town, a multitude of shades of attractive Black patrons filled us past capacity and I could see where Mario must have pulled some of the plastic chairs we kept in the back for the nights where we turned the space for tamboritos and parties.

"Wow, busy night," Genevieve said, impressed with the restaurant as Chichi and Mario navigated the tight space between tables, checking in on people. A pang of guilt hit me to think I'd left my family to fend on their own, but then Claudia popped her head out of the window of the kitchen where they expedited all orders. I saw she was talking to three of my cousins and the guilt lessened, but only a little.

"I've been to several fondas, and this by far is the best decor. I love the mural and the art for the Buenona letters," Genevieve said, her face a mask of wonder as she gazed at the blue, green, and purple wall with an intricate mural of the beach and a curvy woman facing the sea. The letters were blocked, and each of them had native flowers from the area curving around the corners.

"Yeah, that's all Chichi. He's pretty talented. Also very good with graphic design," I explained, proud of my nephew as I rested my elbow on the counter and faced Genevieve. I loved that she was tall enough that I didn't need to fully bend to look down and keep eye contact with her.

"Adri, what you want tonight?" Claudia appeared in the opening, wiping her hands.

"Anything in particular you want to try?" I asked Genevieve.

"If y'all have arroz con coco y guandú, and fish escabeche, I'll be the happiest woman alive."

"It's that easy, huh?" I smirked and Genevieve flushed dark as she fiddled with the strap of her tank top. My chest tightened, and I shifted on my feet, hoping things didn't get hard below. I followed the trail of her finger, my eyes traveling up her neck, then to her lush lips. Genevieve caressed her neck, and she seemed to be caught in the same trance I was in.

"Two days, huh? I'll be surprised if you make it tonight." Claudia pursed her lips in smugness, then turned to Gen. "I have all of that honey, I gotchu. And you?"

"I'll do the same," I said as I noticed Genevieve attempting to find her footing again after Claudia's meddling comments.

"Let's go get somewhere to sit down." I offered her my palm, and she rested her hand in mine. An electric current galvanized where our fingers met. I didn't want to let her go when we reached our table, so I kept holding her. Genevieve stared at our clasped fingers, offered me a goofy grin, and that current strengthened inside me.

"I know I've been acting like a green girl today, but I guess I just haven't done this in a long time," Genevieve confessed, and I nodded in understanding.

"You don't get out much back in the States? All work and no play?"

"What makes you think that?" she said, a self-deprecating laugh escaping her. I tightened the hold of her warm hand, my heart thumping faster at her laughter.

"I had a front seat view of your everyday, at least when you're in a project. Not once did you ask me to make an extra stop or to take you somewhere else completely."

"You don't know my life. I could have been doing stuff after you dropped me off." She flicked her ponytail playfully.

"So, you saved your wild escapades for when I wasn't around. Damn, it's like that?" I clutched my chest, pretending to be wounded.

"Oh please, I wish I had them at all," she mumbled and kept toying with her ponytail. Her hair gradually grew as the day progressed, and I was curious to see how it looked without straightening. When Genevieve had her walls down, and she was fully comfortable.

"You could have asked, I'd gladly have taken you out." Damn, I hadn't meant for that to sound suggestive, but Genevieve didn't seem fazed.

"Really, you wouldn't have felt conflicted about work?"

"I would have asked another driver to keep driving you if things..." If things went the way I hoped these two weeks would go.

"Oh, but I would have hated to lose the time we had together each morning and each afternoon," Gen said.

"We would have seen each other regularly. I was too drawn to you. The truth is I don't do drives anymore. Not since we hired a few drivers. But the guy that was supposed to pick up you up that first day was sick and…" I shrugged.

"Oh, whew… I used to wake up so excited to see you in the mornings I had to temper myself by the time I stepped into the elevator. We'd just been together the night before in the car, but it felt too long," Gen confessed, pressing her palm to her cheekbone.

"We were fools." A pang of regret vibrated through me at the time lost.

"True, but hey, you made your move, and here we are." She squeezed my hand and her plump lips spread in a wide grin.

"Yeah, here we are." I let that bass from earlier really deepen. Her proximity was alluring, and I had to bite my bottom lip to keep myself from saying something out of pocket. Gen's eyes stared at my bottom lip, and her pink tongue traveled the path of her own lush bottom lip. The same way I wish I could right now. I tugged her hand, and she swayed forward, showing me more of her beautiful dark brown skin exposed by her shoulder, begging to be caressed.

"Get a room! I'll be surprised if you can get out of the fonda without jumping on each other. Damn." The group of women at the following table all busted out laughing at my loudmouthed sister's comment. There really should be a support group for aggrieved younger brothers. Claudia placed the fragrant hot plates in front of us, a pitcher of chicha and another of water.

"I was gonna get the plates."

"Really? If I'd waited for you to realize the food was ready, you'd be eating icicles instead of hot food. Enjoy, Genevieve, not for nothing, but I'm the best cook across these areas."

"Oh no, Claudia, don't be so modest; please don't hold back," I mocked and Claudia's hand popped my head. Fuck that hurt.

Genevieve's chuckles joined the laughter from the following table and I felt a spark of happiness I hadn't felt in a long time. I didn't remember feeling this bubble of positive pressure in my chest since...since before I'd made the necessary changes to save myself and my sanity.

"Listen, stop abusing your big sister role. Tell Genevieve about the name of the fonda please." I rubbed the back of my head, as Genevieve brightened at my words. She took a bite of the fish, and her eyes widened in amazement.

"Claudia, you ain't lying when you said you are the best cook here. You put your whole foot in this, girl." Genevieve took another forkful now with rice and stared back at Claudia with an impressed nod.

"My foot? Uh...well, girl, you know I try my best," Claudia said demurely, and I cackled at her act. "So, Mario, whom you saw when you walked in, has been my man since we were in high school. He used to call me La Buenona. Do you know what that means?"

"Bueno is good, right? So the good one?" Genevieve asked and then made eye contact with me and gestured for me to eat. Damn. I'd been frozen with a forkful of food midway to my mouth. This woman had me in her clutches. I took the bite, just as Gen wanted, and saw Claudia roll her eyes. The moment Claudia got me alone, I would hear her mouth about this. And it would be worth it. Being here with Genevieve was worth it.

"Yes that would be the literal translation, but what it means in Panamanian slang equates to 'The baddest one,'" Claudia said, her hand sweeping up and down her side, and she waggled her eyebrows for good measure. Just as she said that Mario popped up right behind Claudia and grabbed a handful of her hip, and planted a kiss on her cheek, making Claudia blush.

To this day, five children later and a few pounds more and fewer hairs, and they both couldn't get enough of each other. It reminded me of our parents. Nostalgia gripped as it often did when they came to mind. Genevieve slid her hand to mine and held it again with a shy smile as if to share a private secret—recognition of how special it was, what Claudia and Mario had.

"Yeah, this my woman right here, and every year she gets better and better. She is truly the baddest of them all, and I let her know every day." Mario smacked another kiss on Claudia, and she melted like putty in his hands.

"Ay, Mario, we have guests," Claudia protested, but made no move to separate herself from her husband. I could only laugh as one of the ladies from the other table hollered, "Get yours, sis!" And Claudia rested her head back on Mario's shoulder letting him kiss her on the mouth this time.

"So that is how the fonda was named La Buenona, and the reason for my five nieces and nephews," I finished telling Genevieve.

"Hey, compa, thanks again for the help with Turito's house. His roof was in bad shape, but with that money you put in the b—"

"You know we good, Mario. That's not my money," I said,

uncomfortable with the topic switch. The family and fellow neighbors never ceased to thank me for the money I'd invested into our little town after things went still with my career, after hurting myself and my family. It had been the best decision I'd made in my life. The decision took me from being part of such an amazing project like the Tropics back to rags. I might not have much now, but together Aguimar was better. And I got to spend time with my family and work on my business in the city with Julín. Finally, keeping a healthy balance.

Genevieve's intense curiosity prodded me, asking to explain more, but this wasn't a topic that was easy for me. Not yet. And that was a reminder of why getting into anything serious with a woman wasn't right yet. Not until I could deal with all my guilt and my demons.

Eight

Genevieve

The walk back to Adrián's cabana carried a different quality than the walk to the fonda. My confidence had increasingly returned as I spent more time with Adrián. He had grown uncharacteristically quiet at the end of our meal, but I coaxed him out of his silence with jokes about my last dates, which sadly had been a long time ago. After a while, Adrián was right back with me, bantering and laughing.

Now we held hands under the moonlight, and I couldn't remember the last time I felt so blissful. No recent date could compare to this, to how open I already felt with Adrián. I could do this for days, weeks, discovering more about him and about myself, as well. Maybe I could extend my time here, taking three weeks wouldn't be so bad—Lissette's commanding voice filtered through me: *"Never lose track of the finish line."*

No. No more thoughts of my mom, or anything but living in the moment. That I could do, I was in the best company.

"Sorry for shutting down on you there at the end of the

dinner. It's just…seeing Claudia and Mario reminds me of my parents. They passed away two years ago. Around this same time."

"I'm so sorry, Adrián. I can't imagine the loss you feel right now." I tangled my arm with Adrián's, bringing our bodies closer together, our hands clasped and fingers intertwined. The night's heat had settled to a warm breeze, and Adrián's cologne and his closeness tempted my composure. It was so easy to be with him when we talked and hung out, but the moment my desire reared its head it came with a nervous excitement I didn't know how to handle. The soft earth and grass muffled our steps as we went off-path taking a different route than before. Soon we were barefoot on the sand, ambling toward two lounge seats directly outside Adrián's cabin.

Warm low lights illuminated the back sides of the family area, providing enough light to navigate. I refused to show the near pitch dark spooked me. Once we lay on the two beach chairs, with the moon's reflection on the churning waters in front of us, all fear dissipated. The stars twinkled bright from our vantage point, live art only for the two of us. Adrián reached out and grasped my hand again. Thank God for the semidarkness because he'd caught me cheesing.

"Tell me about your parents," I asked, ghosting my thumb on top of his.

"They were the best parents anyone could have. I know, I know, it sounds a bit cliché, but it's true. They owned this little hostel here. Before the renovation, it was just five little cabanas, and the main casita was our house. They never had all five rooms full unless it was carnival season, and even then, they sometimes dropped their rates to get people in. This was the type of spot that was very hard to find if you didn't know about it."

"Damn, I can imagine, a little outside of the city but so far away simultaneously."

"Yeah, well they were always struggling financially, but Claudia and I never knew the struggles. I mean, we knew we were poor, but hey, everyone in Aguimar is poor. And we lived in paradise. My parents were always around. My mom helped us with homework, and my dad played ball with us and showed us how to plant a new crop around the perimeter of the property. Every day it was an adventure with them, but we were safe and loved. Their last years… I wasn't as present as I'd liked."

"Mmm, it's hard when we grow older, we go and experience our own lives. I get it. I mean, I wish I could sometimes have some space from my mom." I chuckled trying to chase away the anxiety that crept up at the thought of Mom. I hadn't checked my text messages, but I was certain she'd probably sent a few pointed ones about her thoughts on this escapade.

"You're not close with your mom?" Adrián asked, picking up on my change of tone. Oh, that was lovely. Outside of Gino, I wasn't sure I knew of men being so in tune as Adrián. Having that connection intertwined with our attraction increased the intensity of every word, of each of Adrián's gestures. With Adrián, his perceptiveness sparked tingles in my fingers, and warmth in my chest. And don't get me started with the pulsing between my legs.

How? How was this man making me think with my private parts instead of my head? We were talking about my mother and I ended up lusting after him.

"We are…we are. But our relationship is…she is my mentor, guiding light, and support…and sometimes I'm her biggest disappointment." I shrugged, letting the waves crashing against the sand cover up the pain behind my last words.

"Seems to me like every parent I've ever known," Adrián said. He got it was a sore subject. Based on what he'd just said about his parents, he was trying to be nice; I hated platitudes but again Adrián seemed to be in a league of his own, and I melted by his gentleness.

"Yeah, well, imagine that being your only parent. My dad… he's not much of a dad." That was the kindest way I could describe my sperm donor. As a child I loved his spirit. He was the exciting parent, the one to take me on adventures. But my mother? She was the solid one. The one that made sure food was on the table, and a roof over our heads. I was so thankful that I recognized the family dynamic for what it was in my earlier years, even if I sometimes yearned for the type of carefree energy my father brought to the two of us. "My mom… she's that type of person that can do it all. She's mentored so many Black professionals, especially women. Whenever people find out I'm her daughter it's this 'ohh, aww' moment. You know how parents usually complain about being called 'so and so's mom?' Well, I'm Lissette Raymond's daughter. And I'm so proud to be her daughter, I am, but it's like I'm always striving to break the next glass ceiling."

Saying all of this out loud conveyed way more than I had planned to share. After seeing Adrián with his family, my own relationship with mom felt sterile. No, no, no. No more overanalyzing. More being in the moment.

Adrián sat in his lounge chair, legs relaxed, hands behind his head, his face a mask of serenity. His tongue slid out to moisten his bottom lip, and I held back a groan. He couldn't be aware of how sexy he was. There was no way.

Suddenly we were too far apart. Possessed by Hot Girl Genevieve, I stood up, and changed seats, joining Adrián in his beach chair. I lined up my head close to his chest, my legs tangling with his to ensure we both fit on the seat.

"I was thinking maybe we can cuddle?" I asked once settled.

"I promised you, you'd have the time of your life. If cuddling is what you want. Cuddling is what you get," Adrián said, welcoming me in his arms. Anytime we held hands or hugged, my nerves decreased. My awkwardness receded. I tested the theory now and relaxed my body next to Adrián's, his rich woodsy cologne welcoming me. I laid my head on his chest, and we both sighed, content.

"When I invited you to come with me, I never dreamed I'd lie with you on the same chair on the first night," he confessed.

"Well, I didn't think I'd sleep in the same bed with you."

Adrián's even breath stopped under my ear, and I propped my head to stare at him. To bask in his charm and beauty. His rich beard and pouty lips were the first things I focused on. His proud broad nose seemed to be doing double duty. Might he be feeling what I was feeling? Then his sultry deep brown gaze hit me square in my lower parts.

"If I lie next to you tonight, there will be no sleeping involved," he warned.

That's when I noticed the hardness growing against my hip. I liked how he said that as a statement—a promise.

"Who said I need sleep?" I whispered, ghosting a hand over Adrián's stomach, luxuriating on the ridges of his carved abs. The smooth skin right where his shirt met his pants made my fingers tingle. I caressed him there, making his breath hitch. He had that sexy V, and I pressed there, discovering that Adrián was ticklish.

He barked a laugh that turned into a grunt as I continued my travels, fingers shaking as I traversed the planes of his skin under the shirt. Hot flesh enticed me to follow until I reached one nipple and pinched it. Adrián's groan awakened a recklessness I'd only experienced last night when slightly intoxicated in his company. And this morning when Hot Girl Gen appeared.

"Woman! You haven't even kissed me, and you're tweaking my nipples."

Laughter fizzled out until I was in stitches. Adrián's sturdy arms held me close as he shook with his own laughter. I burrowed, closer, loving how delicious his rumble journeyed through my body.

"I was waiting for you to kiss me," I finally managed to get out between giggles as our laughs subsided.

"Were you, huh?" Adrián's deep brown heavy gaze fired me up in the dim light, and the touch of his golden-bronze skin felt like smooth velvet under the moonlight. His plump, juicy lips were slightly parted as if they divined what was coming. The slopes and dips of his compact arms flexed as if he struggled not to squeeze me, and a rush of liquid confidence settled in my panties.

"Yes. I was," I whispered.

"I needed to be sure you were ready."

The congregation of our lips felt like a burst of pure energy settling into its perfect flow. Inexplicable and spectacular. Air departed my lungs with no signs of return. I'd always scoffed at the idea of being breathless after a kiss, but Adrián

Nicolas hadn't kissed me back then. Now I understood what I'd been missing all along.

When Adrián slowed down our kiss, I whimpered, a deep yearning driving my every movement.

"Wait, wait. Let me take you inside. I want to see you properly," Adrián whispered as I frantically pulled at any piece of fabric available. I needed him, and I needed him now.

"Okay, okay," I reluctantly agreed, watching Adrián stand and offer his hand to pull me up. My legs were unsteady, the force of my desire so inexplicable. It had crashed into me, consuming all my thoughts. Again, Adrián uncovered sides of me I wasn't aware existed.

"Steady…you know what?" Adrián's large bulk came on glorious display as he pushed me into him, hooking his arms under my legs. Air and his arms were the only things underneath me, as my chest pumped fast, adrenaline taking over. Adrián carried me from the beach chairs to the back of his cabana. Still desperate for more of him, I pressed my lips on his neck, making him shiver.

"If you keep that going, I'll have to fuck you right here outside," Adrián's voice rumbled, and I wanted this giddy sensation he created to last forever. With impressive strength, he slid the door one-handed, his large warm hand planted firmly under my ass. I was no wilting flower. I was all flesh, bones, and Sunday soul dinners, and carrying me here was no small feat. And this man managed to make me feel full of helium.

Adrián tossed me on the bed, the softness of the mattress cushioning my fall. Adrián's predatory glint made me scramble back until I met the headboard. Things were about to get real.

"Are you sure you want this?" Adrián asked, and he cupped the length currently printed on his board shorts. Did he even realize what he had asked and what he'd done simultaneously? Because I had and…damn!

"I, well, yes." The awkward shyness tried to sneak into my brain. Nooo, I needed my brazenness back.

"It's okay. I can sleep on my sofa bed." Adrián's face shifted to tenderness, and I wanted that heated gaze on me again. I craved it. Chasing the high before it dissipated, I pulled my shirt and tank top off, throwing them on the floor, then I hooked my fingers on my leggings, bringing them and my underwear down.

Adrián paused midstride and his languid contemplation flickered from the top of my head down to my pinky toe and ended on my face.

"Everything I dreamed and more," he whispered, and my heart short-circuited.

He dropped his board shorts and divested himself of his tank top with equal expediency, uncovering more and more of his beautiful golden-brown skin, then stalked toward me with his heavy dick bobbing with each step, until he ended next to the bed. I couldn't help the gasp that escaped, and I crossed my legs.

Now *that's* what you bring to the table, but could I withstand such a gift?

Adrián chuckled and cupped himself, then ran his hand over his length again.

"Go ahead, touch it. You know you want to." He taunted me, and I couldn't believe his brazenness. Even better, I couldn't believe how much I loved it.

With a dry mouth and trembling fingers, I hovered over his belly button, eliciting a groan from him. Warm, smooth flesh greeted me, and everything in me clenched as Adrián bobbed heavily in front of me. Attempting to alleviate my dry mouth, I licked my bottom lip.

Adrián's desperate growl resounded in the room, startling me out of my lust-induced trance, and before I knew it, he bent over and captured my lips again, proving how wrong I was about the effects of a once-in-a-lifetime kiss.

Adrián's beautiful body weighed me gently down on the mattress, his cologne enveloping me, and I shivered as his warm chest met mine, as our waists aligned together, and as his hand skated down between my legs to discover me wet and open for him.

"I wanted to take my time with you, but... I..."

This time I stole the kiss as his hands wandered all over my body, his fingers awakening something foreign and wondrous in me. I didn't know it could be like this. I hadn't known.

"I... How experienced are you?" he asked into my lips and I stiffened at the question.

"What do you mean?"

"I want to ensure I don't go to the deep end too fast. Is there anything you don't like doing?" What did he mean by that? Was there a long list of things that could be done, and should I know what to remove? I'd had flings and relationships in the past, but it was always similar experiences. I had a limited point of reference.

"Oh, well, just the regular stuff, you know. The regular stuff is just fine."

Again, the rumble of his laughter made me high with endorphins, and the feel of his skin against mine grounded me. All it took was for us to be touching, and everything felt right.

"Okay, we will do the regular stuff for now..." He smirked and pressed his brawny frame over mine. I ogled as he touched himself, again wondering how I'd make this work, but I was determined to go down trying.

"Okay…" *Regular stuff?*

"I have condoms, and I tested after my last person, do—"

"It's alright I'm on birth control, and as we have established, this is not something I do all the time, not since my last test. I'm…good without condoms if you are, okay?" I attempted to hide my face, but he didn't let me.

"Okay, look at me, look at me, Preciosa. I know you're nervous, but I promise I will make you feel good. I'm alright without condoms only if you are truly okay. Remember, best time of your life."

Why did we have to talk so much? I needed him, even though I was way over my head with Adrián, but he silenced my thoughts when his hardness slid inside my core, and for the third time tonight, my breath seized in my lungs.

"Breathe, breathe," Adrián coached me. Fuck, he stretched me so good. I took a breath, relaxing around his length. Already I felt full of him, his dangerous strokes shallow but oh so delicious.

Every time I thought he'd bottom out he gave another inch until I was panting, eyes closed, lost in the pleasure of Adrián's body over mine. We'd been dancing the whole day straight to this inevitable end. An outburst of quivers spread through me, and even then I widened my legs to receive all of Adrián.

"Don't close your eyes. Stay with me, Genevieve," Adrián ordered, and I moaned as he finally bottomed out.

Our gazes locked, Adrián's heated one promising untold pleasure and ecstasy.

And then he proceeded to deliver.

His relentless but measured strokes drove me higher and

higher. I writhed under Adrián, helpless to let him take over with his punishing pace. His stroke was perfection, his pubic bone hitting against mine, stimulating my clitoris for enhanced sensation.

"You feel so good, Preciosa…estás que chorreas. So fucking wet," Adrián murmured in my ear, and damn, he activated the next level in my lust for him. I lifted my legs, wrapping them around Adrián's hips, forcing a deep hiss out of him.

The move opened me up more to him, and his angle shifted slightly; soon, he was pressing against a bundle of pure pleasure. Every thrust galvanized me, and Adrián's rhythm started losing any rhyme or reason as we both approached the end.

"Stay with me, Preciosa. I want you to come first," Adrián urged, his stunning face twisted in pure concentration. His arms tensed up, and he swooped down to kiss me. Vibrations erupted inside me, from where we met to my chest, and the slip and slide of our tongues was the final nudge I needed to fall over the cliff.

"I…yes…yes," I moaned as pure unadulterated ecstasy wracked through me. Chasing his loss of control, I grounded my hips against Adrián, the scent of sex and wet sheets overpowering in the room. Adrián came with a roar that shook the sliding door glass as he pulsed inside of me. The force of his orgasm caused me to come again, and I floated away in a cloud of desire, letting all the hang-ups of the day be gone.

Nine

Adrián

The following days with Genevieve were a feast to my intellect and my senses. The first morning, things threatened to get awkward again. I planted my hardness against Genevieve's back, loving the softness that nestled my length, and talked to her about mundane topics until she relaxed against me, her beautiful brown skin glowing under the early morning rays.

Whatever lay between us, we navigated it better when our skins touched, and we chatted about any topic. Once I figured out the code to keeping Genevieve comfortable, our days became some of the best of my life.

Gen with her walls down was a taste of the finest whiskey. When deep in her sensuality, it was a shot straight to the head. When she opened about her journey, the struggles and the triumphs, the fears and the dreams, she went down like the best smoky old-fashioned. And when she bantered and laughed, when we stayed up late at night talking as if we had been in each other's life for years, she refreshed me like two fingers on the rocks, after a long hot day.

I shared more of my current life, opening up more than I had planned on. The specter of the depth of our connection through our common project, of how we were more alike than different loomed in the back of my mind. I didn't want to add any stress to her stay with me. Work had no space in this retreat for her. And, being honest with myself, sharing with her my connection to the Tropics would have me opening to share way more than I was ready to give.

Healing had not been linear for me, and self-forgiveness of my transgressions still felt out of reach. Sharing my mistake and the deepest regret of my life filled me with dread.

She'd been at Aguimar for a week and had settled in nicely to the beach town life. This morning we planned to go to the shore early and then take a hike around the town. Most of the previous days had been spent tangled up in my bed, as we talked and sexed the day away.

I sat against the headboard, watching Gen walk around the room, holding her bathing suit and moisturizing her body before slipping on the white bikini. I couldn't help staring; her internal beauty translated to how stunning she was outside; the way her curves settled beneath the white bikini had me conspiring on ways to get her in bed again.

"So, you haven't lived with a man?" I asked instead, not wanting to appear too thirsty, following the thread of a conversation we'd started last night before I got lost inside of her.

"No, I have had boyfriends, you know that, but living with someone...never. I mean my mom and then on my own. I haven't found that person," she said as she bent over to rub sunscreen on her thighs, exposing the beauty that lay between her legs.

"Are you trying to distract me?" I grunted.

"What?" she looked back, the view of her even better now that I could see her gorgeous face. Her hair was a cloud of coils around her face. She'd finally let go of her silk press and had allowed her natural hair out, and I enjoyed playing with her strands during our nights together. Of course, I'd asked for her permission first; I hadn't been trying to get smacked by touching her crown. She smirked, then turned around and continued her ablutions.

"Why were you asking me about living with a man?"

"Nah, you just seem to be very comfortable here with me, on my spot. I was just surprised."

Genevieve giggled and covered her mouth, trying to hide her smile.

"Are you making fun of me? What did I say? Did I mess up something?"

"You're good." She smiled again. I was intrigued now.

"No, you're gonna have to tell me."

"Well, I think it's adorable how you have such perfect English but mess up some little things. I'm not trying to make fun. It's just adorable for some reason."

"I'll show you adorable," I grumbled but was pacified when she strolled over to me and pressed an indulgent kiss on my lips. Immediately I ignited, the response to her ingrained in every atom of my body. Her tongue slid languorously between my lips, and I skated my hands past her lavish flanks, down her plentiful hips then grabbed a handful of her generous ass, squeezing it for good measure. She pushed away breathlessly and beamed at my obvious discomfort—the minx.

"Honestly, I'm surprised too, that I feel so comfortable. I'd been so nervous the first day. I thought it would be hard, but... you've made it easy, I guess. Everything with you is just... easy." She stood up, continuing our conversation while I tried to keep up, her gorgeous ebony skin gleaming and moisturized as she put on her bathing suit. The idea of plotting a way of keeping her in bed for a little longer resurfaced, but she'd been adamant last night that my dick and food were no longer enough to keep her entertained, no matter my scintillating conversation and bedroom skills.

Besides, I needed to help a bit more than what I'd been doing around the hostel these past few days. I'd been present whenever Claudia had texted me for assistance but not really proactive with my support. It was hard to ignore the guilt roiling in my gut; Claudia and Mario had assured me they were happy to man the fort while I got some. No respect.

"It's been easy for me too. I... I told you I had had some partners that I cohabitated with, but something always made it difficult to navigate. I think the view you offer is the best selling point."

Laughter escaped as I witnessed the mock outrage on Genevieve's face. But in the back of my mind, I wondered if it was easy with Genevieve because I'd gone out of my way to make it so. I'd put my best foot forward and she, in turn, had done the same. Maybe it was easy because we both wanted it to be.

"Are you planning on getting out of bed and joining me on the beach?" She pressed her hand on her hip, and I loved that she had grown comfortable showing me some of her sass.

"Yeah, I am, but I need to check in with Claudia first to do some morning rounds with the kids helping with some of the housekeeping."

"Are you sure you don't want my help? Nothing I haven't done before," she asked, and I immediately shot down her idea.

"No, you're here to relax and replenish. Claudia would kill me if I brought you over."

"Okay, well, find me on the beach. And you better find me if y'all need help. I'll see you later?" She approached the bed and bent over to give me another kiss, and I took full advantage, pulling her entirely on top of me, my body awakening to her spicy, flowery scent as she laughed and squirmed over me.

"Stop trying to trick me into staying."

"Is it working?"

"Maybe." She pressed one more soft, open-mouthed kiss on me, and I savored her spicy peppermint taste. Gen attempted to detangle herself, but I made sure to make it as hard as possible, holding on to whatever soft curves I could. My hand overflowed with her curves, and I gave her a tight squeeze for good measure.

"Stop! You're a mess!" She separated herself, looking disheveled with one nipple peeking out from one bikini cup and her bikini bottom tucked into one side of her behind.

"I think between the two of us…" I gestured at her, my lower half throbbing in need, as she fixed her bathing suit and threw a cover-up on.

"Bye, sir!"

A cold shower fixed the growing tension Genevieve left behind, and a hot cup of coffee prepared me for the work ahead.

I found Claudia, Mario, the kids, and a couple of the townspeople that worked with them on housekeeping day all gathered in the back of the house cabana, where we stored all the cleaning supplies. Claudia drilled everyone with the steps to follow in cleaning up the cabanas. We divided ourselves into small groups; I got Yiya's helpful company.

The cleaning of my assigned cabana was quick, and the guests in the room were very neat overall. In less than an hour, Yiya and I were back in the house area, where I bumped into Mario and Claudia, who were making out in the corner of the cabana.

"Yiya, go find Mirna, she is cabana #3," I directed her; she just rolled her eyes at her parents and ran away whistling.

"So y'all put me to work, and both of you're here exchanging body fluids?"

Claudia flashed me a finger, and not her ring one, then managed to part from Mario.

"Listen, you have had plenty of time to do the nasty with your guest. We weren't complaining. It was your turn to take one for the team." Claudia shrugged, and I wondered why I ever bothered to try to be right. Claudia's accuracy for pushing my buttons was legendary. All through the week I'd worried about slacking around the hostel. I hadn't pulled my weight and even though she had assured me all was well, I now worried I should have done more.

"Listen I can work for the rest of the day, y'all go somewhere, I don't know... Spend some quality time."

"Que? No! Why would we do that—you have your friend here for a few more days. Besides, anytime you're here you're working, it's okay to relax a bit, you know? I swear you think you took a step back but you still work too much. Relax, hermanito. Enjoy your guest."

The pang of alarm at her implication, that I was still working hard, made me want to push back on her assertions. I took days off. I had learned my lesson, but I had a responsibility to my family. We all needed to pull our weight and Claudia did so much…the least I could do was give her some respite when I was here. I was about to push back but Claudia's fists had moved to her hips and Mario was doing his "now you fucked it up" face. There was no winning with Claudia when she got in this mindset.

"Fine. Yiya and I finished the room. I'll check on the casita, then go to hang out with Gen for the rest of the day."

"Mmm-hmm, see, Mario, I told you these two would end up attached to the hip. I just had a feeling." Claudia raised her eyebrow at Mario, and Mario, dutiful, clever husband that he was, nodded along, sighing in relief at the change of subject,

"I never hid I was attracted to her." I followed along, shrugging as if what I felt for Gen could be easily described with such a benign word. Attraction waved three bus stops behind, and the next stop ahead, longing, awaited my arrival. Better to pretend, because Gen and I had no future together. I'd known this from the first day I picked her up. She was going to be at the top of a very tall ladder someday, and I was happiest here around my people.

"No, you didn't, but to be honest, I know I was all for it, but now I'm a little worried. What happens when she leaves?"

My stomach knotted at Claudia's question, one I'd asked myself several times these past seven days even knowing all I knew.

"Nothing happens. I just keep focusing on living my life."

Claudia's question lingered in the back of my mind, and I took my time before going to Gen. I didn't want to give too much color to the thought of saying goodbye. Every time I imagined it, my brain short-circuited, and nothing but pure static filled my mind.

Attempting to ignore the dread of parting ways, I changed into my board shorts, staying shirtless, and searched for her.

Warm sand cushioned my feet as I approached the family's beachside, away from the guests. Genevieve sat in the middle of the cream sand, close to the water, her stillness reaching me from afar. The crashes of the waves lured me closer to her, the pull inevitable.

Announcing my presence, I ghosted my hand on her smooth shoulder, dark and luminescent under the sun; then I trailed my fingers across the elegant line of her neck. Genevieve trembled at my touch, and my heart slammed around my chest. Damn, less than a month ago, I wasn't interested in any romantic entanglements, and now...

"Hey, you." Gen finally turned her head; her eyes flickered over me.

"You were so still I thought you had no idea I was here."

"Of course, I knew you were here." She smiled and stared at the beach again, a deep sigh wracking her body.

Regardless of my concerns and fears, the only thing to do right now was to hold her close. I sat behind her, gathering her in my arms, and for the first time in the day, things felt entirely right again.

"I missed you, Preciosa," I whispered in her ear, her sweet and spicy scent so intoxicating.

"We were apart less than three hours."

"Too long," I complained.

"Are you pouting?" She turned her head again to stare at me. I took advantage and pressed a chaste kiss on her lips.

Even that soft touch heated my entire being, but I could sense things weren't completely right with Genevieve.

"What's wrong? I thought we were supposed to be having fun today."

"Yeah...well, my mom called me."

"What did she say?"

"She was guilting me about taking time off again... These last days have been magical, but now that I'm halfway through it, anxiety is kicking in. I even checked my work emails," she confessed.

"I thought you said you couldn't check them when on PTO?"

"In theory, I can't, but I know a hack to get them still."

I chuckled at her honesty, but, at the same time, understood her anxiety. Once upon a time, this had been me, unable to fully immerse myself in the present, always working, mind always racing. I'd seen that same drive in her stillness and how she held herself; that relaxation dissipated, leaving a tentativeness I wanted desperately to erase. She had tried so hard to be in the moment this week, her intentionality had been alluring. Whenever work came up, she'd deftly steered the conversation to her aspirations, but not in a way that could cause her to spiral back into her worries. Anything I could do to keep her in that mind frame, to help her disconnect and rejuvenate had become my main priority.

"You know those emails will be there, right?"

"Yeah, I do... I just don't remember the last time I've been this disconnected from my everyday responsibilities."

"Maybe that's something good?" I didn't dare hope for too much, but I wanted to be that space for her, even if for two weeks, her refuge and place of calm. Being with Genevieve had me second-guessing all the doubts I'd had in the past year about being whole to love someone else. She made me want to try.

"Yeah, I thought so, and I was in my feelings, still am, I can't lie. But I decided to get back to focusing in the moment. I want to be present here with you. So I'm going to—"

Before she finished the sentence, I stood up. Only seven days, and already she trusted me to follow my lead without much explanation. I held her warm waist where the sexy folds of hers met and hoisted her to a standing position.

"Adrián! What are you doing?" she shrieked as I pulled her up by the waist, her solid weight feeling like that perfect dead lift in the gym.

"Come, Preciosa, you're over here stressing yourself, and you still have seven days left. I promised you the time of your life."

"Put me down! I'm heavy. You're gonna hurt yourself."

I ignored her pleas, the cold splash of water trickling between my feet, sinking me into the wet sand as the waves pulled back to where they came from. The sun bore down on us, making the cold water feel delightful.

"I could carry you to the end of the earth, Genevieve. Never doubt that." I tightened my hold on her as she squirmed, the water line surrounding me as I moved into the churning waters.

Once the water was waist-high, I dropped Gen into the sea, still holding on to one of her arms, keeping her close.

Genevieve emerged spluttering, her coils escaping from her ponytail and plastering on her face. She never looked more lovely as she growled inhumanly and lunged to tackle me.

"Damn, woman, you have some force," I managed to choke

out between laughter as I scrubbed my face clean of the salty water, enjoying the view of Genevieve in her white bikini, ready to play.

"Oh, you think you're slick, huh?" Genevieve taunted, then launched at me again, the shrieks of excited laughter a melody I never wanted to forget.

Water splashed around us, pure happiness saturating every pore. The summer heat was no match to the raised temperature between Genevieve and me as our slick bodies rubbed against each other, activating my dopamine and giving me a high that lasted the whole day.

A high to mask all the ways I'd hurt when Genevieve was gone.

Ten

Genevieve

"So, this is Costa Arriba, right?" I asked Adrián while we drove along the coastline approaching Portobelo, a town close to his own Aguimar.

"Yeah, all these little towns both on Costa Abajo and Costa Arriba meet the Caribbean Sea. Portobelo was the second try for a settlement to connect the Spanish commerce route from the Atlantic to the Pacific."

We drove slowly; the sun lazily woke up on the horizon, tinging the land with a golden hue that made everything seem otherworldly. I focused on the striking contrast of beauty and poverty surrounding the area—so much potential for the development of tourism to inject into an area of need. I couldn't miss that most of the people awake before the sun, walking to their jobs and duties, were Black, and the whole province was filled with people like me, attempting to live their best lives in an area riddled with potential and neglect.

"Why is this area not developed more? There is so much

beauty, the coastline is pristine, and with some heavy sanita-
tion, you could—"

"I get the instinct of wanting to make this more touristy,
to inject money into it, to bring in foreigners. There is much
history this area has to offer, but how to avoid advancements
from displacing the people that have lived here for centuries?"

I pondered his question, not having a proper answer to it.
He wasn't wrong; gentrification affected us the most wherever we went. But God, there must be a way, a way for us who
had some means to explore beautiful areas like this to inject
directly into the economy of the little towns without disrupt-
ing the culture and the very foundation here.

"It's what happened in other areas in the country…and the
money never goes to those that need it the most. Much could
be done, but I've yet to see projects like what you're thinking
of not displace the people that live here. Close to here was one
of the first, if not the first, settlements of free Black enslaved
people in the continent, we deserve for that to be preserved."

"For real? That is amazing! When did it happen?"

"Damn, now you're putting me in the spot."

I smiled at his mixed prepositions, and he pinched my hip,
making me jump.

"My mama loved to tell us that story. It was told to her by
many before her. A lot of our history has been preserved orally
in these areas. It might not be in history books, though many
are now attempting to discover things we long knew. If my
memory doesn't fail me, it was 1579."

A sensation of rightness went through me as Adrián became animated, explaining to me the story of this area and
his people.

"See, my dad comes from West Indian descent, whereas

my mom comes from Maroon descent from the people that rebelled and raided the Camino Real taking Spaniards' merchandise and money to help free even more enslaved African descendants. Once they were granted the freedom that was always theirs, they built what we call palenques."

"I've read about those remote settlements of free Black people, right?"

"Yeah. Here let's park and walk around a bit."

Adrián found parking on the side of the road, in front of a small fonda, and ran around the front of the car, opening the door for me before I even attempted to reach for the handle. I didn't realize they still made men like Adrián so gentlemanly and polite. He didn't need to do this anymore but still managed to do this little gesture, and every time it warmed my heart. I stepped out of the vehicle and took in the smell of brine and seafood that permeated the area. Small houses and structures of different sizes sprouted along the coastline beside the narrow main road. Everyone made their way to their spots of business and merchandise stands.

"Mama's great-grandma was born in that house, and always led a simple life." He pointed to a red house with ornamental brick-styled windows, the square footage probably not larger than my bedroom in Florida. "Same as my grandmother, then my parents. Then I came, and well, I wanted more, but life has a way of humbling you, and now I love being here. What do you see in your future, Genevieve?"

This trip made me see things I'd never realized were possible. My mind raced to answer the question most truthfully, even though something inside of me made me want to say something different. Wish for something different.

"I want to be the president of my company. Be the youngest Black professional to reach those ranks."

Adrián turned to me and gave me an earnest, sad smile that caused a flash of shame to go through me. There wasn't anything wrong with my dream, was there? The smile Adrián gave me mimicked some of the looks I'd seen in the mirror in the mornings when I practiced a presentation or got ready for a long day of meetings, but then I walked into the office and a surge of energy would fill me, reminding me of what I loved about my career. Wanting to be the president of a company I believed in was a dream that I deserved to pursue without wondering what other opportunities I left on the table, because of the grueling responsibilities of this path. What other experiences I would never have because of the dedication required for my goal. I had decided, and I had to be content with my choice. I *was* content with my choice.

"What else do you want besides the career goal, which by the way, is something I know you will achieve." I didn't need his approval, but I couldn't help the glow at his certainty.

"I...a long time ago, I thought I'd find a partner to share my life with, to do the fun, silly stuff. Wake up on Sundays and drive by the coastline..."

"Like we're doing today," he said with that rumbling, deep voice that always made me think of warm cups of coffee in the morning.

"Like we're doing today. Go sightseeing to new places, discover things about where I lived that I didn't know, and just constantly be surprised. Go out to dance...even though the ancestors played me with all the rhythm but not many skills," I said, not minding sharing this with him. Only Gino knew about these other dreams, and I had stopped reminding him so he wouldn't berate me left and right about giving up on them. But I was a realist. The more I moved up in the ranks the more I realized the time and bandwidth required to stay at that level. Life wasn't fair, nor did I believe in the infamous work-life balance. It was a mirage to keep us believing we could achieve it all.

"All you said sounds like a dream worth fighting for," he said, and the intensity of his gaze singed my skin. I avoided his stare, unable to withstand the heartfelt regard Adrián deployed when I least expected it. I was never ready and seldom said the right thing.

Children ran around a basketball court smiling as two men danced dressed in clothes with colorful tattered rags.

"Who's that?" I asked Adrián as we strolled side by side, and he gently slid his hand into mine, holding it warmly as he guided me across the road. A pool of simmering desire rested in my center, always ready to boil whenever near him. A simple hold of hands and I wanted to start writing my first name next to his last name and list our children's names right below it. I wanted to write his name in every song lyric I loved. It was truly sickening.

"Those are Congos. Many of the people that live in the area, descendants of Maroons, are Congos. They are what I call the living, breathing ambassadors of our culture, our past struggles, and a reminder of all we have accomplished."

"Oh, so they are not just performers?" I asked as we stood side by side in the open space, seeing their dance moves, intrigued; and the music they played from a boom box next to them seemed to be straight from the depths of the sea, a beautiful calling.

"Oh no. They are way more than that. Some people perform Congo dances that aren't Congo, but they don't know half of what being Congo truly means. Right now, we're in what is called Congo season, and during this time, they have rituals and games, for lack of a better word, that re-create many of the ways of the past for the Maroons in this area."

"Damn, there is so much culture here," I said happily, and he squeezed my hand, a tingle running through me at the mere gesture.

"There is so much rich, undiscovered culture wherever we Black people live, don't you think?"

"Yeah, my mom is very 'let's assimilate to survive,' but one thing she always taught me is that we don't share all the recipes outside of us, you know? I guess what you say about the Congos sounds like that." It was awe-inspiring, how our ancestry seemed connected in a way that I wouldn't have understood before without Adrián's stewardship. No matter where we were, where we grew up, the similarities in our diaspora upbringings were much more than the differences.

"Yeah, that sounds about right. Come, let's find you something to eat. I've noticed you're a bear when I don't feed you and get you caffeine early in the morning."

"Excuse me, Señor Adrián. I wasn't the one with the growling stomach yesterday after the second morning sheet tangle."

We laughed our way to the small fonda by the shore, sitting down on the only table behind the fonda with a view to the sea. The Atlantic churned irately, and it promised to be a rough sea day. The owner was an older lady with a weathered smile and hips that told me the food would be delicious, and what seemed to be her adult son sang along to some Spanish song while serving us both hot coffees.

The man was beautiful, with a twinkle in his eyes as he

placed the cups before us. Adrián's attention remained on me, but I saw the admiring glint he'd directed to the retreating man. Mmmhey, I couldn't fault him; the man was empirically attractive.

"So, you always have your coffee black?" Adrián asked me after taking a sip from the whitest cup of coffee I'd ever seen in my life.

"Yeah, always. I sometimes cut it with a bit of almond or oat milk, but most of the time, I need it black, and I need it strong. Gets me going during my long days. So what should I order?" We had started to play this game, and based on what Adrián observed I liked these past few days, he had been recommending meals to try.

"Mmm, today you should ask for the bistec encebollado and tortillas."

"Alright, sounds like a plan. But hold up, isn't encebollado with onions?"

"Yeah." He sipped his milky concoction and sighed in excitement.

"So, will you still give me kisses even after I have my breakfast?" I asked boldly, surprising myself. These glimpses of Hot Girl Gen came here and there around him, but lately, more and more.

"Gen, onions will never stop me from wanting to taste your lips."

"Good to know." I winked at him.

"Would you still kiss me after I finish my cup of milk coffee?" he asked with an impressive rise of his eyebrow.

"See now, why are we taking things so far? I mean...if you like that drink you call coffee, I love it, but—" He sprang from his chair and pressed his luscious lips on mine before

I could even laugh, and I sighed in contentment, tasting the sweet milky coffee drink on his tongue knowing I'd always want more of him.

Always.

Eleven

Genevieve

Everyone has dreams. Dreams of the perfect vacation, the perfect day, the most wonderful weather, the greatest connection with someone, back-blowing sex. Somehow all of this had happened to me in the past thirteen days. And I planned to walk away from all of it tomorrow.

The only thing I could do was ignore the pressure on my chest since last night when I started packing my clothes while Adrián sat on his sofa, his eyes tracking my every move. The quality of the silence between us had matured in the past two weeks from the awkward, nervous type to the "I still want to know all about you, but I'm okay just staring at you right now" type.

Now I sat here trying to capture the highlights of the visit in a notebook I'd bought on the trip we'd made to Portobelo from a street vendor who had offered it. I'd loved the intricate art on the cover. A deep need had awakened in me these past days. Instead of wanting to check my emails, I jotted down moments of the experience that I sought to remember, the feel of walking on the ruins of Portobelo while Adrián explained the history of the port from the appropriator Christopher Columbus to the pirate attack from Sir Francis Drake. The connection that stirred in me when seeing the Panamanian Congos dance in Palenque, their colorful dresses waiving under the sea breeze as women and men undulated their bodies to the rhythm of the handcrafted drums. Adrián attempted to explain more of their world vision, how the matriarchal culture had grown as a mix of Maroons protecting themselves in this area, marrying their West African roots with ways to mock their Spanish oppressors and their religion, creating full new and rich traditions.

In between that, my hospitality brain refused to shut down, and I wrote down observations of what would be ideal for a Black traveler like me to experience. I'd never use it, but who knew, if Tropics decided to do any developments on this side of the country, I would be well equipped to set up a manual for the hotel's concierges. I probably should share some of these notes with Anita for her team whenever they made recommendations to travelers coming to the area for day trips.

Adrián had gone out for an hour to assist in setting up La Buenona for a party tonight, where they would bid a fond farewell to the excursion group that had arrived at the same time as I had. I offered my help as always but was shot down not only by Adrián but by Claudia, as well.

Lost in my musings, my heart leaped to my throat as I noticed Adrián hovering over me with a smirk on his face.

"I love that you've been journaling your trip," he said and sauntered toward the bathroom. Thank God, he gave me time to think because a shirtless Adrián was still a shock to my senses. He emerged out of the restroom with a T-shirt on and his face still wet.

"What are we doing today?" I asked him, ready for whatever adventure he had planned.

"I thought a hike around the area, then I wanted to show you a special spot for me…" Adrián's earnest gaze made me wonder what this spot was about.

"By special spot, are you showing me your sex place or something?"

Adrián's face morphed into shock, then he vibrated in silent laughter as I sat there perplexed at what was so funny. I mean, I had meant it as a joke, but it wasn't that good.

"Better I show you than to explain."

"Oh, I'm…wow, I'm so sorry. I was just joking earlier. I didn't…truly." I was babbling, but what was a woman to do when the man you'd been consorting with in sexual relations for two weeks brought you to their parents' final resting place?

We stood in the middle of a clearing, about fifteen minutes away from Villa Bonita. Low grass covered most of the ground, and palm trees and wildflowers sprouted around haphazardly but with a calm beauty that lured you to breathe in and take the day.

There were wood benches across the clearing, and Adrián sat on one, still, eyes closed as I took in the beauty of the spot.

"Come sit next to me." He patted the space beside him without opening his eyes. I sat and studied his features. His beautiful long eyelashes rested on his golden-brown skin, reddened by the walk here. I wanted to run my hands over his soft hair, longer on the top with its sexy fade. I wanted to snuggle into him and ask him if he thought we could make it past these two weeks. I'd wanted to ask that question, knowing deep down it wouldn't make sense. We both had very clear paths we were following, and I couldn't see them converging.

"We each have a bench here. We carved our names in the benches that sit around their graves. When they passed… When they passed, I promised myself I wouldn't fail my family any more. I'd been so far from them, only available on very special occasions, always busy in the city. I'd send money… thinking that would make up for my lack of time, chasing that next step in my bourgeoning career…then…then they were gone. My rocks. They were gone, and I had no time left. No step left to climb. No money in the world would bring them back…"

"So you moved back home," I asked, not wanting to prod too much. I figured the career was in hospitality, which was demanding as hell, or even transportation, but who cared? In the end, it was about how Adrián had felt. His gaze was shuttered, and the deep wound was clear as day to me. I wouldn't push when my time with him grew short, but I wondered, would I have wanted more? Would I have expected him to open up and bare his soul to me if we had a future? All questions that didn't require answers because our time was running out.

"I did. I rented a little efficiency in the city because of my transportation business. But this is home."

Any thoughts of bringing up a long-distance relationship shriveled in the wind as Adrián explained his deep connection with Aguimar. I'd seen it when we walked together around Villa Bonita or the town; people always came to him, like the de facto mayor. His easygoing nature, quiet assurance, and natural leadership worked like a magnet on all the inhabitants of Aguimar. And I hadn't missed how more than a few people shot me daggers after longingly staring at him when they thought no one was paying attention.

"I understand…" I whispered into the breeze as the warm air caressed the hair away from my face, snuffing away the small flame of hope that had simmered inside for days.

"You make me want things," Adrián said, anguish tingeing his words.

"You make me want things too, but I get it. Let's just enjoy today to the fullest. I'm very rarely able to be as present as I've been here with you these past few days. I don't want to spend my last day wallowing," I said, hiding the fact that I'd probably wallow for days after this. Adrián slid his warm hand into mine, and as always with us, I immediately felt lifted and grounded simultaneously; such an odd contrast but perfect for me.

Adrián seemed perfect for me, and I still would walk away because how could he be the perfect man for me if I had to put my life on hold for him?

We returned to his cabana in silence, the long walk necessary to dispel the sense of helplessness that surrounded us.

"I didn't take you there to make you sad," Adrián said as we stepped into his space. I walked in front of him, seeking the privacy of the bathroom, if only for a few minutes. I was feeling bruised and needed some alone time.

"Why did you take me there, then?" I asked, not turning back to look at him.

"Because I wanted you to meet them, even if…"

The hope and sadness in his voice made me turn around, and my feet acted on their own accord. I crashed into him, our lips meeting in desperation. His taste galvanized me, and

I rubbed my body into his, needy for his warmth and weight. Tomorrow, I wouldn't have this anymore. Tomorrow, I'd be on a plane back to reality, but today, today, this beautiful man was mine, and I meant to enjoy it.

Magic was at play as we pulled each other's clothes off, the actions so easy we were naked in minutes, him on top of me, sprawled on his bed. The brush of his warm nipples against my breasts ignited a whole-body shiver, and his growls in my ear amped up my desperation.

"Always so rushed, I had wanted to take my time with you. Show you how it could be between us…" He groaned as we lined up, and his length glided over my clitoris, my wetness making the move so easy. I didn't know why he was trying to torment me with drags of his shaft against my bundle of nerves. I needed him inside of me in the same way I needed water and air. When he slid between my folds, I jerked up, searching for the fullness only he could give me.

"Take it all, Preciosa. Take me in," he groaned, and I wished his command was true. I wished I could take him all in. I moaned as Adrián's strokes grew in speed, the slick sound of our bodies threatening to visit me on my lonely days ahead.

"Oh, Adrián, I… I…" Whatever temporary frenzy overcame me had me imagining things, wanting to spill all my hidden secrets, making me wonder if my career and my goals were not enough anymore. If only I had dared to dream differently, but none of it was viable. I had a career not only because I wanted it, but because I needed it. Who would I be if I dropped everything for love? My livelihood and my pride would not allow such idealistic musings.

"Stay with me, Genevieve," Adrián grunted and did something with his hips and my eyes rolled up to my head. A deep reverberation emanated from within, where his flesh seduced mine with relentless strokes meant to disarm me. He didn't have to ask me twice. I was fully with him, my orgasm so spectacular that tears gathered in my eyes as my throbbing became full shudders, taking Adrián away with me.

Tears continued to fall as our skins cooled down under the ceiling fan, and I wondered if the tears were not just for how good we came together, but how devastating it would be to be apart.

"This is the town celebration to thank the Americans that came to give us patronage," Adrián explained as we stepped into La Buenona. The merry old girl had gone from shabby dive to an equally ragged nightclub with wooden benches with no backs scattered around tall tables, citronella lanterns around the perimeter of the cement area, and two huge speakers flanking the mural. The kitchen window had become a bar, and Chichi and Mario manned the drinks orders from the patrons.

The Americans—even I'd started calling them that, as if I was a local—were all hanging out in different clusters, the buzz of excitement and slight intoxication evident in the balmy night. Four of the townsmen gathered on one corner of the area pulling out the handcrafted drums of different sizes I'd come to recognize as the drums used for Congo music and tambores. The wooden bodies painted black and white, with hemp holding them together, the dried cattle skin stretched taut on the top of the drums to give them their sonorous quality.

Mario turned off the boom box, and I saw Claudia and other women from the town stand close to the drums. They

had T-shirts and blouses on, and colorful wide skirts for dancing on top of their pants. An older lady whom I'd met in my
walks, Doña Petronila, was seated on a chair with arms, and
she was in full Congo dress, with wildflowers threaded in her
milky-white hair.

That sense of rightness, communion, and kindred experiences ran through me again as Adrián found a seat for me
close to the drums. He squeezed my hand and then walked
toward the group standing next to some men, clapping their
backs and smiling.

Doña Petronila opened her mouth, and a rasping but powerful voice emerged. A cappella, she started singing, then the
drums kicked in, and my blood surged as the women next to
Doña responded to her call with force, clapping at the rhythm
of the drums. The song seemed older than time; the drumbeats
had a sensual cadence that invited the hips to move.

Chichi came out of the bar and approached a young lady
who shyly smiled, then went out to the center of the circle
created by the men on one side and the women on the other
with the drums at the top of the open circle. Her hips and
waist undulated under the song and Chichi shuffled his feet,
his body easily swaying in a similar syncopated sensual move
that I would be hard-pressed to imitate. Every time Chichi
approached the lady she twirled away in a low circle, her beautiful skirt swinging in the air.

The patrons all started clapping at the beat of the drums,
same as the claps of the townswomen singing with Doña
Petronila. My hands matched the claps. I couldn't understand
the song, but it was lovely all the same, and I found myself
humming the response, imitating the words as close as I could
understand them. Different men and women approached the

center of the circle, each couple taking their moment to shine, bringing a new flair.

My heart skipped when Adrián came out, his hips moving with such grace and force, reminding me of how well he moved and surged inside of me earlier. He had no shoes on, the same as other dancers who had taken theirs off, as well. He danced all the way to where I was and I froze, uncertain of what it all meant. Was I supposed to dance with him? I wasn't sure I was ready.

"Dance with me, Preciosa," Adrián whispered, and even though the drums were loud I heard him perfectly.

Hot Girl Gen came to the rescue again. I took off my sandals, stood up, and followed Adrián to the middle of the circle. The excursion guests started whooping and hollering as the drummers beat their instruments even faster, their dexterity and talent impressive. My heart hammered in my chest as I tried to follow the movements I'd seen the other women do—the maxi dress I had on a poor substitute for the beautiful skirts.

I didn't fully understand what to do, but I had noticed the women seemed to lure the men; then, when the men tried to get close to kissing, the women either raised their hand, turned, or danced away. So, with that in mind, I tried to do the same.

Adrián's predatory smirk tempted me as I gestured him to come closer, and Claudia shrieked a high-pitched "yeeeee," nodding along in encouragement. My entire body became one with the music, and even though I wasn't the best dancer, I was giving it my all, my hips and waist moving along the beat of the claps and drums. I grinned with Adrián, his joy contagious, both of us ecstatic to have these last moments together.

This last night together.

When he approached me with intention, my chest tightened, and I froze, missing the beat. My limbs decided to stop moving without my permission. Adrián's scent greeted me, his body heat singed me as his warm lips crashed into mine. The whole party went up in a roar as we pressed together, I threw my hands around his neck, and we let ourselves be taken away by our passion and the beautiful night in Aguimar.

Twelve

Adrián

Without opening my eyes, I knew she was gone. No need for my legs to search for hers, for my hands to feel the coldness of her pillow, fragrant with her scent. I only required the quiet emptiness in my chest, the knots of my stomach, and the ache in my soul to tell me the truth.

Even though every sign of her departure mocked me as I hastily put my clothes on, I refused to accept the truth. What if the empty drawers I offered her to put her intimates away haunted me while I looked for my underwear, or the sad clink of my toothbrush in the holder that used to host two reminded me of how happy we'd been these two weeks?

I refused to accept the truth.

Even when I ran out to find Claudia's eyes full of sad sympathy and a hint of pity, I refused to accept the truth.

"Did she leave? I… I need to talk to her, she…"

"Se fue. Mario and Chichi took her to the airport." Claudia rested her hand on my shoulder.

"Damn it. I just wanted to…say…"

"I know. I know."

Claudia embraced me, attempting to erase the truth that I was finally compelled to accept. Accept the screaming in the back of my head, and the sorrow that had captured me even before falling asleep last night. That my days with Genevieve were a thing of the past. That all I had left were her memories. That she did not want anything else from me anymore.

Thirteen

Genevieve

Starlike particles illuminated the air around me, the edges of the room soft and blurry, the feel of my body cloudlike as Adrián's slick body surged on top of mine, the wet heat just what I needed to soothe my already lonely heart. His golden-brown skin glistened under the moonlight as he pounded into me right there on the lounge chair outside of his room.

Just when I was getting ready to come, Adrián's body shifted. The starlike particles coalesced together creating beams of light. My heart raced, and I fought the restraints around me.

What was tangled around me?

Adrián's hot flesh dissolved in the balmy air. The heat morphed into a sticky cold as I thrashed and turned in bed, waking up from another dream. Or was it a nightmare? My heart disintegrated as I fought to stay in the dream, stay close to him, the memory of his woodsy scent lingering in the air, the last vestige of Adrián abandoning me to my reality.

Fuck, not again.

For three weeks, I'd been dreaming of Adrián and our last time together.

Our last night.

After dancing in La Buenona, everything seemed to happen in a fog of desire and yearning. We drank with Claudia and Mario, chatted with the ladies staying at Villa Bonita, and danced some more. Made out like no one was watching. We made our way back to his cabin in a fit of laughter and heavy-handed petting and kisses; we ended up naked outside his cabana under the moonlight, making passionate love.

I burrowed into my bed now, hoping for sleep to catch me again, to escape into the dreamland where Adrián waited for me. At this point, I wondered if he was haunting me.

I'd asked Adrián for a clean break; he'd reluctantly agreed. Why would I want to stay in touch with the only man in my life who had made me second-guess my plans? I understood what he and I had was unique, but Adrián had a life and a family to support, and I had my own responsibilities. Never had I second-guessed a decision more than I did that night. How could I leave him after everything we had shared together? I'd opened up with him, shared so many fears and dreams, things only Gino knew. The ease of it all, of being with him in paradise, had convinced me if only for a few days, that my life could be different. That I could have this.

But reality had a way of never wavering, of reminding you to stay grounded. And at the end, that is who I was, grounded, determined, goal oriented. Remembering that, what was at stake for me in Florida, I decided keeping the lines of communication open with Adrián would be a mistake. It would be a reminder of a time where I allowed myself to dream too big, reach too far.

So that early morning, I kissed him while asleep, secure in the knowledge I had erased his number from my cell phone, and the same in his phone the night before, then asked Mario and Chichi to drive me to Panamá. They chatted it up all the way to the Tocumen Airport while pretending they couldn't hear the sorry sniffles in the back of Adrián's old SUV.

The sniffles became my best friend for the days to come. Pretending everything was well at work had never been harder. Expecting my knack to compartmentalize to kick in, then finding out I'd lost the ability because of Adrián's absence was a heavy blow. Everything made me think of him, emails from Tropics Panamá reminded me of his pickups and drop-offs.

I started following the *Black Travel Chronicles* accounts where I saw pictures of the last night in Aguimar, of the colorful polleras waving in the night air. In one of the pictures, I spotted Adrián's smiling face, so full of love for his people; I had to turn off the phone, and seriously considered removing my social media apps for a few weeks. Anything to remove the taste of his lips from my mouth, and the feel of his skin against mine. The sense of comfort I felt with him and the wonder lingered on, refusing to depart.

Giving up on any sleep, I changed into my workout clothes and went to my treadmill. After twenty-five minutes, at an obscenely high incline and a speed that required me to wear my hair up in a ponytail today and slick down my edges, I hopped into the shower to get myself ready for the day.

Two hours later, I was sitting in front of my computer, shocked at the email I'd just received.

"I see by your opened mouth you just read the good news." Anibal strolled into my office holding two cups of coffee, looking dapper with one of his bespoke suits, the black fabric accentuating his warm complexion, his soft curls sleeked back, and that megawatt smile that had me considering re-whitening my teeth.

"You knew?"

"Here, drink your congratulatory coffee, future VP of LATAM and the Caribbean." He handed me my cup. My chest tightened, and my shoulders lifted at his words. Words that confirmed what I had just read. The president of operations, Jan Ricard, had invited me to a meeting this afternoon, essentially calling it an informal interview. However, the email stated they wanted to offer me the position. They'd just opened it three days ago, and I thought I'd have to fight for it, but here I was, bursting a ceiling sooner than expected.

"Am I really going to get it?"

"Yes. You deserve it, and I couldn't say much in Panamá, but Ricard had already told me it was almost a done deal. That's why Anita, with her sharp tongue, needs to learn how to…"

"Mmm-hmm. Careful," I harrumphed. I loved Anibal, but he had a few things that irked me sometimes. His weird animosity for Anita, who now would report to me, was one of them.

"What? I haven't said anything." He picked imaginary lint off his suit. Another thing that irked me. He was amazing, always treating me like a partner, always collaborative, but he remained aloof. Never fully opening up. Not that I was an open book, but since returning from Aguimar, I realized a lot of my relationships were more transactional in nature. It was interesting to see usually aloof Anibal flustered by someone. Flustered by Anita.

"Aha, you let nothing bother you...until Anita appeared in your life."

"That makes her sound like a rash." Anibal ran his hand through his curls, and one of them popped up, escaping the sleek hold.

"You know I'ma rat you out, right?" I said, relaxing the way I only could do with him and a few other colleagues in the office.

"Please don't. I'll be your counterpart as I have in Florida, Georgia, and the Carolinas, and I really don't wanna be fighting with her if I have to cover for you."

"Well then, stop antagonizing her. That will fix your problems." I smiled and sipped my coffee, enjoying riling my usually unflappable boss, soon-to-be colleague.

"I stopped by to congratulate you, and here you are, annoying me. I'ma leave."

"Okay, bossy boss."

"Another reason to celebrate, for you to stop calling me that nickname. Oh, your promotion is not effective till next week, so I'ma need that report of the next quarterly forecast for the Tropics Panamá on my desk by Friday."

"Anibal, you're thirty-nine years old, not a hundred. Can you stop talking about reports being on your desk...you know I'll send that electronically. Why are you so annoying?"

"Because I can be. Later." Anibal walked out, and I stared at his back, happy for his support and rolling my eyes at his antics.

Two hours later, I sat across from Jan Ricard, a fifty-year-old mestizo Latin woman with a kind smile, wearing a designer suit that probably would have me eating bread and drinking water for weeks. Her shrewd eyes studied me while I assessed the woman who had taken the company from middle-of-the-road results to the streak of growth we'd had in the past five years. She was a legend in these hallways. Ricard offered me the VP job, giving me a speech about her expectations.

"Thank so much, Ricard, I really look forward to a great partnership. I'm honored to have the position."

Ricard waved my comments away, her bejeweled hand the only eccentricity in the otherwise composed woman.

"You deserve it. And it's too few of us in C-suite positions. Once I retire to a remote beach town in Honduras, I want someone as driven and talented as me to take over. I'm all about the long game."

Her words sparked a hunger in me that had been dormant since I'd returned from Panamá. This was what I had been working for. This was what I wanted. I'd lost track of it in talks of relaxation and recharging, on moping around for a future that wasn't mine, but now that I had accomplished this, I could focus back on what really mattered—the next step in my career.

Right here, Ricard was the best example of why I needed to continue on. She had managed to move up the ladder, and she was planning to bring me up too. That was the only way we women could succeed. Images of Ricard leaving the office last and arriving the earliest filtered through my excitement reminding me of what would come for me. I'd never been afraid of hard work, but with my already meager social life, how would I manage with fewer hours outside of the office?

"But enough about my plans for world domination. We want to continue to foster organic but strategic growth in the area, inviting talented locals to helm each hotel. The main focus for you is expansion. We're seeing great results from Tropics Panamá and Tropics Roatan.

"I want us to add five more hotels in the Central America area by the end of 2027. We have interested real estate owners already. They are willing to be presented locations with similar profit margins to what we see in Panamá. This will be the focus for you, outside of driving results in the region. We want a project as talked about and as exhilarating as Tropics Panamá with a history behind it. Those design features in Panamá have become one of the main drivers outside of the destination itself."

"Absolutely, this sounds similar to my thoughts. The area is vastly underappreciated, and there is great potential for sustainable growth. My vision is to continue to partner with locals and bring economic impact, not to flow out of the areas but into them."

"See, you get the mission. Fantastic. You start on Monday. Your office will move here to the thirty-fourth floor, and you'll get your bonus package, and benefits will drastically change. Mick will provide you with the package by end of the day today, and you can review the offer. I need an answer by Friday. Does that work for you?"

A bubble of excitement threatened to burst out of me at the news. I wanted to whoop and holler. Instead, I flashed my teeth in a poised smile.

"Yes. I can give you an answer first thing tomorrow morning after I review the package in detail," I said with fabricated calm.

"Fantastic. I look forward to seeing you flourish, Genevieve."

I glided out of Ricard's office, transported in my personal

cloud. Who should I call first? I definitely wanted to text Gino; he was probably in mediation right now but would be available soon for lunch. Mom was the obvious choice, but instinctually, the first face that flashed into my mind, was the same one that haunted my dreams and my nights.

"Cheers to you, my friend. You gonna kill it!" Gino said over the bustle of the Korean restaurant that had just made a splash a few weeks ago. It was equidistant from my office and Gino's law firm, the perfect location to celebrate. I hadn't been able to break for lunch, so we decided to meet for dinner instead. I'd reviewed the package in detail and, after hesitating, had sent it to my mom. She'd already sent me bullet points for negotiation, all things I had planned to ask for anyway. Maybe it was time for me to start flying solo, but how disrespectful would that be to her?

"Thanks, babe!" I clicked my Moët glass with Gino. I'd panicked when he had ordered the bottle, but then I remembered I had some wiggle room out of my debts with this new move.

"So, are you gonna negotiate the pieces your mom recommended?"

"Yeah, it makes sense. I'm asking for $10K more than the original offer. I think Ricard would think less of me if I didn't. I also plan to ask for reimbursement for dry cleaning because it's one of the most annoying bills I pay per month. And for them to cover my Wi-Fi at home because you know I'll be working late nights," I said, digging into my spicy beef bibimbap, the umami flavor saturating my palette. Anything not to encounter Gino's disapproving face. Anything to shut up that little voice that told me working late nights wasn't the flex I thought it would be. Insidious thoughts that had no space on a day of celebration.

"Girl, I wish you wouldn't. I'm very happy for you, but I know you'll just work twice as hard, longer hours, and I'll never get to take you out for ladies' night at Kiki's on Thursdays."

"When was the last time I went to Kiki's for ladies' night?" I asked him while taking a sip of the Moët.

"Twenty-fourteen."

"Exactly, the chances were always slim to none."

"Old lady."

"Take it back!"

"I won't. So, are you gonna tell me now what is bothering you about all of this?"

I sighed. Gino knew me too well. I was excited, I truly was, but he wasn't wrong. A lot more pressure and work loomed in my near future, and I always met additional tasks by barreling forward. The thing was, I had been barreling forward for years now. And I'd been able to tell Gino, and Mom, but I wanted to celebrate with the one person that was out of reach.

"Damn, that sigh was deep. What is it, honey?"

"I want to call Adrián."

"Mmmm." Gino kept his face down into his own bibimbap.

"What was that?"

"You deleted his phone number like a sixteen-year-old. Now here we are."

"Yeah. That was a rash decision, but I didn't want to be tempted to reach out, when he was clear there was no future, when I was clear of the same."

"So, you can't even be friends?"

"Remember Joey D from Ms. Ramirez's Spanish class?"

"Yeah, it was everything or nothing. That dude broke my heart. I get it, okay. But, babe, life is too short. You're about to go into overworking mode. Wouldn't it be nice to have your sexy, tall, hunky friend to chat with here and there?"

"Okay yeah, but…how do I reach him now?"

Gino whipped out his cell phone with a flair, and started typing, then flashed his phone on my face, gesturing me to hold it. My heart skipped a whole stanza.

"Go ahead, send the email. This is the business mailbox for the transportation company."

Suddenly my hunger disappeared and the bibimbap decided to start a party in my stomach. My heartbeats were audible, and I tried to pretend I was okay.

"Oh wow, you're down bad," he said.

"I'm no— Yes. Yes, I am. I dream about him nightly."

"Email him, Gen."

"Okay. I will."

And with Gino's help I typed an email reaching out to Adrián, my fingers shaking the entire way.

Fourteen

Adrián

The bang of dominoes on wood startled me out of my thoughts.

"He's gone again," Shakira said and bumped me with her foot as I sat beside her at the square domino table, my hand swimming in my eyes. I couldn't make sense of the game or what to play next.

"Julín, can you sit in for me?" I stood up, and everyone groaned in annoyance. I had warned them I wasn't good company earlier tonight when Julín came through with Shakira, practically dragging me out of the efficiency to come to Shakira's house to hang out and play. I hadn't wanted to leave my spot, even considering getting in the car and hitting the road to Colón to spend the weekend with my family, but Shakira wisely convinced me to stay put. The drive at night not the wisest choice with how my head was right now.

Julín walked by me, grumbling, and sat at my open spot, quickly assessing my hand and banging his chip to continue the play.

The game flowed while the guys and Shakira continued joking. I couldn't be bothered. I had carried a void inside since Genevieve left five weeks ago. That night before, when she told me she was going to erase my phone number, then grabbed my cell phone and did the same, I almost tackled her and kissed away her sadness, begged her to stay. I didn't have much to offer a woman like her. She wasn't wealthy, but she was determined and had carved out a comfortable life for herself in a country full of comforts. I wouldn't be able to offer her that same quality of life she had in Florida, and we both knew it.

So here I was, moping around, sitting on the porch of one of my oldest friends, as I suspected I'd let the woman of my life slip out of my fingers due to pure life circumstances.

"I won!" Shakira whooped, and the guys grumbled their annoyance. Julín said a few choice words and pushed back the chair to get a beer out of the cooler. Shakira came to me, with her bright smile, tanned brown skin glowing, her long braided ponytail swinging back and forth, and Tito and Fufo stayed at the table arranging the dominos.

"So, are you gonna continue to bring the room down?" Shakira offered me a cold Atlas, sat on the bench, and clicked her bottle with mine.

"So supportive."

"This is me giving you support. You've been a shell of yourself for five weeks. The aunties have been asking where you have been every Sunday for the cookouts," Shakira said, referring to her mother and aunts who sold Afro-Antillean food on Sundays. "Julín and I kidnapped you today in an attempt to cheer you up, but I can see we failed."

"Well, I have a lot on my mind."

"Okay, dark and mysterious. I know you like that girl you were driving around. Julín told me."

"Julín thinks he knows all my life."

"Listen, he told me what Claudia told him, and it seems you were pretty sweet on the lady. There is nothing wrong with accepting that. What I don't understand is how in the era of the internet, cell phones, and cameras, you haven't stayed in touch with her."

Shakira had a way of worming her way into the heart of any topic, and I didn't have the energy to spar with her tonight.

"I don't have her phone number. And she doesn't have mine."

Fufo and Tito guffawed at the domino table, entangled in their own one-on-one game, while Julín hovered, watching them play and offering some commentary. On this bench, though, silence reigned.

"So, after spending more than four months driving her and then two intimate weeks together, you both forgot to exchange numbers?"

"No, we had each other's numbers, but she asked to erase them because we both knew we had no future together." A bullshit ask if I had any say, but I wasn't a man to push my attentions on anyone closed to them. But maybe I should have said more, opened up about how much I would miss her, of how she made me hope…

"And…why is that?" she asked in the same tone I imagined she used with her kindergarten students when they did something incredibly outrageous.

"Mira, why are you on me right now, Shakira? I have nothing to give." I shrugged and gulped down my beer.

"What are y'all talking about?" Julín approached, leaving our two friends embroiled in a third domino match.

"Julín, you're looking especially dapper today with those white shorts and blue shirt. They really do make your pretty deep brown skin glow," Shakira cooed.

"Thanks, querida," Julín said and pulled a bench to sit across from them and clinked his bottle against hers.

"Ya'll so queer," I said, laughing.

"You're so queer," she said back, laughing. I was so glad I had my circle of friends who got me and understood me, but right now, I didn't need them to understand me this much.

"What? Is he doing his whole 'I don't wanna talk' thing?" Julín asked.

"You know it," Shakira said, shaking her head.

"Damn. Can I go home now?" I said, annoyed and feeling loved all the way.

"No. Let's figure out how to contact her. Didn't she introduce you to the GM at the Tropics?" Shakira asked.

"She did."

"Okay then, let's see if we can go there on Monday and ask her if she is down to help contact her. I mean, it's been five weeks, and you just work, work out, and eat. Hopefully, you shower…" Shakira said in a wishful tone, and I refused to engage.

"Are y'all trying to contact that woman?" Julín asked.

"Yes," Shakira said.

"No," I said.

"Yes, you are. You're miserable," Shakira insisted.

"Well…" Julín dragged that well a little too suspiciously. My senses heightened at his lack of eye contact.

"Oh shit," Shakira mumbled.

"What did you do, Julín?" I asked, dreading the answer.

"Well, we got this email…" Julín said.

"When?" both Shakira and I asked at the same time.

"Two weeks ago."

"Oh shit," Shakira murmured. My stomach plummeted at the thought of letting two weeks pass on a potential reach out from Gen.

"Yeah, two weeks ago, we got an email from Genevieve asking for your contact information for personal reasons."

"Did you respond?"

"I…might have."

Thanks for reaching out to LasDell. Currently, we are not able to provide Adrián Nicolas's information. I will make sure to share this email at some moment with him.

Kindly,

Julín Ridell

"Share this email at some moment? When is that moment?" I asked Julín, breathing hard as I imagined Genevieve waiting for my response, realizing it wouldn't come. Fuck. A sense of possibility rose around me at the mere thought of Gen reaching out. Was she as miserable as I was?

"Julín…why would you do that?" Shakira asked.

"You were distraught when she left. You told us there is no future. I was trying to spare you." Julín shrugged, then gave me a contrite look.

"That wasn't for you to decide," I told him, wanting to punch something, anything. If this had cost me…

"Just write back to her, explain you didn't see the email." Shakira jolted me out of my defeatist thoughts.

"You right, but fuck, what do I say?"

"What were you planning to say before Julín told us about this email?"

I miss you, Gen. Every morning without you is lonelier than the one before.

"I was just going to ask her how things were going." Both Shakira and Julín gave me a skeptical stare, then Julín offered to get us all more beers. He knew he'd fucked up big-time.

"I know you say he's not into you, but he acts like he is," Shakira said the instant Julín walked away.

"No, he doesn't. It's not that," I replied, tired of needing to have this conversation with my loved ones.

"Then what is it?"

"Can we focus on the email?" I redirected her attention, and just as expected, she clapped, ready to brainstorm.

"Yes! Let's do it."

She grabbed my phone and popped in Gen's address.

"You know, you could have written to her social media…"

"Nah, you know I don't have social media. That's some stalkerish stuff."

"So, you didn't look her up?" Her eyebrow rose, impressed.

"I might have used Chichi's accounts," I confessed.

Most of her pictures had been of her and her friend Gino in different happy hours, sometimes outdoors. She was an occasional poster, months with no updates until she had a new picture. I couldn't see her stories because then she'd have known I was sleuthing, but she was more consistent there. I wonder if it was snippets of her life, or inspirational quotes about achievement. Knowing Gen, the latter.

"So just slightly stalkerish?" She busted out laughing.

"You know what, I'll email her on my own."

"Nooo, don't leave!" she said between giggles.

Shakira negotiated and pleaded as I said goodbye to Fufo, Tito, then found Julín hiding in the kitchen and said bye to him too. Shakira finally accepted I was leaving with a heavy sigh and a hug for encouragement.

Once I got back into my efficiency, I closed the door behind me and plopped on the bed, a spark of hope flickering inside.

I pulled out my phone again and stared at the screen, Gen's email flashing on the top. What would I accomplish by emailing her? Honestly, all the things I shared with her while still here were present in the back of my mind. My family, Villa Bonita, LasDell Transportation, my people. But the yearning for Genevieve became like an open gap in my heart that didn't allow me to concentrate.

For once, after two years, I would do something solely for me.

I typed the email and went to bed.

I slept like a rock.

Fifteen

Genevieve

Genevieve,

Writing this email should have scared the crap out of me, but it was the easiest email I have written in a while. I just found out tonight you had reached out via the transportation company, asking for my information. Here is my email, my cell phone, and the landline of the main house where I stay, just in case. I cannot wait to talk to you. You've been in my thoughts, almost haunting me, to be honest. I wasn't ready to say goodbye. I don't think I'll ever be.

"Gen, how many times do I have to call out your name?" my mom asked as we sat around the table in her backyard. It was Sunday morning after services, and a few of Mom's mentees and I were having brunch with her. Mom sat regally at the head of the table, her brown skin free of wrinkles, her pixie cut straight, and sideswept. Yellow church dress crisp.

Basically, hashtag goals for any Black woman wanting to look good in her sixties. Watching her, I thought of my father and our similarities because the only things I had from my mom were my nose and lips.

I wish I was home, in my huge T-shirt and slippers, binge-watching Netflix while rereading Adrián's email. Instead, I was technically working.

The Black Women in Power Association was Mom's brainchild. She had fostered the careers of many successful Black women during these brunches and one-on-one meetings. Once I started moving up the ranks in hospitality, I'd become the de facto vice president. My Sundays consisted of service in the morning, followed by two- to three-hour brunches spent strategizing different career moves and initiatives and overall being in communion with like-minded women.

"Sorry, Mom, I have a lot on my mind."

"Of course, you do. I completely understand. That promotion entails a lot of new responsibilities," Mom agreed. I forwent correcting her. She was still riding the high of my promotion, reminding anyone of it several times in conversation. I disregarded my embarrassment and smiled at my mom's smug nod to the rest of the table.

"So, is there anything project-wise you need strategizing?" Mom asked, and Johana Bride leaned in over her plate of shrimp salad and quiche.

"Mmm, not right now…" I said, aware that Johana worked with a rival hospitality conglomerate; both of us were very cautious about specifics when speaking about our positions but had a cordial relationship overall. Didn't stop each of us from attempting a leg up from any intel we could gather in these brunches.

"I heard you're all looking to expand in Central America. Smart move. It's an untapped market, there is some uncertainty in part of the region, but Costa Rica and Panamá are smart moves. That is where we're planning to expand next. I've been tasked with finding A.D. Nicholson, the architect for the Tropics in Panamá, for our next project. Such an intriguing story."

I nodded, shocked Johana was in such a chatty mood.

"Oh, I'm sharing because it's a shot in the dark. The real plans of course, I wouldn't mention here," Johana said when she discovered my skeptical expression.

"Oh, I see because I was going to suggest not to hang up your dreams in finding him. I heard of the elusive A.D. Nicholson while working on the project. The rising star pulled out of the architect game before peaking," I explained to the ladies.

"Oh, so why is he so talked about?" Mom asked.

"His most talked about project, and the largest one he worked on before leaving his firm, was the Tropics," Johana explained, nodding at me. I remember being shocked when told the story. Who left their career before reaping the benefits of their success? I had admired Nicholson's work, the structural design touches that spoke to Panamá's known mix of cultures, and many people were lauding his final and only major project.

"True, he did a wonderful job; his practicality, sustainability, and cultural touches made an impact in the community over there and internationally. There is talk about the building getting nominated to the Worldwide Architecture Awards for the hotel category."

"Hmm...interesting," Mom said. Damn. This wouldn't be the end of this topic.

★ ★ ★

"You should try to find that Nicholson guy. Would be a win for your first six months and a leg up against Johana's company." Mom rinsed the last platter and handed it to me to load the dishwasher. The house she bought once she made president of her financial company was gorgeous. It wasn't huge, three-bedroom only, but the neighborhood was very exclusive, and she'd gotten to design everything inside. The decor was a mix of cottagecore and Big Momma's house. A little crowded for my taste, but she loved it.

"No. That's not my plan. My plan is to work with people on the ground in Panamá, maybe tap into a college or two, and see if we can work with young architects. I really want these projects to inject economic impact directly in the hands of people that need it the most."

"You're a VP of Operations, not a philanthropist. Don't lose your focus."

I sighed, speeding up the cleaning process, ready to be on my way. I'd debated between emailing back or calling and wasn't certain what to do.

"I won't, Mom. It aligns with the culture of my company. Trust me," I said with slight chastisement, and Mom whirled about to stare at me incredulously.

"So, you think you know better than I do now?" Outrage. An effective tool in Lissette's arsenal.

"I didn't say that, Mom."

"Mmm-hmm." Mom kept cleaning up and left me standing there, feeling exhausted. I had just started my new position five weeks ago, and the overwhelming excitement had morphed into a determined push.

The drive left me depleted by the end of the week, and this

conversation with my mother was one too many on a week of negotiations and strategizing. I wished that sometimes visiting Mom was just that, a visit, and not an extension of the work I did every day. I understood her need for focus, for structure. Once upon a time, she had the opportunity to be more carefree, but having to be the responsible parent compared to my dad's blasé approach had taken its toll. She'd chosen me, and given me a stable home, and I would forever be grateful.

"I'm going to head out, Mom. See you Tuesday for dinner?"

"Yes. Thanks for coming with me, it will be very beneficial for you too. The financial association has great connections with all industries, you never know," she said, never able to shut her networking brain off, reminding me of the finance dinner she had asked for me to attend with her. Ask was a soft way to describe what Lissette had demanded. And what Lissette wanted, she got.

The drive home was short, and the time from walking through the door to me sitting on my sofa, wearing sweatpants and eating ice cream, was worthy of a world record.

My cell phone burned a hole in my lap, the innocuous device the reason why I was binge-watching beach romance movies and stuffing my face with frozen, flavored lactose. I could call Adrián. I could call him right now. He might answer, or he might be on the road, busy. But I could call, and then the ball would return to his court.

What about this man made me act like a teenager in love for the first time? The cold ice cream rolled down my throat, soothing the intense heat at the thought of Adrián naked on his bed, sheets covering his plump ass, tangled between his thighs as I walked away from him. The temptation to go back to bed and let the plane leave without me had been so strong. But recklessness had never been comfortable for me.

Recklessness wasn't welcome in the Raymond household. Follow your head, and your heart will be satisfied—another motto of Lissette.

Fuck that.

I put down the ice cream and picked up the phone. A cold tingle that had nothing to do with the sweet concoction settled in my belly and made me feel more alive than I had in weeks.

Not since the last night with Adrián.

The phone rang two times, then his euphonious voice greeted me.

"Hello, Preciosa. I'm so happy you called," he said, and I sank back on the sofa, basking in the joy of speaking to him again.

"Me too. I was nervous, but..."

"I was nervous too, that you wouldn't call me," he said, and I could hear the noise of cars beeping behind him.

"Why would you think that? I emailed you first." I twirled a strand of my hair on my finger.

"Well, you left me that morning. I thought I had more time, but I woke up and..."

"I couldn't say goodbye. I just..." I trailed off and shrugged, unable to explain how hard it had been to walk away from him.

"I understand," he responded, and his voice sounded so close I wished he was here.

"So... I emailed you because I got the VP job, and the first person I thought of telling was you."

"Let's go! Look at you killin' it out there in those streets. I knew that job was yours, you're very dedicated, and it shows,"

Adrián said, congratulating me, and besides Gino and Anibal, it was the most sincere, selfless congratulation I had received. I beamed like a kid in a toy shop, and again I wished Adrián was sitting next to me.

"Listen, I have to go, but I want to do this more often. I know we both have lives and careers, but…would you like to have a long-distance friendship?" Adrián asked.

Friendship… I wanted a hell of a lot more than a friendship with him, but I understood his offer and was grateful for it. Oh, if he were one of the men in the shallow dating pool here, things would be different. However, Adrián's goals were as crystal clear as mine, the one space where our compatibility wouldn't be enough to overcome the obstacles.

"Yes, I was wrong to delete your number and mine from your cell. I don't want to say goodbye to you, even if I can't have you near."

"There are always business trips, right?"

"Yes, you're right. LATAM is my region now." Another visit to the Tropics with a weekend in Aguimar haunted me like a dream deferred. Having to see him to then let him go each time…maybe I was a masochist and just didn't know it.

"There you go, so. Can I call you in the evenings?"

"Of course, of course, please call me."

"Okay. Bye, Preciosa."

"Chao, Adrián." I hung up with a silly grin on my face and with decidedly not friendship feelings crackling inside.

A quiet, cold room, furnished by an elegant long oakwood table and executive chairs, a screen with a PowerPoint, and two flip charts with ideas written down in colored marker would be the beginning of my villain origin story.

Another "this could have been an email" meeting. The hour lingered interminably as I attempted to focus on the topic at hand.

"Each of you in this room has an expansion goal, which we will be reviewing every other week together to brainstorm ideas and check progress. My expectation is that you provide a brief overview of the results of your region and then move on to detailing the progress in your action plan for expansion. When we thought of these positions, we wanted them to be nimble. Many other organizations have two people for what you do, one for ops and the other for expansion and acquisition. Here at Tropics, we believe that with the right team and resources, we can accomplish much more in a streamlined structure." Jan Ricard's words resonated in the boardroom where we, the VPs of Ops for the Americas, sat listening intently.

We were a diverse bunch, all due to Ricard's vision for the future. Anibal, Southeast Region with his suave aura but great results; Shelly Allerton, a fifty-year-old, no-nonsense woman, who had a collection of primary-colored pant suits that draped her plus-size body to perfection, who covered the Northeast. Jack Jack Cohen, forty, who asked every meeting to be called Jack Jack, even though Ricard refused to do so, and called him instead by his last name, handled Canada and Midwest/Central. Jack Jack always looked like he had a funny secret and was just here to have a good time. Arjun Suthar, a quiet man who was promoted at the same time as I, handled the West Coast. Arjun only opened his mouth after he'd clearly thought things through from all angles, and I saw an ally in him immediately.

Then there was me.

I'd fought so hard to be in this room; I'd gone above and beyond every single day of my career to be here, in strategic meetings that would shape the company's future for years to come. The sense of accomplishment and excitement had not died down, but Ricard's words lingered as a sober reminder of the workload that was coming my way.

After a round of updates and a presentation of each of our expansion plans, the meeting adjourned, and I braced myself for the barrage of emails waiting for me.

"So, how do you like it so far?" Anibal's long strides kept up with my speed as I navigated the sleek hallways back to my office.

"It's all I imagined, and then another additional pile of work. I wasn't expecting for them to add acquisitions and contracts to our responsibilities." More work. More work seemed to be the recurring theme of my promotion. Do this, but title is the same. Do that, but of course you are a salaried team member. I didn't usually allow dissatisfaction to color my thoughts about work. The only thing I understood was corporate America. My personality suited my work perfectly. My profession was a solid one, reliable even in times of financial concerns because the target market that traveled to our hotels was high-earning individuals. I had ensured I was in a field that would support me and my little savings fund for retirement for the rest of my life. There was no pot of gold waiting for me when I was no longer capable of working. My mom was the perfect example; she'd worked hard and whenever she decided to retire she'd be able to do so comfortably. So complaining about work seemed counterproductive, or at least it used to feel that way.

"Yeah, there was a rumor for months that they were going

to slim down that department. Now that Finn and Thomas retired, the biggest detractors, Ricard made the move," Anibal said as we turned into my office, which I had already made mine with all gold and white office supplies, a few frames from photos I took from Panamá and other islands on the walls, a scent machine and dehumidifier and foot massager tucked in below my desk.

"Interesting, it truly does double our workload. I wish I'd known Finn and Thomas were detractors of the idea," I said absentmindedly as I cracked open my laptop to see any emails. Moving through the paces as my brain flooded with additional to-do lists. I wondered what Adrián would think of this conversation? Of me confronting the load of more work that I hadn't signed up for, but which would be thrust upon me regardless of my feelings?

"Yeah, big-time. They didn't feel the support work required for the field is possible if we are focused on acquisitions. They believe the field is gonna suffer for it. But the compensation packages make sense, and we get bonuses for each acquisition signed."

"Mmm… I don't disagree with them about the field suffering. I have been thinking of that. I haven't been able to get out yet, and it's been six weeks since I got promoted."

"Tell me about it. I'm one of the lucky ones with my hotels being right here. But y'all have it harder. One of Finn's recommendations was to source people from the areas they serve so that at least travel was more manageable, but they continuously hire from within the office or Florida."

I stared at my computer, everything vanishing as the three hundred emails awaited in bold for my review. I snapped the laptop close with dread and attempted to focus on Anibal.

"Mmm, micromanaging much? And…why are you so chatty? You weren't this forthcoming before I took the job."

"I'm not dense. I wasn't about to sell you the nightmare. I needed to market the dream."

"Damn, I thought you had my back."

"I do. And both of us know you're hungry to tackle it all. To prove that this is doable, so…"

Anibal didn't know me. Okay, maybe he knew me a little.

"I mean, it is exciting, right? To establish the ways we can optimize our time and our efforts? I'm working on some special reporting I want to roll out to the hotels in my region to be able to have live results daily so I can quickly pinpoint any areas of—"

Anibal raised his hand and stopped me.

"Two seconds ago, you looked sick when you saw your emails. Now you are over here telling me how you added more work to your day…girl, you need help, honestly. Why don't you go home, take your laptop and work from there? It's six already. We should both head out." Anibal stood up, and I wondered how he managed to keep his suits so crisp through the day. I stared longingly at my cell phone, wondering if Adrián was already home and we could chat, but then I stared at my laptop, and the tug of responsibility had me wondering what to do.

"Hold up…what was that face?" Anibal asked from the door.

"What face?"

"That 'I have a date waiting for me in my bed, and I wish I was rich and didn't have a job' face." Anibal pointed at me, snapping his fingers.

"Okay…that seemed oddly specific… Anibal, you tired. You're imagining things."

"No, I'm not…you have someone. I have worked with you for five years since I joined the company. I know that face."

"Shhh." I stood up, deciding to finish things at home. Home where I had the privacy to get on the phone and…

"There, there it is again."

"Stop. Let's go. You can pick up your laptop and stuff as we pass by your office toward the elevator."

Anibal chuckled, then moved aside to let me out.

"Nah, I'm not taking my laptop. It's Monday. All those emails will be there tomorrow."

As I drove home, I wondered if Anibal had it right and if I was wrong in planning to work through the night to catch up. Then, I thought about how Anibal had had his position for years, whereas I was just establishing myself. This was normal. I would get things under control soon enough. There, that was better. Positive thinking. No more dread about the job and what it entailed. Of what it meant for my social life, or lack thereof. It helped that before checking all my emails, I had that date, even if it was only on the phone.

Sixteen

Adrián

My new cell phone ringtone. The best sound in the world. I only liked this ringtone, the one I programmed when I hung up with Genevieve last night. I put her in my favorites as my emergency contact, and programmed "Tú" from Juan Luis Guerra as the tone. I didn't plan to miss a call from her, no matter the time she phoned. I even saved her phone number on a notepad as soon as I walked into my efficiency, and by Monday morning, I knew it by heart.

Now, it was the evening after a day of dispatching the few drivers we'd onboarded. After the Tropics contract ended, we had a couple of rough weeks where Julín and I wondered if we'd have to let the dudes go that we had just hired, but as my mother used to say, things have a way of working out. And thank God for it because my responsibilities were vast. Whenever the hostel had a bad month, the money I made from the transportation company helped filled in the gaps both for me and for Claudia's family. The fonda usually had steady income, but it was enough for just a bit extra for groceries and the regular necessities. A few sleepless nights had pushed me to engage contacts that had remained unused for a few years. The efforts bore success.

Two days ago, Anita Johnson from the Tropics reached out and asked if we could become their preferred transportation company. Anita was as real as they got, and the offer made in a way that kept our pride intact was appreciated. Since then, we have had a steady request for airport transfers and day trips for their patrons. Enough for me to send money to Villa Bonita, which had seen no reservations since the excursion.

Brushing aside my daily concerns, I hopped in the shower, rinsing the day away. I pulled on my best basketball shorts and my favorite T-shirt, then sat on the small kitchen table and dialed Gen's cell phone number by heart.

"Hi."

Genevieve's voice told me a lot about her day. I wished I was there to make her some dinner and make her smile.

"You sound exhausted," I replied.

"You ain't lyin'." She chuckled.

"Should I not ask about your day, then?"

"Mmm, you can, but it was just another day, filled with deadlines and meetings and…" I could hear the clatter of dishes in the background and imagined her gliding effortlessly into the kitchen, making herself something to eat.

"Have dinner with me."

"Uh…well, you're a bit far."

"I mean, let's video call and have dinner together."

There was a pregnant pause on the other side of the phone, and my pulse accelerated. Had I pushed too fast?

"Well…as long as you don't criticize my dinner, I'm down."

I punched the table in excitement and quickly pressed the video button before she changed her mind. Her face immediately appeared on the screen, the hood of her eyes dropping with the exhaustion I had heard earlier. She grinned, and her whole face illuminated; my breath caught at the sheer beauty of her.

"There you are, Preciosa."

"Oh, here you go, flatterer. You know I look a mess." She gestured at her hair in a messy bun on top of her head, then down to the simple white tee she had on.

"You always are beautiful to me. No matter what. So… what we eating?"

Cereal. Both of us were dining on cereal.

"And here I thought you were gonna criticize me."

"Nah, I keep it simple on nights I'm tired, a sandwich, cereal, crackers and cheese, hey whatever works," I told her, and she chuckled. While we both poured our bowls, she filled me in on her day, then I told her about Anita's offer and how it had been a lifesaver.

"You know… I've been thinking, you could put some targeted ads for Villa Bonita on social media. Those apps have user-friendly platforms. I've searched everywhere online, and besides the website and your little IG account, you don't have much out there."

"I'm clueless with that stuff. I mean, don't get me wrong, I'm good with technology, but I try my best to stay out of social media, so a lot of the new shit don't even make sense to me." Why be behind a phone posting and taking pictures when you could be enjoying instead? Chichi gave me a hard time telling me the new "town square" was online and that I was going to be left behind, but I guess I just couldn't muster the energy to keep up with it all when there was so much to do around me.

"How have you managed to stay out of social media in this day and age?"

"Living life." I shrugged.

"I sense judgment." She rolled her eyes and kept munching on her Raisin Bran.

"Nah, I'm not judging. I know I stay out of the loop on a lot because I'm not on social media. I just worked a lot before, and now, I'm on the road or in Villa Bonita fixing things or helping in La Buenona, and I honestly don't know how people find the time."

I finished my Vitalisimo and waited for her response as she chewed pensively. Just watching her chew stimulated me. I really was down bad for Gen. I could imagine nights like this, the two of us unwinding after a day of work. The same sense of togetherness flowed through us just as it had done for my parents, and for Claudia and Mario. Speaking with her reminded me of my dad telling me of when he'd met Mom and in a day, he'd known they were meant to be married. I always thought he was full of it, but now…now I understood.

"I guess I make the time? I have a lot of people I've worked with in the past and some friends from college that are on social media, and it's a nice way to keep up with them. I'm not on it a lot, but at least an hour a day."

"How do you find that hour, though? You just said you have to clear your inbox before going to bed tonight. When do you do that fun stuff we talked about when you were here?"

"Time…hmm. The concept of time for me flows very differently when not on vacation. I try to squeeze in every minute of the day. But to answer your question, I check it in bed right before going to sleep."

"If I was there…you wouldn't have time to do that," I murmured, helpless to keep my thoughts in.

"Oh," Gen breathed, and her tongue sneaked out to catch a stray drop of milk.

"Yes, if I was there. After dinner, I'd give you an hour tops to check your email. Then I would find you in your office, hoist you up in my arms, and take you to bed, where I would work very hard to remove all the tension from your day. With my tongue, my fingers, and my dick."

Gen gasped and flushed dark in the camera. I bit my bottom lip to keep from saying all the nasty things I wanted to do to her right now. Gen started fidgeting, and I wondered what was happening below, which I couldn't see. Was she rubbing her legs together?

"Are you feeling aroused, Gen? Do you need to rub those lush thighs together? I wish you didn't have to do that. I wish I was between them, my tongue soothing your needs." Shit, at this point, I was just jumping in the deep end. I had told this woman I wanted to have a long-distance friendship yesterday; today I was attempting to seduce her with my words. I wanted more, but…this was as much as I could get.

Gen whimpered, and I hardened fully just with that sweet sound. To be there with her right now. To be able to touch her.

"Oh, I… I thought you wanted to be friends?"

"I think we both know I want more than that."

"Me too but…"

"Gen, how about we let this flow? You and I? We have everything so carefully planned, but what if we jump just like we did that Saturday when you came with me to Villa Bonita?"

Gen's intense gaze searched me, leaving me bare as if there weren't more than six thousand kilometers between us.

"Okay."

My heart rejoiced at her agreement, and I recognized right then and there that Genevieve would change my life.

"So what do you think? Does this look good?" Gen wore a long, one-sleeve, shimmering black gown. Her curves were lush and mouthwatering, and I was certain Genevieve had no idea of her impact on me. Every day I imagined having the honor to be next to her, in her bed, in her room, by her side. If I was there, I'd have removed the dress and shown her how good she looked with only my mouth as an aid.

"Good is an understatement," I said through the camera, lying down on my bed while she got herself ready for a gala honoring her mother.

"You don't think its…too much?" Gen ran a hand down her flank over her hips, and I wasn't shy to say I moaned.

"Define *too much* because I'm certain we have different definitions and connotations."

"Do you always think with your little head?" she protested but grinned, then winked. Okay, so she did know what she did to me.

"Gen, I want to make clear here and now that even though I don't believe in size comparisons, we both know there is nothing little about my—"

"Stop!" She chuckled. "You know what I'm asking about…"

I nodded and sighed. It had been a glorious month. Every day we spoke. First, it was just at night. Then the text messages started one day, when I needed help setting up the ads for Villa Bonita's social media accounts. In between meetings,

Gen guided me through the process and suggested the best markets to advertise to.

We started calls during the day, little check-ins, like the day Gen called to tell me, ecstatic, that she'd booked her business travel for the next month, even though not to Panamá yet, she knew it was just a matter of time.

That night she regaled me with her excitement about her plans for her Jamaica, Barbados, Anguilla, and Saint Vincent tour, where she was going to meet with all the Tropics general managers. She had also planned to do some travel posts based on the journals she'd been canvasing of her journeys, and she beautifully lit up as she strategized her posts. I silently wished I had the means to surprise her but instead focused on her joy.

It wasn't always excitement on our calls, though; one night she called me on her way home, exasperated about her mother's machinations. She'd found out that her boss, Jan Ricard, and her mother had been in the same college back in the day. Even though Ricard had promised Gen she had obtained her job under her own talent, Gen couldn't shake the feeling that Lissette had figured out a way to leverage her friendship. That night I stayed on with her for hours until she finally calmed down enough to eat a bite and get in bed. Her question about her mother did make sense.

"I think your mom might have a thing or two to say, but guess what?"

"I know. I'm a whole grown woman." She laughed.

"That's damn right, and from here, I can tell you it's a good look." I settled on the bed, running my hand down my T-shirt, wishing I was closer.

"Did you just…where did that hand go?" Gen got closer to the tablet she had propped up on her bathroom counter.

"Wouldn't you want to know?" I teased.

"I do... I do want to know..." She sounded breathy; her pupils dilated in the screen, her beautiful face adorned by tasteful makeup, her plush red lips parted. My fingers itched to slide down my basketball shorts, but I refrained.

"I'm going to need you to finish getting ready and get out of the apartment before you tempt me, woman."

"Tempt you to what?" she taunted, spurred by the arousal in my eyes.

"Tempt me to entice you to stay with me."

"I..."

"No, I know you'll be upset if you're late. Go, have fun tonight. I'll be here if you want to call later."

"Damn, I hate when you're right. Okay...okay, but let's talk about this... I...yeah, let's table this."

I smirked as she licked her lips, then blew me a kiss goodbye. Then went to my online buying account and started plotting.

A few days later, I had my plan in place. It so happened that it coincided with her week-long tour in the Caribbean. I made sure to instruct Genevieve to pack the surprise in her luggage.

"How am I in one of the most beautiful areas in the world, and I can't even go out and enjoy the scenery?" Genevieve complained as she settled herself on the sofa in her suite in Barbados. She propped her tablet up somewhere that allowed me to see her sitting on the sofa in her tank top and shorts, hair wrapped under her satin scarf; her luxuriant thighs opened as she sat crisscrossed.

"Did you ask your driver to take you to a cool place for dinner?" I asked from my cabana in Villa Bonita; I lay on the sofa bed, holding my cell phone, watching the night waves come in. I had come for a long weekend to take care of the landscaping, which was out of control. Chichi and Mario had done a little of the work, but with the fonda staying busy, I came up to assist. I'd just returned from taking a plunge in the ocean, and then a quick shower to rinse off. I had needed to bathe twice to calm down enough for this call.

"I should have, but that would have meant me cheating on my old driver."

"Graciosa. You should have. You told me you figured out how to squeeze the minutes of every day…squeeze some for you. You're as equally, actually way more, important than the work you do."

"You're right… I know you're right. But this project about this expansion, it's so time-consuming. I'm starting to think my mom is right, and I should try to find that elusive architect."

I bolted up from the sofa, my heart thundering in my chest.

"What elusive architect?"

"This dude that did the Tropics Panamá? Ricard is hoping that we can get him to do one of the beach resorts they wanna do there. I didn't ask the driver to stop because Ricard called me, yammering about how my mom had mentioned the thought, and it was such a splendid idea, and maybe I could put out some feelers when I went to Panamá. Maybe Anita can help me find him so I can get them off my back…"

"You're coming to Panamá?" My chest tightened; too much activity happening in there as Genevieve dropped bomb after bomb and sat there oblivious.

"Yeah, in less than three weeks. It's wild because I have a lot to do before that, but I don't care because I get to see you.

It's a two-day trip, but it ends on Friday, so I can extend it."
Her eyes shined in excitement and hope.

"I can't wait to hold you, Preciosa." I gave her the truth, or
the only one I could handle giving her right now.

My path to healing continued every day, but the thought
of explaining my relationship to the Tropics and the reason
why I left brought chills. Besides my family, no one understood everything that had transpired. It was so easy to open
up to Genevieve, to share with her my everyday, my dreams,
my challenges. But for some reason this topic stuck in the
back of my throat, bringing cold sweat and palpitations anytime it came up.

Genevieve had become essential to my everyday.

In my quest to divest myself from the relentless chase for a
career, I'd traded a life of lesser comforts but higher returns.
Returns in the love of my family, the time I had for them,
the time I had for myself, the time I had to explore and enjoy
life simply.

If I had met Genevieve before my parents passed away, I'm
not certain I'd have had the time to dedicate to her as I have
now. There were days Gen couldn't talk, and I just texted her
through the time, funny thoughts and observations, just letting
her know she was on my mind while she hopped from meeting to meeting, answering the texts with hearts and thumbs-
up. I got it; I did; her day was saturated with deadlines and
tasks, and her mention of her boss wanting to locate me made
my palms sweat and my stomach cramp up.

Because listening to Genevieve's goals had made me wonder if I could dive into that world again. If we could build a
life together around those goals and beyond. Complementing
each other's strengths.

To produce another project, this time at home…

I hadn't finished doing the work of balance, and it scared me to go back to a world where I knew no boundaries. But I continued to flirt with the temptation of something more permanent with Genevieve, something that allowed me to be next to her every day, even if it upended my life as I knew it…

"Hey, where did I lose you? Are you tired? I…we can talk tomorrow if you like? I think I always take for granted that you're available to speak. Sorry for that." Genevieve jostled me out of my reverie.

"Just imagining having you close again." Again, I said part of the truth. Just not the whole truth. If I did, I would have answered something to the tune of, "I want you forever, to be your man, your partner and I want to spill all my secrets to you." Best if I didn't overshare. She'd probably run away and never call again.

"What's in that package you sent me? I've been uncharacteristically patient with you."

"That you have." I smirked, focusing on today. Whenever I focused on today, I won.

"Should I go get it?"

"Go ahead."

Gen smiled shyly but moved quickly, the camera bouncing about as she took me for a ride around the hotel room. She settled back against a mountain of pillows in the bed and installed her tablet in this contraption she'd bought.

"Okay, open it." I propped my phone against a stack of books I'd settled on my bed.

Gen ripped open the package with childlike delight. Then the innocent glee morphed into giddy lust as she realized what I had sent.

"Oh... I... I've never bought one of these."

"When you pleasure yourself, do you do it fast, just chasing that orgasm, or do you take your time with yourself?" I asked. Her eyes widened, and I could tell I was spot-on.

"I...well, I kinda come fast. I like to think it's my superpower."

"And I love that superpower, I truly do, but sometimes I wish you could take it slower. Tonight's not that night because we both have to go to sleep, but maybe, we can explore that more together. That G-spot massager is the beginning of that exploration."

Gen's chest rose and fell, her nipples clearly hardening under my heated gaze.

"So, we start tonight?"

"You have to go to sleep, though—" Whatever else I was going to say vanished as she shimmied her shorts and panties off.

"I do, but it could be fun to try it out?"

"Yeah, but you gotta clean it first. With the..." I almost swallowed my tongue when a view of her plump ass took over the camera. Resisting the urge to strip, I awaited her return.

"Back!" She scrambled into the spot in front of the tablet and settled against the pillows. I could see her lush legs slightly open and the evidence of her desire between her legs.

"You're trying to kill me, aren't you?"

"No, no, I want to come with your gift."

I said a brief prayer for resilience and temperance. This was for her, not for me. I repeated that mantra as Gen spread her legs wide-open, showing me what I was missing.

"Okay, so today we don't have much time, but whenever you and I were together, you would hold your breath. Try coming this time but breathing through it. Touch yourself as if I wasn't here."

She gaped at me, then hesitantly ran her hands down her belly between her legs. Her moan traveled on a direct flight from her hotel room straight to my dick. My erection strained inside my shorts, but I refused to touch myself...yet.

"I...okay, but I need more."

"You need more?"

"Yeah, talk to me..."

"Fuck, Preciosa. I love it when you relax enough to take care of yourself like this. You're doing such good work."

"Oh, oh..." she breathed as her fingers did the work I couldn't do.

"When you're back home, I want you to pencil in this time for you. Every night, put on some candles, some music, prop up that tablet and give me a call if you need me, but this is for you. All you."

The toy buzzer turned on, and with laser concentration Genevieve pleasured herself. I sat there, hard as a steel pole, showering her with praises as her orgasm approached her like a bandit in the night. When she shuddered in delicious release, I realized the image of her gorgeous brown skin glowing under the bedroom lights—her face, relaxed in pure ecstasy—would be ingrained in my brain forever.

As I attempted to settle into bed after a double jerk-off session that left me drained, I knew I didn't want to be without Gen.

No fear, no healing path would remove the magnetism I felt for her. Opening up still seemed like a daunting process but the rewards would be plentiful if it all went well. After everything my family had gone through, I had learned to appreciate life and all its facets. It was why I tried so hard for balance, but what good was balance if I was not happy with it? Gen made me happy, having her in my life for good and for worse materialized as a dream worthy of reaching. A dream worthy of fighting for.

Which meant I had to make difficult decisions very soon.

Seventeen

Adrián

The plantains were heavy on my back as Julín and I brought them into La Buenona. As heavy as my wondering mind, filled with aspirations, plans, and pending conversations.

Laying my plans for the future, I'd sat down with Claudia and Mario a week ago. The conversation went much better than expected. I'd been afraid they found me selfish for thinking of uprooting my life away from them, but all Claudia's words had been of encouragement.

"Listen, we know Dad proposed to Mami two weeks after meeting her, if they could do it, you can too. Sometimes we can't overthink these things. That is not how the heart works. Sometimes your heart tells you what you need to continue living and you have two options: be miserable or answer the call. No matter what you decide, we are here for you," Claudia had said, embracing me with so much love, it was the confidence boost I needed.

"Damn, Claudia, you look rough," Julín told her as we dropped the bunches in the pantry.

"Oh, you have a death wish, lovely," Claudia said between sniffles.

I approached her cautiously, giving her a pat on the back.

"Go take a nap. I got this. I can stay. I'm alright."

"No, you aren't. You've been wired ever since you decided to propose to Gen."

Here I was, attempting to be a good brother, and Claudia just blabbered my potential plans.

"What?" Julín whirled on his feet and stared at me.

I sighed, knowing what was coming and not wanting to deal with it yet.

"I… I'm considering asking Genevieve to marry me."

"And when were you gonna say something?" Julín crossed his arms over his chest, leaning against one of the kitchen tables.

"Ahh ya vas, Julín. Everyone can see Adri is in love with that girl. And you're gonna have to tuck in your jealousy and deal."

I flinched at Julín's expression of pain, but it quickly transformed into anger.

"What is going to happen with LasDell Transportation? Am I supposed to hold the fort on my own?"

"Ay por favor, you have the drivers now, and Adri can help from afar with all the paperwork and dispatching. Working remotely is the future. Life is too short. We learned that with our parents—" Claudia stopped when she saw my expression. She had zero patience for Julín. Many people didn't, which was why I was protective of him. Claudia meant well, but

I hadn't been able to speak with Julín; my plan was to do it today before we drove back to the city.

"Fine, yes, you're right, Claudia. I'll be out by the car." Julín stormed out, leaving Claudia and me in silence.

"Well, I was right. You should be able to make decisions without worrying about us."

"But I do… I do. And Julín…he's always had my back."

"Oh, honey, I know…listen, I can't imagine how it's been for the two of you in this cruel world. And you know, Mama, Papa, and I, even though we initially didn't fully understand, always wanted the best for you. Julín…sometimes I feel he… he doesn't see you. He sees the version of you he wants to see. That's all."

I stood by the stove, feeling the tug and pull of weeks—the weight of my decision holding me down from what should be the best time of my life.

"Am I making the right choice…we've talked about the next steps, but…there is always that wall. She has a career, and I have you." And the unspoken fear was how would Gen react to such a sudden proposal? She had her life mapped out up to how she was going to utilize her 401(k) once retired. Nothing about my life fit in her plan, but she'd been dropping hints about being open to changes in her trajectory that I hoped I'd read well. We'd spoken of what-if—what if she'd met me on a date in Florida, or what if she worked in the Tropics in Panamá. The feelings of hope were reciprocal.

"And you have us wherever you are. You light up when you talk about her. You're walking around Villa Bonita with a goofy smile and…"

"Okay, you've called me a fool in love enough." I pushed away from the stove and embraced her, letting her love pacify my qualms. She squeezed my cheeks as if I hadn't just told her to stop mothering me and nudged me down to her level. "What if...what if my sexuality..." I reminded her, and myself, that even though I hadn't openly discussed my sexuality with Gen I hadn't hidden it either. It chafed to have to "come out" to people that were heterosexual when they did not have to do the same thing. However, maybe it did not matter to her because we were just dating, but if we were to marry...

"That girl doesn't strike me as closed-minded and cruel. And remember you are in no closet," she insisted.

"I want it to work out." I confessed all the fears and hopes of my relationship with Gen in a simple sentence.

"And it will. Because you deserve love."

The burn behind my eyes sneaked up on me, and her hug lingered as I walked out to find Julín waiting by the car.

"Ready?" he asked and jumped in the car before I had more to say.

"Yeah. You sure you don't wanna stop by your mom's before we head out?" I backed out, the gravel and dust picking up as we left Villa Bonita behind.

"No. What for? She's gonna try to pray the gay away again. Thanks for letting me stay in one of the cabanas," he said, subdued.

"Listen, I—"

"Nah, it's good. I get it. I get that you think you love the woman," he said, cutting me off.

"Don't get twisted. I don't think. I know. The only reason I haven't asked her for more is because of Claudia and the kids and you and LasDell." I tried not to let the annoyance bleed into my tone.

He waved his hand like he was swatting away my thoughts.

"Listen, you don't owe me explanations. If you are happy, I'm happy. But make sure you are happy...that you are doing this for yourself."

Talk about whiplash. Just a few minutes ago, Claudia urged me to do this for myself, and now Julín implied I was considering proposing for other reasons besides my own.

I wouldn't let this exasperation win; I couldn't wait to see Genevieve, who was probably in her meetings right now with Anita. She had arrived last night, and I wanted to greet her at the airport, but she'd known I'd driven to Aguimar three days ago to help Claudia and Mario after the entire family went down with the flu. They were finally on the mend, so Claudia had finally convinced us to head to the city to meet Genevieve.

Last night I'd struggled to fall asleep with the knowledge that only fifty-eight kilometers separated us.

The drive to the city flew by in tense silence. Julín and I hashed out how to move forward with the business if things worked out with Genevieve and things went the way I expected them to go. A cautious excitement built as the busy lights of the early evening sped by us, the afternoon rush of drivers fighting to get home.

"So you're gonna ask this weekend?"

"If things go well...there are a few things she and I have to discuss first..."

"What things?"

I shrugged, not wanting to get into it. Julín wasn't thrilled about my decision, so sharing felt off.

"You and your mystery. Just head on to your house. I can walk from there," Julín offered as he lived nearby in another efficiency.

"I can drop you off, man."

"I feel like walking."

We spotted a vehicle waiting in the driveway with the lights on as we approached my apartment.

"Did the owner of your rental get a new car?" Julín asked curiously.

"No, not that I know of…"

As I parked my SUV next to the awaiting car, Genevieve descended from the vehicle, a vision in a blue wrap dress, a cautious smile as she swiped her straight ebony strands back from her face, and Anita followed behind with a wide grin.

The balmy evening was no match for the heat bursting inside of me. Every muscle in my body vibrated, and lightness crept up as Gen waited as I parked the car.

"Preciosa? I thought we were meeting in your hotel?"

"I know, but I figured I'd come over tonight, and then we could move to the Casco hotel tomorrow as planned…"

"Oh damn, you have money like that? Staying in Casco, huh," Julín mumbled, and I ignored his comment, the same as I ignored the dent on my credit card. Gen was worth the expense.

"So, you came to stay?" I asked cautiously.

"Well, yes, Anita practically kicked me out…" Gen's nervous laughter filled the night and my chest. I devoured her with my eyes, the reality of her, not behind a screen, too much to take.

"Damn, it's like we became invisible. Might as well leave them to it." Anita chuckled, and Julín grumbled.

"So sorry. Let me introduce you to Julín, my best friend." I gestured to Julín, who stood still like a petulant child. With reluctance, Julín approached, barely shaking hands with Genevieve, whose excited smile dimmed slightly at Julín's attitude.

The urge to smack him behind the head was real, but Julín meant well. Even though I'd expected him to treat Gen more respectfully, I let things slide. He stepped back and stood next to me. I whispered angrily, "Don't make her feel bad, ever again."

He sucked his teeth but nodded along in understanding.

"I'm going. Good to meet you, Gen. Anita, good to see you again." And he granted Anita the smile he refused Gen, turned and left us there.

"I usually like Julín, but damn, what happened to him today?" Anita asked, shaking her head. Genevieve's uncertainty flickered until her smile lowered.

"Preciosa, I was going to shower, then drive to the Tropics to see you, so you coming to me takes away one step..." I held my chest and swaggered toward her. Instantly her gaze went from uncertain to that nervous excitement, and my night was complete.

"Alrighty then. I know when I'm not needed," Anita said, and Gen whirled around toward her.

"Girl, I'm so sorry, I'm being so rude."

"Nah, if I had a man look at me the way he looks at you... sis, I'd be ignoring everyone too. Bye, girl. Bye... Mr. *Nicolas*," Anita said and I wondered if I understood Gen wrong about her being engaged; if I was right... What the heck was her fiancé doing then, if not making Anita feel like the most important person in the world? Because now that Gen was here, my priorities were straight again.

I wanted her and only her.

Eighteen

Genevieve

Water. All I needed was a glass of water to alleviate my parched mouth. See, parchedness was what happened when you couldn't keep your mouth closed because... Damn. And water was what you needed to bring down your pulse and calm a speedy heart racing away to reunite with their other half.

"Can I have some water?" I requested the moment we crossed the threshold to Adrián's apartment. His heat seared my back as he followed closely with my carry-on.

"Of course, Preciosa," Adrián responded.

Every day I heard Adrián's voice on my cell phone, and every night I fell asleep with him crooning his good-nights to me, but I hadn't been prepared for the impact of his reality. For the impact of us being in the same room after more than two months apart.

Nothing prepared me for the onslaught of his cologne or the way my pulse skittered at being so close to my person. I hadn't been ready for my body's immediate response, the liquid rush between my legs, or the tingle of my breasts. I didn't know my heart would ache to be held in his thick arms, to sit next to him and talk the whole night.

Adrián sauntered to the little kitchenette and back, handing me a tall glass of water. My eyes took in his small efficiency with a living area/kitchen/dining area comprised of a sofa, a TV on a coffee table, a table for two right next to the stove, and little moving space in between the furniture.

Right next to the sofa was a door that probably led to his bedroom. There was less here than in his place in Villa Bonita, but what impressed me were the pictures of Claudia, the kids, Mario, Julín, Shakira, whom I'd met via video call, and his friends all over the wall. He'd asked for a photo a couple of weeks ago, and now I understood why. There I was part of his inner circle.

"Want to see my bedroom?" he asked with no inflection, and he was probably as equally affected as I was.

"Of course." I grinned at him, trying to chase the nervous rush coursing through my veins.

Somehow our connection still felt new between us. New with a tinge of familiarity, like a recurring dream that faded away in the reality of the morning, then finally came true. Every step and moment embedded in your heart on an unexplored path.

"Thanks for surprising me. I did an hour and twenty from Aguimar to here. That's how bad I wanted to see you." He smirked, leading the way. I could tell he was excited, but he sounded a bit preoccupied; I wondered if he was worried about what I had to say about his place, and I would make sure to alleviate any concerns.

Taking a sip of the water, I followed to find his Spartan

room with a simple full bed with thin sheets, a nightstand, and a chair in the corner. He had a standing dresser and the door to the bathroom next to it. The light from the street outside filtered through the lone, barred window with the obligatory screen, and a gentle breeze blew my hair from the overhead fan.

"I know it's small…"

"It's perfect. That bed will ensure you stay close the whole night." I hesitated for a moment, but saw his face light up. It was the right thing to say. Since I landed in Panamá, I deeply yearned to see him. To be with him. I spent the day in meetings, unable to fully concentrate because of what awaited me at the end of the day. I couldn't stop studying his face with the thick beard and sexy smirk and admiring his thick arms sculpted under his sleeveless tee and the perfect calves… God, when did I start admiring calves?

"You can't do that." Adrián groaned.

"What?" My heart hammered against my chest, and my nipples grew impossibly hard inside of my bra; the breeze from the fan stimulated my heated skin.

"You're staring as if you want to get bent over and—"

My mind knew what I needed before I could get my words out. My breath was lost as Adrián's body crashed into mine, his delicious arms around me calming the raging lust inside. Our mouths smashed, his peppermint taste making me moan. His tongue drove my need in a crescendo as our hands clashed, attempting the same goal.

Zero clothes.

Adrián's beard tickled under my neck as his breath ghosted along my speeding pulse, his hands groping my ass in desperation. My dress lost the battle first, followed by his pants, then his T-shirt. Soon, I was standing in bra and panties, and he was in his boxers, and I attempted the best way to climb him like a tree.

"I thought you wanted to...to take...time." I gasped as he yanked my bra down, exposing my nipples, which pointed toward him in supplication.

"Oh my...fuck did you...did you realize we always do this so fast that this is my first time seeing them in detail?" he said, staring at my breasts, lost in his reverie. Denial sprang to my mouth, but nothing came out because as I ran each moment together, I realized I'd mostly ended up with some clothes on during our encounters.

"Well... I..." I shook as he studied me, this area of mine, abundant and lush, one that had brought me so much satisfaction and grief. I worked in a very safe environment now, but once upon a time... I had learned to cover them in instinct, avoiding being noticed by my chest size versus my mental acumen. I hadn't realized that even in my most passionate moments, I'd neglected one of my most erogenous zones.

"It's okay if you're uncomfortable. I can give you a T-shirt. I always want you to be at ease with me. But let me tell you...you're breathtaking. From each strand on your head to that crooked pinky toe," Adrián said, and I had to pause for a moment.

"Did you just call my toe crooked?"

"It's beautiful, though, with that little curve to the left, not wanting to leave the next toe alone..."

"You a damn fool."

"Yeah, I am, for you...listen, your breasts...they are...gorgeous. Can I touch?" he asked, and I nodded wordlessly, trembling as his hand coasted along my soft skin, his rough palm dragging along the skin, causing all sorts of riots inside.

"Can I...can I lick now?" he asked, and I whimpered in consent.

His tall frame bent like a palm tree in the wind, and his heated breath touched one nipple; my knees buckled, and he took advantage, sliding an arm around my waist and running his big, juicy tongue over the tip as if it was a cherry on ice cream, and I melted.

"Oh, Adrián, oh please. Please."

"You beg so pretty, I guess this is just another night where you win, and we do it as quickly as you want."

"Yes!" I begged carelessly for him inside me.

With economic moves, Adrián removed the last vestiges of clothes on both of us, and I stood there unable to do anything but take deep breaths before I passed out of unrealized lust. And if I ever wondered if that last piece of the cookie was one too many, Adrián removed the concern when he carried me effortlessly and deposited me gently on the bed.

Mind in a fog, body on fire, Adrián took me with one swift stroke, his length the thickest, most delicious intrusion. Then Adrián followed my screamed instructions, urging him faster, harder until his bed creaked under the pressure of our passion. I didn't lie there taking it, though; I gave it back to him, with all the yearning and lust built from days and months apart. Our flesh smacking against each other quickly became my favorite sound, causing ripples of joy in my chest.

I finished first in delicious abandon because Adrián made sure of it, his thickness flooding me in warmth, my heart and my core in harmony, rejoicing at our reunion. Adrián crested soon after, his orgasm stunning as he trembled in my arms, his neck tense in fierce pleasure, his groans all full of my name.

Thank God for standing fans.

I lay sprawled, limbs skewed, shoulder and arm on top of Adrián's sweaty chest, legs tangled—the thin sheet draped over our private parts and nothing more.

"You good there?" He chuckled.

"For a second, my heart felt like it was gonna escape forever and never return." I grinned as I followed the wings of the fan.

"You came to Panamá to kill me. Now I understand your true intentions." He groaned, gliding his palm over my belly, resting it gently there.

Oh…my heart.

"I didn't. I came because of work and because I missed you so much. Anibal was so annoyed at me the last few days that he suggested I should take a week. I was so tempted, but I couldn't. There is so much happening between the expansion plans and results, and…ugh. Who would have thought that reaching most of my career goals meant I had no time to enjoy life?"

"Mmm, I wish I lived close to you. I'd ensure you relaxed sometimes."

"You sure would…" I ignored the simmering heat and cuddled up into his side. His arm immediately cloaked over me, and I never felt safer.

"Preciosa…have you thought about how things would be if we lived in the same place?" he murmured, his velvety voice caressing my soul.

My heart had been working overtime since I saw him, and I couldn't articulate the rush of rightness that suffused me at his question. We'd joked around about it but there was seriousness now that hadn't been there before. But there lay a pipe dream. I understood the importance of his family, and he comprehended the meaning of my career. Besides, who moved in together after just a few months of knowing each other? These types of decisions took time, but with Adrián? With Adrián, I didn't care about timelines.

"I have, but…"

"No buts, just, let's imagine, for now…"

"I've thought of moving here with you…working remotely. I know how Aguimar is important to you."

"I've thought of moving to you…but it would require…"

"I've looked at fiancé visas," I confessed, and he squeezed my hip and rumbled in laughter.

"So, we've both done that internet search, huh."

My chest tightened in excitement. "But wouldn't you prefer for me to move here? I mean, it would be hard. This job doesn't want any remote work, even though I could very easily do this work anywhere."

How funny that when I finally got to the pinnacle of one of my career goals, the goal no longer satisfied me. The job at the Tropics remained challenging and important, but every day I pictured myself doing something different. Hospitality was in my blood, helping people plan their trips, giving them the resources, it all resonated deeply within, but maybe there were other ways of going about my dreams. Such thoughts would have felt blasphemous just a year ago, but now I could only see the vast possibilities.

"I know your work's important, so I'd be willing to move…"

Air whooshed out of me, everything held still, then I remembered…

"This is us imagining, right? Honestly, it would be the perfect dream," I said, pressing a kiss on his chest.

"Mmm-hmm. It is the perfect dream. Another one to add to our collection."

Adrián drifted to sleep shortly after that, and I lay next to him, wondering again if I was following my brain or my heart when it came to Adrián.

"I was here for four months and had no time to come and visit," I said, my hand warm in Adrián's palm. Purple, blue, and gold splashed on the horizon as we wandered around the city's Casco Antiguo.

The area brimmed with restored buildings from the 1600s, standing as the second established city founded by the Spanish colonizers. Ever since we reunited yesterday, I indescribably felt at home. When I met Adrián that first day, what initially drew me to him was his confident aura, then he opened up slowly during our drives until every morning and evening were the highlights of my day.

His dedication to his family, passion for life, silly humor, love for his friends, inquisitive mind, and sense of pride lured me until I fell in love. By the time I was ready to leave Panamá, the infatuation was so intense the steps to love were a hop, skip, and jump. Now I couldn't imagine my life without him.

"I know, all that time, you had me—a sexy, debonair brother—at your disposal, and you didn't take advantage of my services."

"Sir, you are making it sound like your services were different from driving."

He chuckled as we crossed the cobbled street into a little coffee shop. The scent of coffee beans greeted us as we entered the space, and I closed my eyes in satisfaction.

"The hotel has a restaurant facing the bay, so I figured we'd dine there, but before that…" He gestured at the shop, and I realized how quaint and similar the decor appeared to one of the fondas where we'd had breakfast in Portobelo. Not the same architecture, but a feel of homeyness and belonging that I couldn't shake.

An older woman with flawless ebony skin walked out from the counter and greeted us warmly, inviting us to sit. No one else was in the shop, and from our seats, we had the view of one of the plazas with an obelisk and a rooster on top. The area was surrounded by pristine white archways and stairs that led up to a pathway with water views.

"You've brought me to have your evil milky concoction that you pretend is coffee?"

Adrián's delicious rumble infiltrated my ears, traveling straight to my stomach. I didn't need any warm drink. All the comfort I needed resided here with him.

"I…" Adrián started, then closed his mouth again.

"Are you alright? And why are you sweating? It's nice out for a change." I took a napkin from the table and wiped his forehead. He leaned and allowed me the gesture, and that bolt of rightness hit me again.

"Yeah… I'm good." He nodded forcefully. Odd.

"Don't tell me you're nervous?"

He frowned then smiled, but still no words emerged.

"When we leave here, do we have time to go and take pictures in that plaza? I want to write in my journal tonight. It's been enriching to document my travels. And I know your thoughts on social media, but people have really been liking my tips for Black women travelers. Is it wild to say it excites me sometimes more than doing Tropics work?"

"Mmm-hmm." That's all I got from Adrián as the lady brought our drinks, setting them in front of us.

Okay. Something was definitely off. He'd jump on that comment any other day; he'd been encouraging me to lean more into my travel journaling passion. I'd even considered starting a blog. Maybe changing topics would snap him out of his trance.

"So, Ricard asked me to do some reconnaissance for that dude, the architect. At first, I refused, thinking they were a big-time, privileged person, but apparently, he's from humble beginnings and Afro-Panamanian! Now I'm intrigued, and I emailed his old firm to see if they can put me in contact with him. It's exactly what you and I were talking about that day…"

Adrián's face went ashen at my words, and a cold finger ran from the back of my neck to the bottom of my spine.

"What's wrong?" I murmured.

"Nothing. I was going to… I was… I need to tell you something before I move on." Adrián cleared his throat, straightening on his chair.

Our relationship felt like an unattainable dream, but I thought we had time. I thought we were still basking in how different and unique it all felt between us.

"I'm bisexual," Adrián said and took a scalding gulp of his coffee.

I guess this was when I had to say something, but I was perplexed. I thought…

"Yeah… I figured."

"You figured?"

"Well, sometimes when we are together, you admire the same men I do…it's not overt. It's just a quick acknowledgment of beauty. Hey… I do it too. Then there is Julín." I shrugged.

"Julín is gay, yes, but… I don't have feelings for him."

"I didn't think you did, but him, on the other hand." I turned my gaze to the plaza as night settled over the last vestiges of daylight. The hot cup felt warm in my hands, and I held on to it, attempting to tamp down my nerves.

"No, he doesn't. I know everyone thinks so, but…he's just overprotective."

"And he needs to protect you from me?" I asked, hurt that his best friend saw me as a threat.

"No…to be honest, he thinks he needs to protect me from the world. It's tough for me to explain…" Adrián's supplicant gaze made me soften immediately, my hands extending on the table to feel connected again. It worked at the beginning, so why not now?

"Okay, I have never had to tell someone about my sexuality. It's always implied, so I cannot imagine having to come out to someone. Please know that you're safe with me. I see you, Adrián…" I grinned, and he leaned in and pressed a sweet kiss on my lips.

"There you are," I whispered, then he took my mouth with sensual swipes of his tongue, the taste of his milky coffee the best I've ever tasted. Time stood still as the lamps outside the plaza turned on, and night blanketed everything. The cool breeze reached us as our kiss grew incendiary.

"Marry me," Adrián gasped the moment our lips separated.

"Wait? What?!" A rush of adrenaline shot through me, my hands shook in Adrián's large palms, and the prickle behind my eyes couldn't be contained.

"I want to spend the rest of my life with you, Genevieve Raymond. Life is too fleeting…that I know. I thought I had the rest of my life mapped out, but then you came with your powerful aura and dedication. Many men would have been intimidated, hell I was that first night, but in a couple of days, you started showing me the real you…and I was captivated. Captivated with your brilliance, sweetness, and burgeoning sensuality, with your reserved nature and your inquisitiveness. All the things that make you, you. With you, I can be still, I can be loud, I can be sexual, I can be—just me. And even though our paths are very different, the similarities make it all possible in my eyes. You make it all possible. Would you marry me?" Adrián shifted from his seat and dropped down on one knee. In my periphery, I could see the owner of the coffee shop holding Adrián's cell phone, and it stoked me that he had actually planned this.

He had wanted to propose. This wasn't a spur-of-the-moment thing, but he'd ensured it was an intimate gesture, just for us. He'd taken the time to bring me to a place that reminded me of our first explorations together, ushering our short story to a new chapter. No public proposal, no great fanfare. Just him and me with his explanation of why he wanted to take this step with me. An explanation that resonated deep inside because he had also captivated me from day one. From his thoughtfulness, his courteous gestures, to the way he saw the world. His love for his family, and his care for me. Hard worker, goal oriented, but still deeply grounded. Self-aware and insightful. And oh so sensual. Handsome and just…

He got me.

With the backdrop of the plaza behind us, I accepted his pledge.

"I'll marry you!" I shouted, even though it was just the three of us in the coffee shop. Tears streamed down my face, and everything looked blurry until Adrián kissed me again. When he pushed back, I saw the tears falling down his face too, and I wiped them with my thumb.

"This is my mother's ring... Claudia had already married before they passed, and..."

He slid the warm gold ring on my finger, a twisted vine design with small glittering diamonds on the top. A bubble of air caught in my throat, and I couldn't speak, so I did the only thing I could. I embraced Adrián, the race of our hearts meeting as we both cried in joy.

The walk to the hotel was a blur, and even though it tempted me, the three-course dinner he'd planned for us full of Afro-Antillean delicacies wasn't enough incentive to convince me away from my goal. To get Adrián naked and in my mouth in record time.

The hotel room's old feel was a feast to the senses, or at least it would have been if I'd had the time to enjoy it. The bolt of serotonin made me high on love and lust, and I shoved Adrián inside the room, ready for him.

"Damn, woman, let me take my pants off first." He laughed as he removed his clothes, and I did the same with mine. Adrián stood bracketed by the view of the city and the bay behind him, an image of glittering night lights and the magnificence of his burnished brown skin. With confidence usually only present in boardrooms, I stalked toward him, then it was my turn to drop to my knees.

Adrián's deep groan filled my ears, and his salty taste flooded my buds as I explored his smooth length with gusto.

I might have done mostly regular things in bed, but this was one thing I excelled at.

"Uh, mmm. Gen, bebe, no puedo…ahhh me vas a ser venirme muy rápido." Every rumble of his traveled straight to my core until I wept in emptiness. But I could bring him back after he came for me. My single-minded goal remained to have him spill inside of me.

Whatever Spanish I understood told me he was fighting not to come too fast, but as always, I got my way.

Salty warmth poured down my throat as Adrián shouted his satisfaction.

"You did come to kill me," he accused as he collapsed to the carpet beside me, and I giggled in happiness.

"I didn't because I'll need you again tonight."

Adrián, the good man he was, delivered over and over until I had to beg for him to stop.

We fell asleep in soft white sheets, the promise of our future bright. No concerns would mar my happiness.

Nineteen

Genevieve

Brightness dislodged me from the land of dreams into reality. A reality where I had agreed to marry a man I met less than a year ago without minimal thought for the next steps.

The clock announced I had two more hours before my departure, and a pang of uncertainty hit me, leaving me paralyzed next to Adrián, who slept beside me, oblivious to my panic.

Marriage hadn't been part of my life plan. How, when love had never been fair to my mother? All my references were of men too intimidated by her intelligence and success. When I was younger, she tried to open herself for love, but the results were never favorable. I hadn't seen a successful marriage in anyone close to me, not anyone as successful as I aspired to be. Diligence, ambition, and drive required sacrifices... Sacrifices that seem to weigh heavier and heavier on my shoulders.

Then there were the concerns about our lifestyles. I was not high-maintenance but a creature of comfort. Adrián could fall asleep on the floor with a blanket on him. He wasn't trapped by any need for status; his only goal: his family's well-being and health. I envied that. There was nothing wrong with my view of life, but would it align with his? Would our everyday merge comfortably? And what would he do for work if he moved to the States? Was it wrong for me to want him to have a more solid plan?

Next to me, Adrián stirred in his sleep, his obnoxiously long lashes flickering open until his adoring gaze rested on me.

Oh yes... I could definitely see our everyday merging. I had forgotten how special he could make me feel with just one look.

"So, is this the part where you start freaking out?" He propped his head on his fist, swinging a leg out of the sheets. The ripple of strength all of that movement displayed made me study the clock again, wondering if I had time for a...

"Focus woman...no debauchery today," he said in mock outrage.

I flushed at his admonishment, then saw the white sheets and how they rose on a particular area of his anatomy.

"I think there'll be some debauchery today."

"Who am I kidding? I can't deny you a thing." He chuckled and lay back, staring at the ceiling. The beautiful lines of his lean muscles stretched, illuminated by the early morning sun. The struggle to ignore the tent under the white sheet was becoming an epic battle. "But for real, were you freaking out on me?"

"Well, aren't you? We have no definite plan."

"Step by step. We can look at the visa paperwork first. Then take it from there."

"So you are moving to Florida." I studied the planes of his

stomach and the thick arms I loved around me. He lay pensive on his bed but then turned his face to me.

"I know it's a lot, and if you need time…"

"No!" I blurted and studied the reaction. No, I didn't want to take time. This felt right. Every time I was with him, it felt right. I wanted this. I was tired of overthinking, analyzing, and seeing how marriage would fit in my fifty-five-year career plan. I just didn't know how to achieve this particular goal. But oh I had never wanted something as bad as a future with Adrián. That goal deserved the same type of determination I'd put in my career, didn't it?

"Okay, so we do the paperwork. With the visa, I can get a work permit so I can work there. I will find something to hold us over until…until I figure out my long-term plan, then we decide from there. I'll contribute to the finances of your apartment. Don't think I'm planning to come and wait for you to be the sole provider."

"I never thought that." But Mom, on the other hand…that conversation would be interesting. Having to defend maintaining Adrián while he received his work permit would be a hard conversation to have. Mom didn't rule my life, but to be honest, some of her concerns would have mirrored mine if this was any other man. Was I jumping into this too fast? Letting the high of love take over rationality? The pendulum of my thoughts was making me dizzy.

"Okay." He nodded and bolted out of the bed. "Come on. I want to take you to have some breakfast before the flight."

The grumble in my stomach approved of that plan.

Two hours would never be enough to plan the rest of our life, and the minutes fell through my fingers like sand. After some quick debauchery in the shower, we headed out for breakfast. I continued to "project manage" the upcoming months while Adrián patiently let me spiral while holding my hand.

"Where should we get married?"

"Can we decide that when I am in Florida?"

"Fine, but we need to decide, because if we are doing a big wedding then I need to plan the event…"

"Do you want a big wedding?"

"Uh…" A few days ago I wasn't even thinking of a wedding, how would I know what I wanted?

"So, let's pencil that in as things to consider," Adrián said gently, his sexy smile making me wish we'd just ordered breakfast in bed instead.

"What are you going to do about LasDell and Villa Bonita?"

"Any admin work I can help with remotely, and I do plan to find more work as soon as that permit arrives in the mail."

"Do you want us to move? I have a nice apartment, but it might be too small."

"Let's live together first and decide if we need to change that."

And so along we went, me in a slight panic while Adrián exhibited an annoying amount of patience. Not going to lie, it was very sexy to me. Maybe we could have a quickie in his apartment before the airport… I looked at the time and realized that wasn't possible and almost wailed out loud. After stuffing my face with hojaldras and chorizo, I hopped back in his vehicle, forlorn to leave him behind.

"So, you feel comfortable with this plan? Are you moving as soon as you get the visa? Are you sure? And…"

"Breathe, Preciosa. One step at the time. This will work. Trust me." And Adrián enveloped me in a hug calming all my nerves. Now if only I could calm my racing thoughts.

Twenty

Adrián

The sweltering heat surrounded me immediately when I stepped out of the airport in Miami.

Time had accelerated the instant Gen and I decided to move forward with our lives together. The visa process, from all we had gathered, could be a swift or lengthy one. Expecting months, we had filled out the paperwork, secure in the time we had to make the needed changes in our lives to join them successfully.

I hadn't been expecting less than two months. I received the invitation to the embassy a month into the request, which set a chain of events that brought me to this hot Florida morning waiting for Gen to pick me up.

My chest vibrated with mixed emotions, just a tiny sample of the myriad of physical reactions since I got the visa. Pain to say goodbye to my family and Villa Bonita, and not sure when I would return. Chills with excitement as I packed, imagining placing my clothes next to Gen's. Indigestion as I dealt with Julín's cold shoulder. Nostalgia-filled goodbyes with my friends and family. When I traversed the security checkpoint to go to my gate, my throat closed up, and I could not look back to see them all waving one last time.

The exhaust of vehicles burned my nose, as droplets of sweat trickled down my back, and I tapped my feet to the invisible music in my head that had kept me together through the walk out of the airport.

A white car beeped loudly startling me out of my fog, blinding lights flashed in the darkened underground arrival area, and then a door popped open.

"Hey! We gotta move fast. Let me open the trunk." Gen jumped out of the car in a whirl of cream clothes, sleek hair, and smiles. She threw her arms around me, immediately settling a question that had moved in, niggling in the back of my mind.

Was this the right move?

My chest expanded, taking in her familiar scent of cinnamon and honey and her softness soothing all the turmoil inside. Yes… this was the right move. I had left a crying Claudia and a pissed Julín behind for a worthy reason. This was why I had to trust that Villa Bonita would be okay and that Julín would thrive without me there. I had to trust because holding Gen close felt as right as I had felt in a long time.

"Okay, let's go," Gen whispered in my ear, and I entered her vehicle, finally excited for the future.

White, beige, and pink.

An abundance of the first, contrasted with the second with splashes of the third. I took in my new home, an apartment on the fourth floor of a small building in an area she had described as nice but not like "nice nice," but that to me felt way more than what she described.

I wandered to the living area with its comfortable seating, with a pink throw over beige furniture. The coffee table had an assortment of travel magazines and hidden behind the main sofa I spied fuzzy slippers, which made me grin. Her kitchen opened up to the living area, and the dining room stood right by the window, with an open plan that made the space feel larger than its reality. Gen stood by the door, watching me with apprehension, and I winked at her.

"I got the mortgage when I became director. It was a bit out of my range but... I fell in love with it when I walked through that door," Gen said proudly.

"It's beautiful, love," I said, meaning that.

Everything in the space screamed Gen. She had pictures of her with her mom, assortments of prizes declaring her best team member or best manager, showing her progression to the top. Her kitchen was oddly bare of any fruits or produce on the counters, and when I peeked at the fridge, I found oat milk, eggs, bacon, and a few packs of salads.

The space smelled just like her, and there were books about building your career, being an effective leader, and much more.

Then right in front of the sofa was a large flat-screen TV.

"I bet that TV sees you asleep more than you see it on." I chuckled, and she laughed.

"No lies. Damn. You know me too well."

"I do...now show me the bedroom, Preciosa." I smirked at her and she rolled her eyes but gestured for me to follow. I took off my sneakers and gladly trailed her.

"This is my...our room." She gestured as we entered the

large chamber with a king bed in the middle of more beige, this time mixed with lavenders and pinks. A sizable dresser and mirror sat on one side and on the other the bathroom door and a small bookcase filled with more books about hospitality and success. A comfortable fussy white chair sat in a corner with a big blanket on top.

"Wow, you really like pink, huh?"

"I didn't envision myself living here with anyone else, so I leaned into my design side." She interlaced her fingers and started cracking her knuckles. Shit, we were back to the nerves. I got it. I felt nervous as hell too, but it was to be expected. After dropping my backpack I crossed the large bedroom to her, taking her soft hands in mine.

She blew a sigh of relief, our gazes connecting.

"Missed you," she whispered.

"I missed you too," I said, pressing my body against hers. Her cream pencil skirt and silk blouse taunted me, a package ready to be opened to reveal the beauty that lay within.

"We should redecorate, make the space ours," she whispered calming my thoughts before they were even a concern.

"We have time, we can do it slowly."

We stood close, our breath matching as we relearned each other through touch, sight, and sounds. Our mouths met in a relaxed exhale, reminding me that we no longer had to rush because we had forever. Our tongues intertwined, and her taste traveled straight to my growing erection. Maneuvering by feel, I guided her toward the bed, where we collapsed in a tangle of limbs, passion building, without breaking the kiss. Gen moaned and attempted to throw a leg over my hip; then as if water had been splashed over us, she parted in a frustrated groan, scrambling up to stand.

"I have to go back to the office," she whispered, looking down at me, while my hard dick strained inside my jeans.

"What?"

"Yeah, I have to go back. We have a staff meeting this afternoon that I can't miss. But I'll be home early."

It took a second to register that she had plans to return to the office. I had flown in early, and this was technically lunchtime, but I had assumed...

"Oh, don't look like that, you know I would have stayed, but this meeting is...it's important..." Shaking off my disappointment, I nodded, flipping my perspective. This would allow me time to settle and unpack. Get myself comfortable and familiar with the area. Take a walk around the block. Yes, this was okay.

"Come here," I growled, standing to gather her close, my hands full of her abundant ass.

"I'm gonna let you go, but tonight..." I bit her neck, and she threw her head back, moaning, her hips pressing against my groin. I couldn't help myself; I trailed kisses down her chest into her cleavage, getting lost in her velvety skin.

"Tonight Mom's coming for dinner, but after yes..."

It was my turn to jerk back, causing Gen to whine in disappointment.

"Your mom?"

"Yeah, we...we're having dinner with her. I figured you could meet her the first night. Then in the next few days, you can meet Gino."

I had no qualms about meeting Gen's mom. None, but she'd curated this image in my mind with her love and her complaints that had me feeling a certain way about having to do this meet and greet the first night I arrived. I wanted time to get used to us, in our space, before anything else. But her mom was important, and I understood that.

"Alright. Okay, you want me to cook?"

"Nah, that's why I'm coming home early. To cook and for us to have a little time before she arrives. I'll be home at four, and dinner is at seven."

"Now you're speaking my language." I pulled her close again and made sure she left to work with a significant incentive to return.

Genevieve was late. Dinner with her mom was set for 7:00 p.m. It was 6:15 p.m. and she hadn't arrived nor texted. Once I'd realized around 5:15 she wasn't on her way, I'd ventured out to the supermarket a block away, buying some simple ingredients to get dinner going. An hour later, I had diced peppers, garlic and had a pot of rice on the stove. Oil spattered hot in a frying pan, ready for the sliced plátanos I had for the tajadas and I had a salad of lettuce, tomato, and cucumbers sitting on a plate.

The shrimp had been way more expensive than anything I had ever paid for in Panamá, but I wanted to impress Lissette, hoping to make her fall in love with my cooking. Her approval wasn't necessary to me; Gen's need for that approval was what fueled me.

The smell of shrimp al ajillo sizzled on the pan as Gen finally made her entrance at 6:45, throwing her heels to the side as she padded into the kitchen.

"Oh my God, I'm so so sorry, I didn't realize I left my cell in the car, and by the time I realized, I couldn't leave the meeting, which ended up running so much later than expected." She sighed getting right next to me. "What do I do?"

"You can set the table and pull the plates and cups. The food is almost ready. You told me your mother was punctual so…"

A knock stopped my words.

"Yup. You were right about that. I love that you remembered." Gen kissed my cheek quickly, then sped to the door. I pursed my lips and girded myself for the upcoming hours. I followed at my own pace as Gen opened the door.

"Mom, hi," Gen said as a woman taller than Gen with the same dark brown complexion entered the room.

Lissette Raymond was imposing; I could see where Gen got that aura of command and self-assurance she usually exuded. But where Gen was often vulnerable around me, Lissette currently showcased an impenetrable shell.

"So, this is the young man you have decided to marry impulsively?" Lissette glided into the house, not bothering to remove her heels, until she posted up right in front of me. An aggressive, simmering energy emanated from her, and I realized this night would not go as Gen expected. I gained nothing from antagonizing Lissette, so I kept my calm, unwilling to match her intensity.

"Mrs. Raymond, I'm glad to meet you finally. Thanks for coming tonight," I greeted her, extending my hand. No hug would be coming, so I didn't try.

"Mmm-hmm, I come whenever I like. This is my daughter's apartment," she claimed and put down her purse on one of the sofas.

"Mom." Gen's forceful reminder made Lissette smile, then as if she hadn't just come into the apartment with fighting words, she sat on the seat at the head of the dining room table.

"It's alright." I squeezed Gen's arm as I walked past her back to the kitchen to finish serving the dinner.

This would be a long night.

★ ★ ★

We ate silently for a few minutes after a begrudging "this is good" from Lissette.

"So, young man, what are your plans now that you're here?"

I'm unsure what exactly I'd done to earn her skepticism. But I'd promised myself to keep the peace, so I was honest. I sat across from Gen, whose frown was so loud, I could sense it whispering her displeasure in my ears.

"Not certain yet. I want to find a job that provides me balance to continue to grow our relationship healthily." I extended my palm to Gen, who grinned apologetically and placed her hand on mine.

"Mom, Adrián owns a small business in Panamá, actually two. They are both…growing, but they are still both his, and together we're working on ways of expanding them from here too," Gen explained. Well, that was news to me. She helped set up ads, which had helped get more bookings in Villa Bonita, but I hadn't realized she wanted to be more involved. It warmed my heart, but the skeptic in me wondered if this was to appease her need for constant success. I wanted the business to provide for my family, while she was using words like expansion. I squeezed her hand in acknowledgment, tucking in my concerns for another day. We had time. We had plenty of time.

"Oh yes, that little motel he has on the beach? Isn't it just your family house and you rent some rooms? That won't be enough to maintain a household in this country. As you know, Genevieve works hard, so I want to ensure you plan to do the same." Lissette stared at me with a challenging glint in her eyes.

"Whatever plans Gen and I have, they are ours, and as long as Gen is good, then we are good."

Gen's nervous laughter hit me like a warning bell. She slid her hand away from mine and focused on her meal.

"You know, I had another great meeting today, speaking about expansion. We reached out to the architect company in Panamá where A.D. Nicholson used to work, we're hoping they reach out to him."

Fuck. Of all things, this was what she segued with? This whole dinner was a disaster. I should have told Gen before proposing about my relationship with the Tropics, but something continued to block me, and I seldom ignored my gut. There was still healing to be done, for the wrongs I had wrought, but it was my past, and I should be able to tell it at my pace.

When I had proposed to her, I had wanted to tell her before, for her to understand me even better, and now with it dangling over us, I knew it was time. It allowed Gen to make decisions if she needed to.

I hoped she understood my hesitation in telling her because sometimes, her goal-oriented hunger came out and made me wonder if she would ever comprehend the steps I took to move on from tragedy.

But it had to wait until we were on our own, this night needed to go well, for Gen's sake and even for Lissette.

So I stayed chill, polishing my shrimp, the savory flavors flooding my mouth, making me think of home. I kept my shit together while Gen and her mother discussed A.D. Nicholson and how it would a boon for her career to find him.

"Tropics wants to retain him for exclusive work. The numbers they're thinking...unprecedented."

My heart skipped at the kind of money I could make

again...but no, there was a reason why I had left that side of my life behind. Look at Gen, she barely had any balance. The Tropics wouldn't be a suitable environment for me.

I pushed myself with no help from anyone, no boss needed to ask me to work late, or do more, I believed in hard work. However, when Gen told me stories of how additional responsibilities had been added to her plate post accepting the job, it raised a flag. How could I explore a future with this company where I could keep a balanced life, if this was common practice?

"Mmm-hmm. I hope you find him. It would be such a windfall for your career. See, young man. When I ask about plans, this is what I mean. Gen is very successful. She deserves someone who matches that energy. I would know. Her father was another man who thought love and vibes would fill our pantry. So, while I worked hard, he just...did odd work here and there...needless to say it didn't last long. And I don't regret it one bit."

At this point, my mood had grown from curious annoyance to feeling disrespected. I stared at Gen, who glared at her mom then turned an apologetic gaze at me.

"Mom, that is unfair. This is not like my dad. And you forget he was an artist. You knew it when you got with him, and he asked you to..." Gen took a deep breath and then shook something off.

"Mom, I've got an early day tomorrow, and it is Adri's first day here. Maybe we do brunch another Sunday, huh?" she said gently, and I wondered if this would be how it would always go. If her mother's personality would overpower our need for unity as a couple.

★ ★ ★

"Babe… Adri, I'm… Shit, that was bad. I'm so sorry."

Gen's mattress felt like pure heaven underneath me after one of the most challenging days in my life. I stared at the ceiling, arms crossed behind my head, wearing basketball shorts as Gen sat up with her laptop on her legs, wearing a cute pink tank top and shorts that made me look twice when she got in bed.

In the span of fewer than twelve hours, I'd said goodbye to my kin and country, had walked into uncharted territory, and was greeted by hostility and a lackluster welcome. I tried my best to give Gen grace. She couldn't control her mother. I understood that, but why, if she knew what Lissette was on about our marriage, had she invited her to the apartment on our first night together under the same roof? None of it made sense.

"What exactly are you apologizing for?" I asked, and she tensed next to me.

"Well, my mom can be an asshole, but she's like that at first. She'll warm up."

"Gen, I…listen, I can't lie. Your mom was rude and disrespectful, and she doesn't even know me. But my main worry is not that. I didn't have any high expectations from her, but you…well, last I knew, we were both grown. Why does she have such a hold on your life?"

"Excuse me?" The temperature on her side dropped by several degrees. Shit, I was messing this up.

"Look, I get it. I was close to my parents. Shit, you can see I'm close to Claudia, but there is this hold she has on you…"

"Like Julín on you?"

"That's not fair. I'm here, am I not?"

"And I'm in this too! Why would you…ugh." She shoved her laptop off and stomped off to the bathroom. A few minutes later, she returned with a full-body onesie, white with pink bows scattered all over, and I stared. That shit looked... fuck, I was mad right now, but that onesie looked sexy on her. And it was such a contrast, I loved that she could show me all her facets.

"Uhhh...what just happened?"

"Well, this—" she pointed at herself "—is what I really wear at night when I'm by myself. I was embarrassed and, also I thought we would have sex, but if we are gonna fight on the first night, I need all the comfort I can get." She threw her hands up.

"I don't want to fight, Gen. I'm...this is a lot okay, I just... I truly don't want to argue." I sighed and stood up, helpless to her magnetism. Her eyes brimmed with sadness, and I wanted to erase that look, even if I needed my own balm for my feelings.

"So, this is what you wear to bed?" I asked, ghosting my arms around her hips.

"Yes..." she whispered.

"It's sexy as fuck," I murmured in her ear and loved how she trembled. Now that we were touching...it was easier. The soothing calmed me.

"How can we navigate your mom so that we fulfill your needs but respect my boundaries?" I asked, my hands full of her ass, itching to do more, but my mind needed reassurance, that, and my heart.

A heavy sigh wracked through her body, and she pressed a soft kiss right above my nipple, making me shiver.

"Stop playin'," I chastised her.

"How can I when you feel so good?" She burrowed deeper

into me, waking my lower body up as I met with her soft goodness.

"We need to talk…"

"Yes, I know." She sighed and pushed back from me. My dick protested the lack of her softness, and I concurred, but if we were going to move forward, we needed these conversations.

I took her hand and brought her back to my side of the bed, settling her on my lap, her long legs surrounding my sides.

"Dad asked Mom to move when I was really young. She is very picky with what she shares, but it seems he wanted them to move back together to Panamá with me. She was spooked but considered it, but then he changed his mind last-minute. Left without us. Broke her heart. I remember some of this because I had to go to my grandma's house before she passed because my mom was severely depressed. Lost her job, her first manager job, and had to be institutionalized…" She sighed again. "Once she was out…it was like…a switch was flipped. Her career and I were her only focus."

"Wow, I'm sorry, Preciosa, that must have been hard on her and you." My chest caved to know her mother had endured such challenging times. And Genevieve, she might have been young, but to see her mother navigate those difficult periods on top of her dad leaving…

"It was…and she still deals with depression. Structure, goals, challenge…they keep her centered. It's her defense mechanism."

"Damn."

"Yes, which is why it is the way it is with us… I get that it seems a bit dysfunctional, but it allows her structure. And I'm driven too… I was young, but I remember how it felt not knowing what the next meal would look like while she clawed her way back to normalcy. I...don't ever want that for myself."

"I get it." I pressed a kiss on her forehead, then another on her lips, tasting the uncertainty there.

"And I get her concern about you having work..."

It was my turn to sigh. I had that concern too; just the prices at the supermarket had jolted me to the true reality of living here. I couldn't have expected her to carry the load on her own—and hadn't—but my work with the transportation company would maybe be enough for a utility bill or two here.

That didn't cut it.

"So, let's accelerate getting married."

"Are you sure? We have the ninety days. We can plan a little celebration in a couple of months..."

"We need the marriage certificate for me to get a work permit." This whole process was maddening. I wanted to be a true partner to her, and carry my own load, but I depended on Gen for every step of creating a life here. There was no path that didn't include her sponsoring my way forward.

"You're right...okay, okay, let's do it." Gen's watery smile told me this wasn't her vision, but we knew this process would be rocky. I'd figure out how to make it up to her. I would.

"There is something else you need to know." After everything she'd just shared with me, I couldn't keep her in the dark anymore. A metallic flavor flooded my mouth, and my stomach cramped up. I squeezed her hips in the reassurance of how real she felt on top of me. She snuggled closer, clearly exhausted but willing to listen.

"I...know A.D. Nicholson...shit, there is no way to ease into this. I'm A.D. Nicholson. Adrián David Nicolas."

Twenty-One

Genevieve

Sleepiness threatened to take me away, but this conversation with Adrián was meaningful. Now that we had both established what was essential for us, we needed to move forward, but apparently, he had one more thing to say.

He tensed up below me in preparation for what he had to share, but I was so tired I didn't brace myself.

"I...know A.D. Nicholson...shit, there is no way to ease into this. I'm A.D. Nicholson. Adrián David Nicolas."

I should have braced myself.

"What?!" I screamed, breaking the soothing vibe we had created together.

I attempted to get off of him, but he held on to my hips as I watched him, stunned. Adrián locked his jaw, but his eyes... they pleaded for me to understand. Something about how he watched me softened me enough to relax in his lap again.

"I've told you how I used to be a workaholic..."

"Yeah, but I guess I always assumed it was something to do

with transportation or even hospitality, and that you had pivoted to what you do now." How oblivious was I not to even ask? This man had the ability to scramble my thoughts and my acumen. Around him, I was a lovesick girl with no malice.

Naive, that is what he made me. I knew we had a lot of past to still explore together—I didn't expect him to regurgitate all of his life events in a night or two—but this was a very significant thing to leave out. Why would he keep something like this from me? We'd been nothing but open with each other; I thought everything we built together was on a solid foundation of mutual trust but now...now I didn't know what to think. What to expect next.

"It's not on you, and I never meant for this to become a thing. I just... I don't talk about my career that often, actually never."

I paused, flabbergasted at his explanation. *He didn't expect this to become a thing?*

A thing?

He was the man I've been searching for, for weeks. I should have known; how did I not put two and two together?

"Why the pseudonym?" Maybe if I focused on small details, I would avoid the encroaching fear mingled with anger threatening to take over.

"I went to school for architecture for my parents. I wanted to redesign Villa Bonita. You haven't seen pictures of what it was, but it was a mess, falling apart. It needed so much work. And we didn't have the money. I'd always had an artistic side, loved to draw, and I had a good eye for design and was handy. It all made sense in my eighteen-year-old mind. Then it took me years to finish my studies. Years because I kept taking time off to help in Villa Bonita or help Claudia and Mario with the kids. My grandpa, Dad's dad, was the one to encourage me to finish. He had me stay at his place in the city to focus. By the time I was close to graduating, he had passed, and... I wanted to honor him, so I started signing my designs with our family's old last name and my first two initials. It stuck, and those designs got me in at my firm."

"Oh...but why...why the secrecy?"

"There is none, at least not in my circles. My old colleagues have been respectful of my need to leave my career because they know what happened. I think people made the situation more mysterious than it was."

"What happened?" I rested my hand on his chest, where I could feel his heartbeat the strongest. Whatever it was...it was life-changing. I could see it in his haunted gaze. My fear hadn't diminished, but it had taken a different color.

What about us two hadn't allowed him to open up about this? I had to trust we could avoid something like this in the future. Here I was thinking of an *us*, while finding out he kept something so big from me. I really was gone.

"I had a very important presentation of the Panamá Tropics project that evening...it was my birthday, and I usually went to Colón, but I decided to stay in the city. Too much work. It had become the norm. I hadn't been in Colón for months. The only time was when they came to Panamá City. Mom, Pops, everyone would pack up the car and head to my place. They decided to surprise me. Two cars in a caravan on that dark road..." His voice broke, and he shuddered under my touch. Suddenly I didn't want him to say it; I knew what was coming.

"Oh, Adrián."

"Yeah. My dad lost control of their car. We aren't certain

how. Chichi was riding with them, but miraculously he was okay. All the damage was in the front of the car. They were probably gone on impact. They hit a pole on the side of the road."

Tears gathered in my eyes as Adrián got emotional. He wasn't over the hurt, but how could he ever be? And without asking, I understood he blamed himself. I understood why he'd kept it from me. Not because he wanted to hide it, but because he had not fully processed it all himself. That didn't excuse him keeping things from me, but my heart broke to hear what he'd been through.

"I'm rational. I promise I understand the danger of the blame game, but objectively, they wouldn't have been on that road if it wasn't for me. If it wasn't for me prioritizing work over them. The sense of pride I felt every time I put money in my parent's bank account was my driver, but pride was my fall. I was getting great projects, being pulled in different directions. I was exploring my sexuality in the city where there was a little bit more open-mindedness, not that my parents ever made me feel less, but others…they just didn't understand."

The download of so much between the two of us had drained me of all semblance of delicacy; I wanted to comfort him and sleep. That simple.

The rest I would sort out tomorrow with a clear mind. But understanding that the name of A.D. Nicholson was so connected to the trauma he was still healing from…it made sense. It made sense why he had separated himself from all that reminded me of how he had neglected his family in his eyes.

"Adri…let's go to sleep. I get it. I do. I can't imagine what it would be like to have experienced losing my parents like that and… I even understand blaming yourself even though you know you had no control over what happened that night. Whatever shortcomings you think you have, you are your family's rock, and now that we are together... Maybe I can be your support too? We will figure it all out tomorrow. But for now, let's rest."

"Are you upset with me?" he asked, his voice already trailing off as I plopped next to him, and he gathered me in, his arm draped over my waist, hand on my belly. My heart settled securely, knowing we would figure out the next steps together.

"Anger filled me at first, to know you'd kept something so big from me. It took all of me to keep levelheaded while you spoke. Now...I don't know. I...I'm not. I... I wish you'd told me, felt comfortable opening up. What does this say about our mutual trust?"

"No, no. That was exactly my fear. Every day that I didn't tell you who I was I feared what damage I could be doing to our trust. I just... I justified it all in my mind, at first I thought we wouldn't last the two weeks. Then it was too new, we were getting to know each other, I figured I had time. But then once Tropics started looking for me... I should have said something, no matter how hard it was. No matter the fear I felt about the proposal they wanted to give me... I should have been sincere. Because I do trust you, and I want you to trust me. I mishandled this and I'm so sorry for the hurt and anger I caused. I don't want this to become what breaks us."

Ugh. This man. He even apologized perfectly. No matter how much I wanted to hold on to anger and indignation, I just didn't have it in me. I knew he was dealing with grief from the time he showed me his parents resting place. To now know how deeply embedded his career was to that grief... I couldn't imagine. If I lost my mom tomorrow due to work, how would that impact my mental health?

"I don't want this to break us either. So we won't let it, it's that simple. We knew it would be bumpy at first…" The tinge of fear of the unknown resonated an alarm, but I ignored it. I'd always gone into my decisions with a full deck of information, everything studied. Pros and cons detailed. Not this time, and I wouldn't let the fear take over. Even if our first day together in Florida had been less than desirable.

"I love you, Preciosa." He said it so simply and I felt every impact of the weight of his words. I didn't need anything more than that.

"And I you," I said because, with us, it was that straightforward. That easy.

We both fell asleep seconds later, the first night of the rest of our life.

No more snoozing.

I jumped out of the bed and had exactly thirty-five minutes to get myself together and out of the door. The vestiges of anger, fear, and determination lingered in the back of my mind like pesky flies that refused to go away.

Adrián lay sprawled, the laugh lines next to his mouth showing slightly more than the last time I saw him. I couldn't wait to see how time would mark him gently and for me to be the person to catalog each and every change. It was a privilege I wouldn't have had if I hadn't taken this risk and for that I was thankful. With all the chaos of our lives converging, there wasn't a moment I didn't feel unvarnished joy being with him. My doubts were not of our compatibility, nor our love, but of every other practicality that surrounded our everyday life.

They said love conquered all, but that was the movies and books. Here I had the sexiest, most beautiful, kind man I had ever met, inside and out, and love was working overtime to ensure we could smooth over all the little fires that kept creeping up around us.

I dashed to the bathroom where I took the most efficient, shortest shower ever—then dealt with my makeup while the flat iron warmed up so I could smooth my hair. I hurried out to put the coffee on, but a warm sturdy body collided with mine.

"Hey, where you're rushing away to?" Adrián said, sliding one arm around my waist, his hand finding its favorite spot on my ass. I didn't think I'd be ready to face him after last night, but now that he was awake, I couldn't have been more wrong. His embrace soothed all the worries away. If only I could bottle this feeling and take it to work with me, I'd have an outstanding day.

"I have to finish getting ready."

"Okay, but why are you running?"

"I wasn't running." I frowned.

"Wow, you don't even notice it anymore." He planted a kiss on my forehead, and I puckered my lips, ready for the next one.

"Nah, I gotta brush my teeth first." He shook his head, winking at me when I pouted, and he swaggered into the bathroom. I stared at that firm ass under the sweatpants, then shook myself, remembering I had thirteen minutes left.

I was pouring my coffee into my travel mug when he walked out, all that dick I hadn't enjoyed the night before taunting me as it bobbed inside his sweatpants.

"Hey, eyes up here, woman," he said, laughing.

"Sorry." I shrugged, my cheeks heating, but honestly, I had no regrets. Well, I had one, the fact that I was leaving without a ride on his—

"No, you're not because you are still staring at me like that. And if you continue, I'm not gonna be nice, and you'll end up late for work," he promised, and I was startled when the alarm on my watch went off, letting me know it was time to depart.

"I expect to see you tonight, ready for my arrival. It's Friday, so hopefully…"

"Don't hope, Preciosa, just make sure you get here on time. Because he and I will be waiting." He ran his hand over his length, then grabbed right under, showcasing exactly what I was walking away from.

My paid time off bank is full again, isn't it?

"Oh… I know you probably want to tell your boss about A.D. Nicholson… I need a second to wrap my mind around it all, and it doesn't mean I can't…" He shrugged, opening the door to a conversation I feared would take a lot of finesse and diplomacy. I tampered my excitement. After anger and disappointment had their way with me, a cautious hope had bloomed. Here I had A.D. Nicholson, in my house, ready for duty…but only if he wanted it. And with everything he told me about his parents last night, convincing him would be difficult.

"I wasn't going to say anything until we spoke, but…this would be good, no? For Claudia and the babies and Mario and even Julín?" I really tried not to growl his name, but Adrián's headshake told me I was unsuccessful. "I got no beef with him, but…the man don't like me."

"I know…but he has his reasons, no matter how wrong

they are. And I know you think this is all good, but…have you thought what it would mean for us?"

I had. It would mean stability, security, and I'd get to see my man at work. All wins in my book. But clearly I'd missed something. "What are you saying? I know you're still a hard worker, and I can see your steps to healing, so it would be just like working on Villa Bonita or LasDell…"

"No, it wouldn't. I was very strategic about what I decided to do after the crash. I worked with my family, not away from them. Taking this job…it would put us with conflicting schedules all the time. I would probably be traveling a lot to different countries for projects and…" Adrián grabbed the back of his neck, eyes clouded, and I tried to see things from his perspective.

I was failing, though; we had already done the long-distance thing, so it couldn't be worse than that. Whenever he was in the office, he'd be a couple of floors away. And I could probably manage some trips to my own territories to coincide with his. This was a good thing. How could he not see it? Not wanting to get worked up before work, I filled my lungs, expelling all anxiety and animosity.

"I…hear you. Let's talk about it more, okay?" I wondered, if I deployed my skilled professional persuasion, what would happen? I left that Gen out of our dealings, but…it was part of me… I didn't disagree with him that we would both have long days of work ahead of us if he accepted.

Just weeks ago, I was wondering about new ways to think of my career and my future, and here I was asking him to go back to something that clearly did not serve him anymore. But… I couldn't shake the feeling that he did love it. Adrián had just equated everything that happened before the accident as this "big bad thing" and maybe, with his newfound balance, he would be able to make it work. I could deploy my negotiation tactics, I was tempted to, but then my watch vibrated again.

"Shit, I gotta go. Love you." I yanked my door open, but it bounced back and closed. In some ninja move, I would have to study when I had more time; Adrián had reached the door frame, his body pressed over mine, one arm braced over me. I forgot how his sturdiness was the perfect contrast to my tallness, and I avoided the urge to purr in satisfaction.

"You don't walk out of the door, ever, without kissing me goodbye first. Understood?" His hooded gaze studied me.

"Yes…" I moaned, and he captured my mouth in a savage but short kiss that left me breathing heavily.

"Now go, you'll be late." He opened the door and turned me around, giving me a swat on my ass that made me jump.

"Remember, be here on time."

Oh yes, Adri.

Damn, the end of the day couldn't come fast enough.

"What was that cryptic message you sent me?" Anita's beautiful face popped up on my screen with an eyebrow raised. I had tried to see if she had known who A.D. Nicholson was, and she had always been vague with her responses. Now… I wondered…had they known each other all along, and she knew who he was?

"Have you been keeping secrets, Anita Johnson?"

"Girl, if you don't tell me what you wanna know…"

"But I have! I have asked you several times, and you always give me the runaround!"

"Ohhh, you figured it out, didn't you?"

"Ahhh, so you knew A.D. Nicholson is him?!" I whisper yelled at the camera. My voice carried enough that Anibal burst into the room with Arjun, who followed behind, looking mildly amused.

"What are you screaming about and...mmm, I should have known... Anita Johnson." Anibal strolled over to me to face the camera. He crossed his arms, glaring at the camera while Anita returned the favor. Arjun sat across my desk and shrugged apologetically.

"We were just coming to invite you to happy hour," Arjun explained.

"Ah." I nodded.

"So, did I just hear right? Did I hear that you have known A.D. Nicholson's whereabouts and did not share?" Anibal accused. What the heck? He had no bone in this game. LATAM wasn't his region anymore. And he barely cared about the expansion plans anyway; he was effective but always with that laissez-faire vibe.

This indignation was...interesting.

"Oh please, here you Americans go again. If I knew, I wouldn't say anything. Clearly, the man retired from that career, and you all know there was some tragic reason why and you still haven't given a flying fuck about it. Still trying to figure it out. He was never hiding. He just wasn't doing that work anymore. I have no regrets." She glared back at Anibal, who scoffed, but he looked chastised.

My stomach curdled at Anita's words. All through this, we had been adamant about finding more info about who he was but...never cared to examine why he had removed himself from his career. Adrián's words flashed through my brain and guilt prickled at me.

"Whatever. You act like you don't like working for the Tropics. It is one of the best companies in hospitality in your country, and you know it," Anibal retorted with a satisfied grin. Arjun and I just followed along, spectators at a tennis match.

"You really think the Tropics is the end all be all? How sad. I'm about to leave a bit early to go on a weekend trip to the beach with my fiancé. Let me guess, Anibal, will you put in some extra hours tomorrow to impress your bosses? Yeah, I thought so. You're arguing with me when I don't care what you think. I'm proud of everything I do, but this is my job, not my life. Tomorrow if I become a seamstress, I'll be as proud to do that job as well. You, on the other hand… Chao!"

Anita ended the call as the winner because clearly she was unaffected, compared to Anibal, who stomped to the other seat across from my desk and threw himself there with a growl. The chair creaked under his robust weight and his frown spoke volumes. Anita's words affected me too. To be confident that no matter where your career took you, you were proud of your accomplishments. I don't think I've ever had that conviction. My sense of self has so long been tied to my career path that if I needed to detangle both, I was afraid of what I'd have left. The realistic side of me asserted that I'd done everything right. I was successful, climbing the corporate rungs, and soon would be in a position to expand this world for other people like me. The pang of envy that resonated inside of me at Anita's last words told me that deep inside, I wanted more. I craved more. Good for Anita for knowing what she wanted unapologetically.

"Damn. She really is leaning into you not being her boss anymore." I grinned, attempting to lighten things up.

"Man, I always thought you had your shit together...until today." Arjun clapped Anibal on the back. "Now I know you're human like the rest of us. And with that, I'm going to head out to meet everyone else for happy hour. See y'all there?"

"Nah." We both responded at the same time, and Arjun chuckled and left.

"What the fuck was that, bossy boss?" I rounded on Anibal as soon as Arjun walked away.

"I have no idea." He ran his hand over his curls, clearly flustered. Anita's words lingered in the back of my mind, and I couldn't wait to get home and speak with Adrián.

Once Anibal left the office, I started packing up to go home when Ricard stormed into the room.

"We need to have an emergency meeting. I just caught Anibal in his office. The executive office wants the GM meeting's focus next week to shift to expansion."

My heart sank as Ricard walked me through the changes, knowing it would be a long night and a long weekend.

Years ago, I'd have been thrilled by the challenge, excited to work the long hours to come but now... I didn't know if this was what fulfilled me anymore, and it filled my heart with fear and trepidation.

Was this Adrián's influence, or was this in me before him?

I texted him the news and went into the boardroom to work with the team, who all looked pissed to be there on a Friday night.

For the first time in my career, I was pissed to be there too.

Twenty-Two

Adrián

A weekend to spend in my thoughts while supporting Genevieve. Her work demanded all her attention, and knowing how mind- and body-consuming working long hours could be, I made sure to be her cheerleader during the quiet times.

"So, you're just gonna spoil me the whole day?" Gen asked on Sunday as I brought her a plate loaded with mini sandwiches, chips, and grapes. I set the obligatory cup of black coffee next to her and planted a kiss on her forehead.

"Yes, I know how working through the weekend without breaks feels. But you must promise me you'll stop before it gets dark tonight. You need to reset before the week starts. What are you wearing tomorrow? Do you need me to press it?" I strolled away to the kitchen to grab my own plate but turned back when her keyboard clacking stopped.

"Are you real?" she asked in awe.

"Stop it. I'm home until we get my work permit. Did you

think I would sit on the sofa and surf channels?" I brushed her off and kept approaching the kitchen.

"I just wish I could take time off to spend it with you."

"You still can," I said, trying to keep my tone relaxed. Genevieve sighed but didn't respond, and I didn't push. She'd shared Anita's words of wisdom on Friday night, and they weighed heavy on her.

Same as the A.D. Nicholson situation.

Not knowing what the right step forward was, I understood my mental block with the entire situation wasn't healthy either. I'd been turning the idea in my mind over and over, wondering what was the right step to take. Something that honored me and my additional needs.

So, in an attempt to keep all my options open, I agreed to meet with Gen and her boss later this week. The money I could canvas for us and for everyone in Panamá was a strong motivator.

"We will find the time," I said, attempting to cheer her up.

"Sure, yeah. I know," she responded, but there was no conviction in her voice.

The alarm woke me up before Gen, just as I had planned. After putting my plan in place I slid back into bed and Gen curled up, her warm back and booty pressed against me, and I skated my hands down her hips, today's onesie blue with palm trees all over. She'd confessed she'd bought it after returning to Florida after our two-week idyllic time. I loved how passionate she'd been about our time together, and to find she had filled her journal with detailed accounts of those memories, including the time in Casco, made me wonder how I could support her to have time to lean into something that gave her so much delight.

Gen stirred, and her breathing changed until her eyes fluttered open.

"What happened? Did my alarm go off?" she asked, confused.

"No, not yet. I woke you up a little earlier than usual, but I want you to disregard the clock for now. I know when you like to leave the house. Can you trust me? I'll make sure you're on time."

"Oh...okay," she agreed, filling me with determination.

"Okay, come. I have the tub ready for you." I stood up, gently tugging her until she stood next to me.

"A bath? At this time?"

"Trust me...remember?"

"Time of my life?" She grinned as she trailed behind me. The scent of lemongrass and green tea infused the bathroom; the internet was a great resource for finding the perfect mix for a wake-up bath. Gen's giddy but confused energy was amusing as she stripped and got into the bath.

This time was for her, for her relaxation, for energizing before her day. Still, I couldn't front, witnessing Genevieve's stunning body sinking under the clear water, her ebony skin sleek in the places not submerged, the tip of her dark chocolate nipples goading me to taste; her closed eyes as she allowed herself to relax... It was a transcendent experience. I would be privileged to do this with her for the rest of my days.

"Are you gonna stare? Not that I mind," she said, then smirked.

"Nah, I need to make sure to keep you on track," I said and

stood up. "I'll be back. No need to look at the time." I cautioned from the door, and she nodded, eyes closed.

I finished the porridge I'd made for both of us, one of my grandpa's old recipes from the islands, which would make sure Gen had something more substantial than her usual coffee.

I played some mellow reggae as I guided Gen to them, leaving her there to finish getting ready.

Whispers and soft words, that was all we used as she finished her makeup, then sat with me to eat breakfast. When she was done, I held her hands and asked her to close her eyes again.

"What? Are you sure I'm going to be..."

"Shhh...this is my routine, without the bath, during my regular mornings after my parents passed away. I needed connection with myself... I felt lost for a while. Meditation in the morning and evening helped a lot. I had stopped doing it for a minute, but being here..."

"Do you feel lost?" she murmured, pain coloring her question.

My eyes shot open to find her wounded gaze.

"No! I mean, being here has inspired me to want to build new routines together. I don't feel lost, but I don't want to lose myself when my well-being could affect you. I gotta be well to be good for you. And the same the other way around. Maybe if we do this together...think of it as preventive maintenance," I finished hoping she understood.

"You're right. I...adjusting to living together has been exhilarating but, not going to lie, overwhelming. I realize now I'm responsible for more than just my goals and my work and... I fear I might be falling short already." She sighed, voicing her fears.

"Nah, I know how determined you are, and I've always

respected that. This is us marrying what we know of each other to create something new." The deep certainty of my words resonated in the apartment as we did our five-minute meditation together.

The soft kiss and hug Gen gave me lingered in my mind as she left unknowingly ten minutes before her usual time, both of us in an uplifted state of mind.

The rest of the week we continued our new morning routine. Always ending with a soft kiss and hug that Gen gave me. The rest of the days I spent attempting to remove the small fish in a big pond sensation I'd had since moving to Florida. Everything felt enlarged, and overwhelming. Thankful for the small town feel of the area we lived in, I took it upon myself to walk every street and corner, visit every store until the owner of the convenience store knew me by name, and the cashier for the groceries called me a regular.

With the impending meeting at the Tropics looming over me, I needed a pep talk. I craved the connections with my friends.

Sitting in our living room in the afternoon while I awaited Gen's arrival, I video called Shakira.

"Manito!! Miss you! How's Los United States?" she greeted with a wide smile. My chest tightened at the sight of her excitement. I could barely contain mine. I could hear the squeal of happy children playing in the background. She probably was doing her after-school duties.

"Miss you too. How are the kids?"

"Oh, you know them, they swear they know more than I do, their teacher." She smiled then turned around to call some kid's attention who was climbing one of the picnic tables for lunch.

"I hear that, and you, how's everything?"

"Mmm. Good, but I'm glad you called because I was working up to send you a nasty text asking why you forgot about your friends now that you are about to be American." Her eyebrow rose so high it left the camera frame.

"Here you go."

"What, am I lying? You have a new girl and a new life and you forget about us peasants."

"You know I miss you. It's just been…" I sat back, uncomfortable now that I had her on camera, about sharing how things had been.

"It's a lot isn't it?" Her face relaxed into a sympathetic expression. The pang in my chest widened at the sight.

"It is, but I'm making it work. Listen… I need advice. I have this opportunity to take a job here, that would…it would take me back to architecture."

The silence elongated after my news. Even the noise of the children dimmed as Shakira turned the information over in her brain.

"So, what do you want to do?"

So simple… What did I want to do? I wanted a healthy life, worth living. I wanted to be passionate about my work; I wanted to be an equal partner to Genevieve. I wanted my family to live comfortably.

"I want to do the right thing," I answered instead.

"Come on, manito, you know what the right thing is, and before you answer back, what I mean is, you know what the right thing is…for you. You just want to do the right thing for everyone else but not serve your needs. It's okay to look out for yourself in order to be able to do the same for others."

"Why are you so wise?"

"Because I am a teacher, and teachers are the real superheroes of the universe," she boasted, then hollered so loud that my ear rang.

"Hey, Pablo, no, I told you not to climb there! No...listen I gotta go these childr—"

Shakira hung up, leaving me with true silence, only the sounds of my thoughts making my ears ring.

"Mr. Nicholas! Such an elusive man," Ms. Ricard said as we shook hands. All of Gen's descriptions had prepared me for the short, determined woman, the aura of power emanating from her. Gen strode to the chair next to mine and we sat across from Ricard, her poised and collected energy helped my overall nerves, but outwardly I had my calm mask on.

"It's interesting that I'm considered elusive when I've been employed by Tropics all this time." I sat back into the armchair crossing my leg over my thigh.

"True, true. What a wonderful coincidence. To think you have been part of the project all this time. From day one. We want that type of collaboration in an extended manner. To work with you in all of our expansion projects to create new hotels all over Central America and the Caribbean."

"What is your plan to avoid gentrification and ensure the townspeople maintain control of the areas?" I asked, and in my periphery, I saw Gen's grin before she began speaking.

"Adrián, as you know, the project I have presented for Tropics Colón has a full environmental, community-based study request to be presented alongside the architectural plans. No project should be larger than the ecosystem around it can sustain. For the most part, from our preliminary studies, the projects need to be less than fifty rooms. My overall expansion presentation to Tropics is to create hotels that not only speak to the area's history, but that meld organically with the region without promising the hotel owners that the real estate of the zone will change in any number of years. The idea is that the towns don't change unless the people want them to. Also, I have proposed that the purchase of land is injected directly to the economy of the people as some of these land grants are coming from the governments. I've insisted that Tropics add this to every contract with clear contingencies to avoid gentrification. Every decision should include a referendum approved by the townspeople."

This woman.

She'd listened to everything we'd discussed and every fear I'd shared with her. I still had my concerns, and she understood them well, but that she had found ways in this expansion to take so much into consideration was warming. Every day I fell irrevocably more in love with her. The shy, goofy woman that was an effective silent sniper in her work. The determined daughter, the kind friend, the inspiring partner. I loved all of her sides.

"Thanks, Genevieve, that does ease some of my concerns. As you know, I don't fully believe that outside developments can remain that altruistic. I also understand the financial decline in our areas, and the need of the many can't be dictated by one, so I'll be open.

"The other concern I have, Ms. Ricard, is having a good balance between life and work. My time with my partner and my family is essential for my well-being. Having the autonomy to dictate my work schedule and overall project load while ensuring results is nonnegotiable."

Genevieve's impressed gaze washed over me, giving me hope.

Ricard promised to present me with a comprehensive package that I could review before making my final decision, and with that, Gen and I left the room hand in hand, the hope of the future secured.

Twenty-Three

Adrián

Moving away from the only home I'd known for my thirty-six years of life hadn't been an easy decision. Gen's love and my family's support carried me through the hard days as I assimilated to a different world, a different culture.

Time used to be a slow friend that allowed me space to enjoy my day and bask in the wonders of it. Now it had become a foe, leaving me breathless as situations happened to me without my control. Unwilling to worry Genevieve I settled for our routines, which helped a bit.

We'd just finished our meditation, and Gen stood by the door, giving me a kiss and a hug that promised to become more until she gently disentangled herself from my arms.

"Fine, leave me like this," I grumbled.

"Oh my God, why are you acting like we didn't just have sex last night, and during the early hours this morning and…"

"Okay, okay, you made your point." I escorted her out of the building with a farewell kiss while I went on my morning walk. Enjoying the unusual cooler breeze, I took my cir-cuitous trek around the block, ending in the grocery store at the corner, where I selected a few chicken breasts and thighs to cook with assorted vegetables for dinner.

Knowing Genevieve, she'd be late today. She'd been most days since I'd moved in with her. Now that everything was in the open, I wanted to share my worries. I respected her drive, and would never impede her career path, but anyone with two eyes could see she was running herself ragged. If she came home inspired every day, that would be one thing, but lately, it was more grumbles than wins when we snuggled under the covers at the end of the day.

After setting my purchases in the fridge, I went to take a shower, enjoying the warm water easing the tension in my muscles, worries for Gen's well-being and mine swirling with the water.

After taking care of my skin, a task that now was more important than ever with the dryness I experienced from all the air-conditioning, I settled to work on the accounting for both Villa Bonita and LasDell.

Thank God for the Tropics account because it was what was keeping the coffers somewhat stable. After a few hours of numbers swimming on the screen, I paused, needing a break from the artificial lighting of the laptop.

With lunch in my mind, I rummaged through our fridge, looking for cold cuts for a quick sandwich when the lock on our door turned.

Who the fuck could it be at one in the afternoon? Gen was at work, and no one had a spare key. I'd asked her if her mom still had one the other night and she'd assured me that was no longer the case.

Springing to action, all the hairs of my body lifted, and my muscles tensed up prepared for anything. I snatched a cast-iron pan and a knife for extra protection.

By the time Genevieve walked in, I stood in a defensive pose, ready for anything.

"What in the world is happening? Why are you holding my cast-iron pan, and the chef's knife?"

Breathing hard, I placed the pan on the kitchen counter, followed by the knife, inhaling and exhaling to remove the chest pain from the adrenaline. Then I returned to Gen whose lips had disappeared as she pressed them together. Her shoulders were rigid, as she held her laughter in.

"Go ahead, let it go," I drawled.

She doubled up, her adorable giggles fizzling out and filling the room with her contagious humor. A few minutes later and we were both doubled up in laughter.

"What...what are you doing here?" I managed between chuckles.

"I took the rest of the day off."

Arching back in surprise, I followed her as she went into our bedroom, removing her shoes and pencil skirt in the process.

"So my lovin' advances this morning inspired you to return for more?" I asked, hopeful, as she removed her silk blouse, revealing her smooth dark skin, and her pink lace bra.

Genevieve turned around in her panties and bra with a quirked brow.

"What advances?" Her eyes twinkled in mischief.

"Graciosa." I leaned against the door frame, watching her put on an olive jumpsuit over a white tee. It looked like overalls on top with wide legs at the bottom. No words were said between us and it felt absolutely comfortable. For all that I was having a hard time adjusting to living in a new country, this? This was perfection. Being with Genevieve, actually fulfilling the simple wishes I had for our lives together?

Perfection.

She pulled her hair in a messy bun on top of her head, then added some hoops and a Cuban link to the ensemble.

"Ready?" She turned around. "What you are wearing is perfect for what we are doing."

She gestured at my mustard-colored shorts and white T-shirt and gave me a thumbs-up.

"Oh, that reminds me of our drive to Colón that fateful day," I drawled, mimicking her awkward face and thumbs-up of that day.

The thumb tucked in, then another finger made its way out.

"Damn, it's like that now?" I asked, laughing.

"You, sir, are not jumping for joy at my adventure."

"What adventure, Preciosa? You just came in, gave me the quickest striptease of my life, then robbed me of the opportunity to thank you because you put your clothes back on. That's all I know," I protested.

Her brows scrunched in exasperation, morphing to a satisfied grin. Her beautiful dark cheeks plumped until her eyes crinkled with triumph.

"I'm taking you sightseeing."

"I realized I hadn't really shown you around since you arrived," Gen said as she maneuvered her car on I-95. Even though it wasn't rush hour, there were so many vehicles on the road. In that regard Panamá and Miami were the same. Never a time where you could enjoy empty roads unless late at night, and even then you had to be wary of partygoers.

"You haven't, but you've been busy I get it," I said, touched that she'd prioritized this time for the two of us. It felt good to be out and about with her, during daylight.

"It's no excuse, I've been an atrocious host, but no worries Señor Nicolas, I'll be guiding you around today."

"Oh, so you are my driver?"

"And tour guide." She smiled as she focused on the road. Genevieve's joy was infectious and damn sexy. After getting off the highway, she deftly took us to an area I hadn't seen before.

"Where are we?"

"Overtown. Here let's find somewhere to park."

We drove down a street with short trees adorning the edges. The area had smaller buildings, some well painted, some dilapidated, and in every block there were Black people either catching public transportation or walking about their business. Miami was a very diverse city, and everywhere I'd been so far I'd seen a mix of races and cultures, but here, here it felt closer to home. Closer to Colón.

"Why are we here?" I asked her when she parked her vehicle in an open parking spot. As soon as we got out of the car, I was glad for the shorts. The sun beamed over us, heating my skin.

"I am probably going to mangle a lot of the story, but, this is Overtown, which used to be Colored Town back in 1896 during the Jim Crow era. Many Black people from the Carolinas, Georgia, North Florida, Alabama, and the Bahamas came to work for the railroad and the rich land in Coconut Grove, but when Miami became incorporated as a city, because of segregation laws, they needed a colored area."

We walked down the same street we'd driven, with some

parking lots, what seemed to be smaller apartment buildings, and enclosed lots with fences. This was more of how I had imagined living in the South would feel based on movies I'd seen while young. I admired the low-hanging trees casting cool shadows to hide away from the sun, and the slower pace, as if this street stood in a time capsule.

Gen walked with purpose until she paused in front of a white house.

"See when Flagler, as they say, founded the area, Black folks helped alongside everyone, but the moment it became a city...it was a wrap. No longer could they live where they worked. We were given this area northwest of the developed city. At the beginning...it was rough, but you know us," she said, taking out her cell phone and shooting a video of the house ending with a close-up. She was brilliant at it, and I wondered what her post would be on social media after our visit. Her tips to Black women travelers were gaining traction online and her following had expanded. I stared unabashedly at her, in awe.

"We always find a way." I nodded, following her thoughts. I studied the two-story old wooden house behind her with ivory walls and brown roof. Easily spotted were the areas that had been modernized, from the windows to the upper balcony, but the structure still maintained that older feel.

"My weekends with Mama, after Dad left, were mostly about doing homework. But sometimes she'd bring me here to walk around, when this area had not one spec of gentrification, and it wasn't updated as it is now. This is the house of Dana A. Dorsey. Mom and I would stand in front of it, and she'd tell me that he was the first Black millionaire in South

Florida. She'd explain how he was also a civic leader, creating housing for Black workers here in Colored Town, which in the 1920s people started calling the Harlem of the South. He had a dream and he never stopped chasing it. People like him opened the doors for people like you and I, she'd tell me." Gen shaded her eyes from the powerful sunbeams and watched the house for a while.

As she watched the house, I watched her. Her dark skin gleamed under the sunlight, as she shared a glimpse of what and who she was. Every little morsel delicious and exhilarating.

"So, since you were little you've had dreams to be a millionaire?" I asked, curious, grinning when she gave me a "really?" look with a tilt of her head and everything.

"Mmm-hmm. Maybe at that age I dreamed of the dollar signs, but soon it was about the work itself, about opening doors and opportunities. To better our worlds. When I think of Colón, and Overtown, I think of what Colored Town used to be. A Mecca made by Black people for Black people. Here, come, let's cross." Her soft hand grasped mine, and together we crossed to stand in front of a two-story building with tall cement pillars creating arches on the front.

"This is the Ward Rooming House, it was for out-of-town Black travelers and Native Americans who couldn't stay in Downtown Miami back in the 1920s. It is now the Ward Rooming House Gallery. A group of Black intellectuals called the Hampton Art Lovers worked on restoring it. Want to see some art?" Her eyes shined with pride and excitement, and her exuberance was so infectious, my heart tripped and restarted as we walked hand in hand together to the art gallery.

"Let's do it."

★ ★ ★

"This is delicious…mmm, my God," I murmured while I took another bite full of creamy mac and cheese. Our plates were similar with both mac and cheese, collard greens, and corn muffins, but I'd ordered the oxtail and she had the turkey wings. Everything was great. The spot she'd picked was unassuming but had great pictures of the history of the area and the restaurant.

"I know, it's good, right? Some good soul food, and it's been here for ages." She grinned and took a sip of her flop.

"So, the area around us, is being gentrified?" I asked.

"Yes, it has been, but many of the historic landmarks we saw today, it's Black Miamians working on their preservation." After going to the art gallery, we'd walked over to the Lyrics Theater, which she'd shared had seen many of the greats perform back in the day, from W.E.B. Dubois, Marian Anderson, Langston Hughes, Paul Robeson, and Whitney Houston. She'd made fun of me when I *fanboyed* when hearing Whitney Houston's name.

"Was this really about sightseeing or are you trying to send me a message?" I took a sip of my flop, comically squinting my eyes at her. Her passionate recounts of her mom's words, her delight about what Black people did with Colored Town, and what the new generation was doing with Overtown had inspired me. Now more than ever I understood her drive and her passion. It came from a similar place to mine, our love of our people, her in a macro level mine in a micro, but she was challenging me to think bigger. To be more. It was a scary but thrilling proposition.

"Am I that transparent?" She chuckled, then waggled her perfectly arched eyebrows. I got lost in her brown gaze, realizing there were some specks of amber in her eyes. God but she was gorgeous, and persistent. No wonder they called her the Silent Sniper at work—she was relentless. That knowledge made me want to take her home and finish what we'd started in the morning.

"Ah… I think I lost you." Gen smirked, and I shrugged, snapping out of my trance.

"Can you blame me? Look at how carefree you've been today, and the videos you took. You're challenging me today, so let me pay you back in kind. Remember how today felt. How making time for yourself made room for this. I'm thankful for you showing me around your city. It makes it feel more mine now too." I reached out and squeezed her hand.

"Oh, you good…you really…" She chuckled, shaking her head. "Okay then, I guess you have things to think about and so do I." Her brown eyes zeroed in on me, willing me to agree. I returned the impassioned plea, kissing her soft hand, savoring the silky, salty skin, never breaking the connection. Pressure built in my core as her tongue slid out of her mouth to moisten her perfectly plump lips.

"I guess we do," I murmured, recognizing that gauntlet for what it was. We soon departed the restaurant, our hands and fingers interlaced, carrying the heat and the promise of what would happen the moment we crossed the threshold of our apartment. But even in the maelstrom of desire that had swirled around us, I couldn't stop thinking of Genevieve's message, and the things we could do in Colón if I only dared.

Twenty-Four

Genevieve

The steps Adrián and I took together to secure our life were a source of happiness I hadn't experienced in a long time.

Adrián's speech to Ricard, and our day in Overtown were the fire I needed to start thinking strategically and boldly different. My goal had transformed to include me. To include my needs and my passion. My family and my well-being. Encouraged, I planned to demand more flexibility in my schedule, and the ability to work from home.

All through the day I'd fretted about opening this conversation, practicing counterarguments in the mirror. The ask felt simple, but it was a momentous occasion for me. I'd lacked imagination before, of what things could be for me.

One path, one way, one goal.

With my requirement of security, it had been so easy to fall into this structured mind frame, where vacations were not resets but rewards, where extra work was expected, and balance was eschewed. Now, that mind frame no longer served me, but the passion for the work hadn't diminished. That was why I'd struggled so much with these last weeks at work. How could I influence my field, while being true to myself? Adrián opened the door to how that could look, and now I didn't want to look back.

"I want flexibility, to work from home at least two days a week."

Ricard studied me while I explained my stance, how the scope of the work that had landed in my lap required some pivoting, how constant travel for acquisitions would erode my ability to maintain balance, and how the possibility of working from home would provide a more holistic approach to my weeks. She let me speak and speak, then delivered a chilling message.

"You should have negotiated that before you took the job. We have a vision of what the VP roles are about, and collaboration is a must. This is why the regions are all under one roof, which *will* not change."

The message crushed me. Her lack of compassion disappointed me, draining me of all the energy I'd canvased for the day. I walked away, discouraged and disillusioned. I needed to regroup. This couldn't be the end of it?

Battling a deep annoyance, I reminded myself of what I signed up for when I graduated college, even before that. My goal had been simple, and the vehicle had been diligence, ambition, and drive. Somewhere along the line, though, the goalpost had transformed, and I no longer desired the next best role.

My mind and my heart had never been in opposition, but lately, my heart's desire challenged me to look at my plans and really examine what I wanted in life.

I wanted Adrián.

I wanted health, travel, a fulfilling, balanced career, and family time.

My ambitions transformed as I expanded my view of what was possible.

Those thoughts circled my brain as I entered the global cuisine restaurant where I had agreed to meet my mom.

"I can't believe you're not at that general manager conference networking during lunch," was my mom's greeting.

"Well, hello to you too, Mama." I embraced her and sat at the table. I could imagine the striking picture we presented. Her in her crisp black suit with just a hint of pink on the collar. Me with my pencil skirt and structured blouse. Impeccable makeup and hair. Power women in a power lunch.

Your appearance is your best calling card. It was one of Lissette's mantras and possibly the one that had sunk in the most. Right now, though… I wished we could just be mother and daughter. No armament necessary.

"What? What's wrong? You know you should be networking," she insisted while I sat there wishing for the impossible.

"It's the closing lunch. It was optional. I needed to talk to you."

"Why? Everything is going well now that that boy has shown he actually has drive. Imagine the power couple you'll make in a few years!" This had been a recurring message from the moment I told her of Adrián's past career. I sighed.

"That's not what I want. I'm sure as fuck that's not what he wants either."

"So vulgar. No need to curse, child. Come, let's order," Mom commanded as the server approached our table.

I'm not sure what I was expecting of her, but I wanted her advice.

Once the entrees arrived, we settled in to eat; I tried again.

"I asked Ricard to be able to work remotely. If Adrián agrees to the position, I want to have flexibility. She shot me down, and I need advice on approaching it again."

Mom's fork slowly clacked against the plate.

"Girl… You asked for what? Were you even in a position of influence when you entered the bargaining table?"

"Well, no, but Ricard told me she wanted change."

Mom pursed her lips in disappointment. The sight didn't make feel me the need to prove myself any longer, but it saddened me nonetheless.

"Change for her is moving from all white males in the room to what she's hired now. That *is* the extent, and…listen, baby girl. I… I'm proud of you. For pushing the boundaries. And your relationship with that boy, he…he makes you happy, don't he?" My heart soared at my mother's capitulation. With shaking hands, I nodded, too moved to do much more than that.

"He does, Mama. He makes me realize there is more to life than the chase."

Mom's gaze softened, and she reached out and cupped my cheek. I took a deep breath, enjoying the rare gesture of affection, a balm to cherish for harder days.

"Good. I know you and I have been at odds. I wanted to blame it on that boy, but I've been taking stock. I pushed too hard. All I've ever wanted is for you to stand on your own two feet."

My eyes burned as I let my mom's word wash over me. She hadn't been that oblivious to our recent rift, and in her own way she was trying to fix it. I breathed a sigh of relief. The tension of many disagreements and conversations ending in disappointment dissolved. Knowing my mother's past, I'd utilized all my patience to deal with our dynamic, but I was so glad to have her acknowledge it wasn't sustainable anymore. I loved my mother. No matter how hard she could be, Mom was so important to me and being at odds with her as I started this new path…it hadn't felt right.

Her silent blessing of my marriage to Adrián mended something I hadn't realized was broken inside.

"I know, Mama… I know, and I love you." I didn't know how we arrived at this place of introspection, but I was so thankful.

"So enough with the mushiness. If you want something, you must approach it from a position of power. Go back and bargain when you figure out what that looks like."

Now that I had the backing of my mother, you would think things should feel better.

My career woes loomed over me, threatening the balance I was achieving in my personal life with Adrián, and I had no idea how to make it all work. I'd studied to be a career woman, successful, but no one had taught me how to manage the personal side that I now so desperately wanted to master.

With my head in turmoil, the date of our wedding crept up on me, silent and unexpected. I tried not to bemoan the fact that work, life, and everything had prevented me from focusing on what should be the happiest day of my life.

I should have had time to plan, maybe host a little reception in one of the hotels for Anibal's region, but instead we were doing the bare minimum because of the need for speed. We'd agreed we'd prioritize getting the paperwork, then revisit the conversation about any type of ceremony. It was the logical, mature thing to do. So why did it feel like a gut punch any time we discussed logistics of our wedding day?

The marriage certificate process had been straightforward. Almost too simple.

Anticlimactic.

"So, we go to the court on Friday. We're gonna be together anyway after your convo with Ricard," Adrián said as he scarfed down the greens, mac and cheese, and baked chicken I made for him while I tidied up around the kitchen. Our Saturday so far had been fantastic, sprinkled with some work I couldn't leave for Monday.

"Yeah, yeah. That sounds like a plan," I murmured, the clank of silverware against the sink masking my disappointment.

"Hey, what's up? You sound sad? What happened?"

Drat the man for not letting me wallow in peace. I refused to say anything about the court plan. He'd been adamant about wanting to be equal partners, so planning a reception even if small wouldn't be possible. Right now, I paid all the bills and he paid for groceries with whatever money he received from LasDell's partnership. I couldn't and wouldn't burden him with my newfound princess white dress wedding dreams. It was silly. It was all just, silly.

"I shouldn't have cooked so much, especially with tonight's dinner cruise," I answered instead, turning around and regaling him with the biggest smile I could muster. He studied my face and I sighed in relief when he finally looked back down to his food.

"Are you kidding? This is good, Preciosa. I promise I'll

pretend to like the food tonight half as much as your cooking," he joked.

"You're gonna be stuffed. Are you sure you want to go? I
thought it would be better to stay home...chill."

"Nah...if we stay home, you're gonna work. You did that
plenty last weekend. Besides, remember your dream?"

"I said exploring new surprising things, not hanging out
on a sunset cruise with a bunch of octogenarians." I folded
my hands over my chest.

"No worries, I won't tell the crew what you said about
them," Adrián deadpanned and stood up to clear the table.

"You got jokes." He knew I wasn't referring to my friends.
Gino and his boyfriend had invited us to this dinner cruise,
apparently a favorite activity to do for the two of them. As
Anita was still in town after the GM conference, I invited
her to come along. My mistake was extending the invitation
as Anibal and Arjun were walking by, so now it had become
a thing.

I just wanted to lie down and chill with Adrián. Let my hair
down and let go of my worries about work, and our wedding,
and his pending decision. I just wanted to relax. Maybe ask
him to show me some of that slow loving he talked about. I
wanted to show him some tricks I had searched for, the Google
search becoming way steamier than I had bargained for.

Tonight, I planned to seduce him.

I couldn't help myself; I could sense he was a bit more ad-
venturous than me, and I wanted to explore. Surrender myself to the passion ever simmering between us, and for once
take my time with him. No rushing. Sweet steamy sex until
the morning found us tangled in our sheets.

"You want to stay?" he asked as we got ready together side

by side, startling me out of my horny thoughts. I flushed, attempting to act put together while my plans for tonight teased me.

"No, I think it will be fun. And you're right. If it was just me, I'd already be in my onesie eating ice cream and binge-watching streaming service reality TV."

"I mean, if you're wearing one of the onesies, I might be persuaded to stay." He inched closer to me, his woodsy cologne lingering around him.

"Behave!"

"That's not what you said last night when you were bouncing on top—"

I covered his mouth with my hand, and he kissed my palm, further eroding my resolve.

With a great deal of diligence mixed with teasing seduction, we managed to head out with enough time to feel comfortable and not rushed. Adrián and I cut a striking figure. Him wearing a white guayabera shirt and cream linen pants, which miraculously had no creases, and his gold chain that gave him that extra swagger I so loved about him. Me with my white jumpsuit with plunging cleavage and flowy pants that accentuated my curves. I couldn't wait to get home and strip us of it all and enact my steps to seduce him.

The beach town just north of Fort Lauderdale boasted a mix of white art deco buildings interspersed with modern newer developments. People walked on the sidewalks, some still in their bathing suits, others dressed for some form of entertainment. The eternal vacation feel lingered here and I wistfully thought of Villa Bonita and the habitants of Aguimar. I wondered how things were in Adrián's little town. With everything with his papers, I wasn't certain when we would return together. Gratitude and sadness mingled, putting in perspective again everything that he had put on the line for me. Adrián smiled at me, and just like that, he transported me to the present with him. I could and would leave the worries aside for the night and enjoy our time together. He deserved that. *I* deserved that.

"My man!" Anibal boomed when we approached the deck area before embarking.

Adrián clapped Anibal on the back, then embraced Gino and Mark. Anibal and Gino looked like two burly body-guards next to lean and shorter Mark. The cruise waited for us—a three-story extravaganza with windows everywhere. A group of five elderly Black women passed by, clearly having the time of their life.

"See." I tugged at his sleeve, and he smirked.

"Don't start," Gino admonished me, and I threw up my hands in surrender.

Just before I turned to check my phone for Anita's where-abouts, she descended from a hired ride, flawless in a yellow sundress, which contrasted beautifully with her dark skin and opulent curves. The muttered curse to my right, where Anibal stood, told me all I needed to know. Arjun descended right after her and Anibal cursed yet again.

"Wasn't she engaged?" Adrián murmured in my ears, and I shivered at his touch.

"Why would you assume…" Adrián gave me a look and then stared at her finger. No ring. I sighed. "Things are not looking too good. Different views in life," I whispered back.

Shit, I needed to connect with my girl. I hoped she was okay; her wanting to stay behind for a few extra days in Flor-ida made more sense now. Her relationship woes bubbled up some of that discomfort I hadn't been able to shake even when things were going so smoothly between Adrián and me.

Anita and her fiancé had known each other from Sunday school back in the day. If life circumstances had overpowered their relationship, what hope was there? *No, no, no, Genevieve, focus on the present.*

Maybe I needed to resurrect Hot Girl Gen. She made things happen, she went for what she wanted and left no prisoners. My life was richer due to her efforts.

Where had she been these past months? Hot Girl had deserted me the moment shit got real, just when I needed her dearly.

Adrián squeezed my hand, and I gave him a stilted grin, my cheeks feeling unnatural around the gesture. *SOS, Hot Girl Gen!*

"What's up, y'all," Arjun said.

"Hola! So is everyone ready for this cruise?" Anita grinned and we all followed.

"Yo, I see the appeal of these dinners!" Anibal said as we all chatted. The buffet had some okay options, and some wins enough for me to be satisfied after dinner. Now we were all relaxing, watching the houses of the rich and famous as we commandeered a comfortable area with plush leather seats surrounding the rear of the boat.

The Florida breeze was kind to us, cooler than usual for a summer night.

"Yeah, that conga line during dessert time was epic," Adrián said straight-faced. And we busted out laughing.

I gasped. "Take it back!" I cuddled into him as we all dissolved in giggles.

"Damn, what's wrong with them? I love a good conga line."
Anita chuckled. "And did y'all see Anibal? All the older ladies
were dying to pull him to do the electric slide."

"I'm not inviting y'all to anything ever again," Gino scoffed
in between chuckles.

I was dying of laughter, my stomach hurting from all the
jokes flying between us. The conversation flowed as we all
discussed different topics. Here was another proof of the things
I had put on the back burner for my career. This type of ca-
maraderie was something sorely lacking in my life. My lunch
and dinner dates with Gino were fantastic, but this? Having
a group of friends and the actual time to be with them was a
luxury that felt difficult to achieve with all the work I had in
front of me. Even now, the mountain of emails I had left un-
read mocked me, reminding me of the extra hours I would
have to surrender this week.

But I had no logical answer for my dilemma, no brilliant
idea besides having another conversation with Ricard, and
the odds of that going any different settled like acrid dread in
my stomach. Attempting to keep the emails in the back of my
mind, instead I focused on my travel tips. Maybe that would
resurrect that trifling girl who had abandoned me to real life,
and real-life problems.

Pulling out my phone, I took a picture of the horizon as
the sun disappeared into the darkness.

"You're gonna post that on your social media? You should
put one of the captions from your journal that you showed
me last night. That topic of planning a staycation during the
weekend? I thought that was brilliant. I love that you're leaning into your girl travel vibe," Adrián whispered in my ear.

"Really? I thought you didn't like social media?"

"For me, but for you…it's lovely, you light up when you do it."

Oh, be still my heart. My man was the perfect cheerleader. *My man.* A thrill bubbled up from my stomach, lodging into my chest and filling me with the joy I had been searching for all day. His ability to make me look at the bright side was astonishing. I grinned at him, cupping his cheek, raspy with his growth, leaning into and getting lost in the luxuriantly soft lips of my man.

"Who lights up? What are y'all whispering about? No secrets!" Gino said, and I flushed, attempting to rear back from Adrián, but he didn't allow me to pull back until he was good and done with the leisurely kiss that stirred things down between my legs, and deep in my chest. He finally let me go, pulling my bottom lip with him as if he never wanted the kiss to end. I sighed after our lips parted, and wondered how much longer this boat would keep us here.

"Genevieve has been doing a travel journal, and I'm encouraging her to post online as well," Adrián said, much more composed than I was. My cheeks were hot to the touch, and I pulled out my fan to reduce some of the heat gathering around me.

"Those posts you made during your last trip to the islands were unique, and did you see that? *Black Travel Chronicles* shared it on their account!" Anita pointed out, and I grinned shyly as everyone gassed me up.

"I know the owner of the publication. She went to school with me at FIU," Anibal shared.

"What? I didn't know that?" I exclaimed, an odd excitement rushing through me. I wasn't shy to share that what the owner had done with her publication had become a main point of admiration for me. What a creative way to marry your passion for travel and business acumen. I'd been sleuthing a bit wondering how I could find a way to partner with her and her team for some opportunities, but I was still conceptualizing.

"Do it," Adrián whispered in my ear, so in harmony with my train of thought, it was eerie. The warmth of his woodsy scent, so close to me had me fanning faster, to keep my temperature regulated to acceptable socializing levels. I turned a mischievous gaze at Adrián, then tried to change it to an admonishing one when he slid his hand down my waist, past my hips and close to my ass, but he just smirked and winked. Oh, he knew what he was doing. He tapped my behind and nodded toward Anibal. "Go ahead," he urged.

"Anibal, I'd love to connect with them. I have ideas on what we could do for Villa Bonita and the Tropics hotels in Central America and the Caribbean. Maybe some feature of special events in those destinations. An intimate wedding in Villa Bonita. We could get an influencer couple to get married there…"

"Oh." Adrián's surprised murmur reached my ears, and I turned to watch him. What did he think I had in mind? I searched his surprised expression, but he shook his head, shrugging then gifting me that beautiful smile of his.

"Thank you," he mouthed, and I realized he hadn't expected me to think of Villa Bonita, but how could I not—Villa Bonita was the place of my heart; one of the concepts I had was an intimate tropical wedding, and Villa Bonita shining in the background of a couple saying their vows…

A cold chill raced through my veins as the couple materialized with faces. Adrián and me saying I do in the place where we fell in love. My unease, my dissatisfaction with a judge of the peace marrying us… I wanted more than a court procedure. I want time to explore with him after our wedding, I didn't want to be worried about emails piling up in my inbox, and disappointing anyone. I didn't want the tension gathered in my shoulders every Sunday afternoon when I realized it was time to go to the office Monday morning. But more than anything I wanted to go back to Colón with Adrián and say I do. Hot Girl Gen had spoken, and I wasn't ready for what she had to say. None of the things she wanted made sense in my current reality.

We couldn't travel.

Adrián could not leave the States until he had his green card, which could be a year from now. I had a career that required diligence, ambition, and drive. I'd built a life based on those tenets.

An ache settled in my chest, but I was being fanciful; at the end, marrying Adrián was the prize regardless of how we did it or what came next.

Twenty-Five

Genevieve

The beauty of a sunset cruise was we were home by nine. The car ride home was filled with ideas of how we could showcase Villa Bonita online. I told him all about my concepts, of the things I had been journaling and that now had become my dreams, and Adrián received it all with such a bright grin he magically lifted my spirits.

At this point, I was convinced I could sell those smiles as pick-me-ups in the pharmacy and make a fortune.

Thoughts of what our wedding could be taunted me with vivid images of Adrián dressed in white, the warm sand under my feet, the breeze rustling around my hair as I held his hands, but I let go of that dream for now to live in the present.

Whenever we were in Aguimar, and I had focused on the present, I opened myself to the most wonderful memories of my life. I had stopped doing that. I'd been living in my head, full of troubles and worries, pending decisions and changed lives. Adrián had guided me through a softer way of living, but none of that would work if I didn't embrace it physically and mentally.

So, refocusing on the present, I turned all my attention on my plans for the end of the night. Before we sat on the sofa, I deployed part one.

"Adrián, so sorry. Could you get us ice cream?"

"Ice cream? We ain't got none in the fridge."

"I know." I tried pouting to avoid the smile that threatened to come out. He hadn't slipped in a minute. Holding my smile didn't feel comfortable, so it probably came out as a cringe smirk. Great, real hot girl behavior.

"What's that face? No need to do all of that. You know I got you." Yup, sexy, I was really putting it on right now.

Minutes later, Adrián was out of the apartment, and I sprinted to get things in place.

He'd learned to navigate this part of the city pretty well, so I had limited time.

Twenty minutes later, the scene was set. The door opened, and in walked my future husband, looking scrumptious in his outfit.

"Hey, Preciosa, I have... What is this?" he asked in awe.

The living room glowed with many lanterns, an amber hue transforming it into a magical hideaway. In the middle, I had removed the coffee table and layered blankets and pillows. I sat in the middle of the blankets with spoons on one side and oil on the other.

"A night where we take our time, finally," I said.

"Yes, that, yes." He gave me a mischievous grin that hit me right in my feelings and other areas. "What you're wearing is...wow," he said, removing his shoes and approaching me.

"You like?" I stretched my legs, showcasing my onesie.

Black with gold hearts, a little tighter than my usual, with a zipper in the front for when things got steamy, and another surprise left for him to figure out.

"Do I like it? Listen, you could be wearing a burlap sack covered in angry ants, and I would love you. When you grow gray in your temples, and your laugh lines become wrinkles, I will love you even more."

Waterfalls, waterfalls everywhere.

"Come here." I pulled him, and he settled on the blankets bringing the ice cream. We sat facing each other, me criss-crossed, and him sprawled on a mountain of pillows. Even though he was familiar with every inch of my body and I his, he still sparked a firework show in my belly.

"So, did you really want the ice cream?"

"Do you *not* know me?"

He opened up the butter pecan, the only right flavor, and grabbed one of the spoons, feeding me.

"Today was unforgettable. Outside of my trip with you, I don't remember enjoying my time, unbothered, relaxed, just having a good time—zero stress. And how our week panned out with our new routines, and…it's all just *right*. You always say I'm rushing through things, through life, so I want us to take our time tonight." I wanted to embrace it all—mind and body—leave all the worries behind while we were together. But I didn't need to say it out loud. He understood.

"You know I'm all for that." Adrián pressed a butter pecan–flavored kiss on my lips. Our tongues met in a sensual play, a give-and-take, a leisurely exploration that left us with me on top of Adrián. His hard body supported mine, my heart beating so fast in complete abandon, ignoring the slow pace I was trying to achieve.

Adrián's hand slid up my thighs, up my ass, and he pulled back from our kiss, leaving a trail of goose bumps in his wake.

"Excuse me, señorita, what's this?" Adrián groaned, his hooded gaze making my belly swoop.

"Easy access," I said to him and dissolved in needy laughter as he nuzzled my neck, the heat between our bodies increasing as the passion between us crescendoed.

"You're wearing too many clothes," I complained.

"Says the woman wearing a full-body onesie," he joked but complied when I glided my hands up his stomach as he unbuttoned his shirt. In a concerted effort, Adrián ended up in his boxers, just as I wanted.

"I want to try something. I want to…" I slid down his body raining kisses, as he lounged against the pillow fort.

"Whatever you want, it's yours, Preciosa." He couldn't know how that sounded. He couldn't know how delicious he looked with his flexed arms behind his head, his mahogany skin smooth to the touch.

Hooking my fingers in his boxers, I removed them, the final frontier between me and my ultimate goal. He bobbed out magnificently. I never had such a need to taste, kiss, and indulge.

And indulge I did; I went in, raining pecks on the head of his erection, encouraged by the moans and groans coming from Adrián.

"Mmm, yes, Preciosa. I love how you love me with your mouth," he moaned, ghosting his hand over my hair. Any other time or person, I would have disliked it, but right now, it made me feel powerful. Gathering my courage, I caressed his balls, then traveled farther. Taking a brief detour, I grabbed the oil and moistened my hand, anxious for what I planned to do. I took him in my mouth again, savoring his salty skin and cupping his balls. When my finger pressed *that* spot, Adrián's erection grew harder in my mouth, his hips jerking upward in what I hoped was excitement.

"Wow, okay…we ready to explore?" he asked, giddy.

Without pausing, I swirled my tongue around his frenulum, taking time to massage his perineum.

"Fuuck, Preciosa, you're gonna have to stop. You're going to make me burst. Please," he begged, igniting a bolt of electric heat between my legs. I kept going, my pace matching Adrián's heavy breathing and his hips' movement until all he did was gasp, growl, and moan.

"Preciosa, I'm about to come, ohhhh." Adrián exploded in ecstasy, his taste flooding my mouth, his body trembling under me.

"Mmm." I wiped the corner of my mouth and yelped when Adrián pounced on me; my adrenaline went from a five to a ten. He drugged me with his kisses, the sensual swipes of his tongue loosening my muscles and widening my legs under him. His blunt hardness pressed on my belly, and I loved the contrast of his solid planes against my yielding flesh.

"Okay, it's my turn now to drive you wild," he whispered between kisses that had me searching for his lips for more and more.

With impressive dexterity and some help from me, Adrián arranged us so that we ended up with him sitting against the pillows and me between his spread legs.

Adri dragged a finger of each hand in a maddening path from the shells of my ears down the side of my neck. His breath kissed my pulse, teaching it to accelerate kinesthetically by his will and desire. His digits kept trailing down my collarbone, down the vulnerable skin between my breasts, then the sound of the onesie's zipper pulled straight to the tips of my nipples, making them tingle.

Anticipation swirled in the room as our breathing synchronized, the pull of our love at the forefront of every sensation he created. Adrián's warm palms tickled my nipples, stealing a gasp.

"Let me worship you, show you how much I love you," Adrián said.

"Yes," I moaned, helpless to deny him anything.

The teasing touches built up to deliberate caresses on the undersides of my breasts. He weighed them in his hands, attempting to cup them, but they overflowed. I shivered, my breasts heavy, in need of his firm touch. His sensual massage made my skin prickle with goose bumps, the throbbing between my legs becoming an insistent anthem I could no longer ignore. He plumped, tickled, pulled my nipples, and caressed until I squirmed. Every nerve ending seemed to connect to my tits directly, and I couldn't take it anymore; I rubbed my legs, chasing the building orgasm.

"Let it take you away. You're so magnificent, Preciosa. Your tits on my hands are a work of art."

I sneaked a peek at the amber glow of the candles, which made our skin glimmer bronze under the touch of the light. In searching for my nirvana, I undulated my hips against his hard dick, which had risen again. The scent of our arousal lingered, alluring in the air as I inhaled, attempting to slow down. Being in the moment, being present here with Adrián, not chasing the next high but allowing every sensation to sink in was overwhelming my senses. My breathing accelerated, my heart tripping in my chest, unable to hide my body's trembling under his touch.

Never had I been so stimulated by breast play; only Adrián, sorcerer extraordinaire, with his encouragement, love, and his sensuality, could accomplish this feat. Now I understood his comment on our first time. This wasn't just sex. This was a communion of minds, intimacy enhanced, a marriage of hearts. This wasn't just scratching an itch; this was vulnerability, trust, and raw emotions.

"Breathe, Preciosa, take a deep breath. Let it course through your body. Surrender," he coaxed me. He flicked my nipples, then pinched them. The pain-pleasure activated a new level of sensation I wasn't ready for, and I whimpered at how good everything felt. A rush of liquid heat invaded my veins, and wetness gushed from my core. I took a deep breath, and the buildup of the orgasm transformed into something else.

"Open up your legs, Preciosa, let it take you," Adrián instructed, and when I didn't react right away, he nudged my thighs apart until I hooked them over his.

Levitation was the best way to describe it all; every hair in my body stood at attention, my brain fogged, only dopamine driving me now. Without any stimulation on my pussy, my orgasm exploded through my body. My legs shook, my belly contracted, then released; everything relaxed as the climax commanded my body; light flashed in my eyes until I had to close them, and all through it, Adrián continued to talk to me.

"Fuck, Preciosa. So good. Mira como te dejas llevar. You're a champ. Yes," his voice growled deep, and as I gathered control of my limbs, he completely unzipped the onesie. Cold air kissed my flesh as he sank his finger into my soaking channel. I hadn't realized how empty I felt until he easily glided three fingers inside; his other hand pressed my lower belly. Something clicked, and I proceeded to ride his hand with abandon.

"Dale, Preciosa, give me another one, one more for me." His deep voice did unspeakable things to my sanity. I liked micromanaging in every aspect of my life but this one. Here I wanted him to lead me through every step, cheer me through every win, take me to another climax as my body was wracked by pleasure, my vagina clenching his fingers, desperate for more.

"More, please more," I begged, and Adrián didn't disappoint.

"Remind me to get you ten more onesies with this flap thing," he growled, then pushed me forward to undo it so that my lower part was more accessible.

Before I could take another breath, he lifted me as if I was made of air, then plunged inside of me as if I was composed of water. Close enough—my pussy was dripping wet, and his thickness glided effortlessly in and I shivered as I accommodated his length. Somehow, he felt more...*significant* than usual, and that was saying something. I'd never had sex in this position, but there was always the first time on the saddle.

"Remember, slow, grind on it, Preciosa. Make me beg for it," he coached.

Say less. At this point, I had come enough that I could take my time. Remembering the beats of the drums in Aguimar, I let a faraway rhythm guide me, letting the spirit of my love for Adrián lead the way.

We got lost in the most intimate dance; every undulation of mine met with a deep thrust of his, every one of my moans mingling with his desperate groans. The melody of wetness surrounding flesh reminded me of how well Adrián fit me in every regard. Time became unmeasurable, nonexistent as we gave each other the pleasure of a thousand lives together.

"Genevieve, te amo. Take me, Preciosa." Adrián barely got the words out, more a grunt than anything else. I rested my body against his chest, one hand of his on my neck, his mouth pressed against my shoulder, his other hand on my clit. The mental fog returned, and I knew what to do. Relaxing it all, I gripped Adrián's length one last time as he drove inside me with abandon, and I faded away in the most glorious orgasm as Adrián imbued me with his warmth.

"Such a magnificent girl. Mi amor."

Twenty-Six

Genevieve

Monday arrived too soon; after a weekend of relaxation and disconnect, I again found myself leery of returning to the office. I hated this feeling; I'd never had it before, but now here I was, second-guessing my motivations. What exactly should be my next step? I felt I had a few loose ends that didn't allow me to enjoy what should be an exciting time in my life.

Prepared for a grueling day of meetings, I focused on this morning's meditation, attempting to clear my mind of all the unanswered questions. What to do about work? What to do about my disappointment about our wedding? How to balance my drive with my wish to prioritize my personal life?

With Adrián involved, the meditation instead led to a quick make-out session that required reapplying my makeup. Even with all of that, I left with a smile on my face that started to fade as I walked into my office.

"What's wrong?" Anita asked me as she sat down in front of my desk. She'd planned an extended stay this week after the general manager's meeting to visit some of the Tropics hotels in South Florida. I'd offered to go with her, but that idea had been quickly squashed.

"Nothing, just wanted to stay home and frolic with my man."

"Oh, excuse me, girl, now that you have a fiancé, you're not desperate to come to the office?" She chuckled.

"Listen, don't start with me, why are you still here in the States? Any other time you'd be rushing to go back to be home with *your* fiancé."

Anita's eye roll and full-body shudder were as telling as anything else.

"I know I'm your boss, but I want to believe I'm your friend too...this is me asking as a friend, is everything okay?"

Anita sighed, then pushed back in her chair. After a brief hesitation, she scoped the office and got up and closed the door.

"First of all, that man stays in my business...and now he jumps in, on my hotel visits, talking about it's my region, so I have to go," Anita scoffed, and I wondered what I had missed; she and Anibal were always on each other's throats for some reason, but it had gotten worse lately.

"Are you alright?"

"Yeah, I'm... Calito and I decided to take a break. He's having some doubts about the direction of our lives... I hate that it's come to this. He and I have known each other since we were kids." Her saddened gaze prickled at me. I wanted to tell her it would be okay, that things would work out with her fiancé. I had to believe that. That love could conquer the differences and fill in the areas where things didn't fully align.

"It's going to be okay. You and Calito have weathered so much together. I have faith in y'all's connection."

Anita smiled unconvincingly, then shrugged.

"At least that's one person that is rooting for us."

"I'm sure others are…" I murmured, unsure of how to proceed, her sadness was palpable in the room, and it fed into my fears for Adrián and me. Right now, things made sense between us because we were being intentional, but when he accepted the job here, and I continued to travel and get busy…what would our everyday look like? What did we want our everyday to look like? I didn't want to be counting pennies daily for love, but…the alternative was equally as scary. I shoved the thoughts aside, wanting to focus on Anita, and comforting her.

"Girl, enough about me. I hate being down. The break is a good idea, and we said whatever happens over the break is fair game. I mean, he's the only man I've ever been with so… yeah, maybe I should lean into that."

Oop. Okay, I wasn't touching that with a stick.

Accepting her change of topic, I gathered my courage to ask her something that had been on my mind for a minute. With Adrián not having family or close friends yet for our ceremony at the courthouse on Friday, I'd been hesitant to bring up the conversation about witnesses.

"Okay, girl…you do you! But know I'm here if you feel like talking. If you're around after lunch, I'd love to have you join my call with *Black Travel Chronicles*. I'm pitching them a full collaboration. Oh, and… I'd love for you to be our witness for our court appointment on Friday." I rushed to the last part nervous about her answer.

Anita, with her tough persona and boldness, instantly melted.

"Of course, I can. Oh, that would be lovely," she said, smiling, then growing pensive. "Promise me you'll never let any external forces fuck with y'all. Make time for each other… prioritize each other. I think that was Calito's and my miss… but hey, now that I know, maybe there's time to fix things." She grinned, and I couldn't help the pang of alarm that traveled through me at her advice.

The call with *Black Travel Chronicles* went flawlessly. The owner was Latoya Jenkins, Black woman in her late thirties just like me, who was deeply interested in my pitch of collaboration with organic partnerships for marketing. Latoya loved the idea of having our Tropics properties, and I made sure to plug Villa Bonita, be the hosts to different Black traveler influencers, highlighting our hotels and experiences through the eyes of their correspondents. The main hook that really resonated with her was our plan of opening properties in Black towns but owned by people of the area, or with heritage from the area, connecting the traveler with experiences that were authentic and keeping dollars in the surrounding areas. We ended the call with plans of meeting in person in the next couple of weeks.

"Hola, Preciosa, I missed you today. I've been moping around without your company," Adrián crooned through my cell phone as I finalized my last task of the day. I sat with no shoes on, feet in my massager, my ergonomic chair pulled away from my desk. Just the sound of Adrián's voice and my body was on high alert for all the pleasure and love.

"I missed you too…work clothes feel so sensitive on my

skin now…after all that naked time we had on Sunday," I murmured back, my finger going to one of my coils that had sprung free. After such vigorous activities during the weekend, I'd forgone the silk press. Who had time for a salon appointment when you have an all-day inclusive pass to Dickland?

"So, will you be home soon, or should I see to this fellow who's been hard all day?" he asked, and I chuckled.

"Nah, tell my friend there to hold firm. I'll be home soon to take care of—"

"Genevieve, I have news for you." Ricard waltzed into my office, making me jump.

"Hi," I said while Adrián kept telling me about his dick and the despicable things he planned to do to me tonight. I turned down the volume of my receiver, afraid Ricard could hear.

"Babe, babe, Adri… Ricard is here. I gotta go, okay?"

I hung up, uncomfortable with my ruined panties, as Ricard sat before me.

"So, I need you to pack a bag and head to Panamá first thing tomorrow morning. There is a prospective owner interested in the Colón project. Now that we almost have your fiancé locked in, this is an opportunity we cannot pass. He is Afro-Panamanian, just as we wanted, but lives in New York. He's in town for other business and wanted to meet."

Shit, another trip, and with such short notice… I'd jump for joy for going to Panamá, but right now Adrián couldn't travel with me…he'd have to stay behind while I went for a couple of days. My chest tightened at the thought of giving him this news, but I couldn't let this opportunity pass me by.

Buoyed by the reminders of my call with *Black Travel Chronicles* and how interested they'd been in partnering with projects that were connected to the land and offering experiences for Black travelers looking to avoid making a negative impact on the areas they planned to visit made me fill with a new sense of purpose.

"Okay… I'll get home and ready for that. I… you know it's hard now to just up and jump for travel. It was manageable for me before, but I'd love to discuss when I return how we can minimize these instances now that I have my family—"

"Let me stop you right there, dear. This is part of the job. You signed up for it, besides once Adrián is on board, he'll probably be doing tons of travel too, of course, he has a bit more control than you." Ricard gave me a kind smile that didn't match the message. She really had the best intentions, but was so far removed from the type of balance I was looking for that I couldn't help but deflate at her words.

"Still… I want us to meet, maybe when I'm back Thursday or…" I trailed off when Ricard shook her head.

"You won't be back 'til Friday night. He wants a private meeting tomorrow, then a full presentation for him and his executive committee on Friday afternoon. You can maybe jump on the last flight that night."

A sharp pain lanced my head, an eerie coldness running through my body.

"I cannot be there on Friday. It's my wedding day."

"Oh, child, please. Your mom told me it's just a formality." Ricard waved a hand at me. "A quick visit to the court and done. Y'all can reschedule that for another day. I'm sure Adrián will understand."

My heart ached at the decision in front of me, my feet heavy as I ambled through to the end of the day. If I refused the trip, would that hurt our chances with this investor? This was the type of developer I was hungry to work with; it would be the right thing for the areas around Aguimar, and it would even be great for Adrián. It would set his first project close to Villa Bonita. And if it meant us postponing our wedding for a few days well…the end result was for the best. For all of us.

I knew what I signed up for when I took this job; I understood the type of sacrifices it would take. Missing family celebrations and such was never a concern because I had tailored my life to mirror my career, but now with Adrián it was different. I had to think of him.

I packed up my laptop to go home. My heart raced—my brain clouded in what-ifs, and alternatives to make it all work, but in the end the only variable that was fully controllable by me was changing my wedding day.

Our wedding date.

My stomach crumpled to the floor as I realized what I needed to do and hoped to heavens Adrián would understand.

Dread infused every step as I walked into our apartment.

Adrián, the goofball, was sitting on the sofa, no clothes on with a huge black velvet bow covering his crotch, his brawny arms and chest burnished warm brown, begging for my touch. Next to him was a bottle of lube. When he noticed my gaze shifting to the bottle, he wiggled his thick eyebrows and winked. That wink was deployed to cause a riot in my panties, and it worked damn it. Even while my hands were sweaty and my chest hurt, he could make me yearn for him with just a wink.

"I was thinking we could do a repeat of Saturday, maybe your finger ventures farther than—"

Oh no, I couldn't handle his cute banter right now—I needed to say what I had to say or I would lose my courage.

"I'm so sorry, I really love all of this, but I have to pack. I... I have to go to Panamá on the first flight out," I blurted out, donning a self-assured mask. Maybe if I sold it as a done deal, it would be better. It would sound official and inevitable.

Adrián sprang from the couch, still holding the bow over his middle.

"What else aren't you saying, Preciosa? I can see you think-ing a thousand thoughts a second right now," he said with such tenderness I became undone. He started walking toward our room, which now had less pink and more signs of our life to-gether. Pictures of Aguimar and our travel. Adrián's books next to mine.

"We have to postpone the wedding," I whispered as I fol-lowed him. The view of his plump ass a consolation prize to being apart for the next few days. At my words, Adrián froze, his ass clenching as he slowly turned on his heel.

"Excuse me. We have to what?" he asked with a sinister calm.

"I... I have to go to Panamá to meet with a potential buyer. Just the type of person you and I dreamed of aligning ourselves with for the Colón project. He is a native of Colón, Costa Ar-riba. Everything I have researched on him gives me the best of vibes. He now lives in New York but is going back home and requested a meeting. I have to fly in and present things to him first, then to his executive board on Friday. He's fly-ing them in if he likes the preliminary presentation." With-out wanting to, I said those words poised and collected. The Silent Sniper had entered the chat, leaving Hot Girl, vulner-able lady, and in love Gen aside. I stood tall as Adrián's gaze flickered from bewilderment to hope to resignation.

"How can Ricard be okay with sending you on our wedding day?"

"Well, it's something small, isn't it? Could we postpone? We can ask the court for another date…" I shrugged, but inside, vulnerable Genevieve was raging, pleading for me to let my guard down. But how could I? I needed this job, this was the culmination of all I had accomplished, and I had never had to compromise. Ever.

"Wow…okay. Well, it seems you have made the decision." Adrián's shoulders slumped, and he dropped the bow on the floor, leaving me to stand on the threshold of our bedroom feeling bereft.

Was I wrong to go on this trip? I wanted the best for him and for us; this was beyond my job, this would secure the right type of owner for Tropics Colón. I wasn't naive, no matter how great Tropics was about inclusion, working with the communities where they opened projects, they were a business first and foremost. If I didn't spearhead this, then who knew what route they would take? The work was important. Damn it, even Adrián depended on it going well.

With that renewed certainty, I stormed farther into the room while Adrián pulled on basketball shorts.

"This is going to secure your future and mine."

"The only future I want, is one where we get to live our lives, not work ourselves to death."

"It will get better!" I pleaded, dropping all my poise, showing him all of me again. I wanted to believe it would get better. Wasn't that the promise? If you worked hard and pushed and persevered then on the other side, you would get the life you always dreamed of? And why had my dream morphed into soft living, with my husband and my family at my side, with travel and a project I was passionate about? Why had the dream of corporate excellence forsaken me?

None of this made sense. And the dream of soft living was a pipe one at best. I had no money in the bank past six months. If I didn't work hard, none of it would be possible. Why couldn't Adrián see that?

"Will it? Does Ricard work better hours than you? Does her boss? Preciosa... I will support anything you want. If that is your dream, I get it. I really do, but in order for my dream to also come true, that means one of us would have to take a step back. And I am okay with it being me," Adrián said; a clang of danger resonated in our room. No matter how gentle we attempted to be with each other, the tension in the room was pervasive.

"Nooo! I don't want that! You negotiated a hell of a good contract that allowed you to have balance and be able to help your family and us financially. I want to say I could live in squalor with you, but I have to be honest, that is not what I want. I guess what I want is impossible, but..."

"It's not. I can get another job. Maybe open a transportation company here, something with a couple of drivers, something that allows me flexibility, but I don't want to jeopardize us. Our time together. My parents..." Adrián's deep voice trailed off, and I sat beside him on the bed, holding his hands.

"I don't want this to be the type of marriage where we barely see each other. I couldn't live like that, and I don't want to live without you, so...something has to give."

"Adrián...please," I begged, but what was I asking him to do? Why did my heart feel like it was crumbling in my chest? We were not saying goodbye, so why did it feel like our marriage felt so much further out of reach than it had just a few hours ago?

"Go to Panamá. If you have time, please go hug Claudia and the family for me, then when you come back, we finish this talk."

"You were supposed to say yes to Ricard on Friday. I need you to say yes to Ricard on Friday! That's our plan...it's the plan..." I pleaded.

"I'm not saying yes, Gen," Adrián said with a finality that closed the conversation.

The rest of the night, we moved like ghosts around each other, going to bed in silence.

It felt as if something irreparable had broken, and I had no idea how to fix it.

Twenty-Seven

Genevieve

Sand and spikes had taken residence on my eyelids. Sleep had clearly become my enemy. Every honk from the taxi cabs outside irritated me as I waited for the arranged transportation from the Tropics Panamá.

My flight here had been smooth but riddled with emotional triggers. When the flight attendant asked me if someone was joining me, gesturing at the first-class seat next to me, I teared up. Immigration in Panamá was a breeze. When a gentleman approached me as soon as I left the plane and explained he was friends with Adrián, I agreed to follow him. Adrián had set up for me to get VIP service where they took care of all my immigration, customs, and baggage claim transactions and I just had to wait in a well-appointed lounge with snacks and drinks. I sat in the VIP lounge, alternately sobbing and mad at I don't know what.

I texted Adrián to let him know I had landed well after he asked about my status, and he replied with a heart. The damn man couldn't even be one of those who got prissy while arguing. He was all, "Did you arrive well, Preciosa?" and "Text me when you're in the hotel" when all I wanted to do was curl up in a corner and cry.

I was being dramatic. We just needed to postpone the court date to Monday. Adrián had promised to take care of it, and I had wanted to rail that it wasn't fair that we even had to push it. But clearly, I was in my Oblivious Genevieve era because I was the one boarding a plane four days before our wedding. Come to think of it; I hadn't even bought a dress. The only attention I'd put to the date was getting Anita to witness so that Adri had someone there for him.

"Fuck," I exclaimed as I waited.

On the periphery, I read a sign with my name, and I whirled to find myself eye to eye with my driver.

"Oh fuck."

Julín took my carry-on and guided me to the waiting vehicle. Beyond "Good afternoon, Ms. Raymond" no other word was exchanged until we got into the car.

"Hello, Julín."

"Hello, Genevieve, imagine how surprised I was to find out we had a person from our Tropics contract that required driving…over the same dates as my best friend's wedding."

"Julín…"

"I'm not getting into your business. I'll drop you off at the hotel and that's that," he said and then stayed quiet. What were the odds that of all people he would pick me up? I should have thought of this; I would have told the Tropics not to worry and that I would rent a car. Now I was stuck with Julín. And why hadn't he assigned another driver? Great. Besides leaving my fiancé at home before our wedding, I had to deal with his best friend, who clearly hated me.

I descended from the car, thanking Julín as he helped me with my carry-on. The hard slam of the vehicle door told me all I needed to know about how Julín felt about this situation. Had Adri called him?

Putting my game face on, I checked into the hotel and freshened up, ready for the meeting with Danilo Morrison. I couldn't stay in this moping state while I had business to conduct.

Diligence. Ambition. Drive. I kept repeating my mantra to keep from crumbling into pieces.

A few hours later, I sat across from a tall, debonair man with the most striking eyes I'd ever seen, with a beautiful ebony complexion, a face that should be in magazines, and a build that said super heavyweight.

"Mr. Morrison, such a pleasure to meet you. Thanks for taking the time today," I started.

"No need to thank me, I should be the one grateful. I called Ms. Ricard on such short notice. I would have understood if the meeting couldn't happen until another time."

Huh.

"Of course, we were ready to meet. We have been trying to gain your attention with this project."

"That you have, and I'm very intrigued. I've always been hesitant to build in that area because I'm protective of what it is and needs to remain. Sacred to our people."

"And that it is. Let me tell you more about our plan."

The meeting with Mr. Morrison was such a great success I felt giddy at the possibilities. He, like Adrián, had an aversion to gentrification for the sake of gentrification and was willing to make the type of moves to protect the area from additional developments that did not aspire to the same goal.

"So, tell me, Ms. Genevieve, are you looking for work? I hate to be that person, but you're a very effective saleswoman, and the passionate way you speak about the experience for the Black traveler is fascinating. You'd be the perfect ambassador for one of my old investments, *Black Travel Chronicles*."

My heart tripped in my chest.

"Well, funny enough, I was in conversations with them yesterday about a partnership with Tropics."

"Hmm, I'll hit Latoya up and ask her thoughts, but she probably saw the same thing I did."

"I don't know if you can afford me." I laughed but inside I was eager to hear more. The excitement I used to have about work took over and I sighed. I'd missed this feeling. This was the type of job I'd never have considered in the past, but now...now it would be the perfect job that encapsulated my new goals in life. Everything that I had shared with Adrián and it would probably offer much more balance.

"They probably can't. The publication just bought out my equity ownership, but it's an amazing project with fantastic people. I'm telling you. You'd thrive there."

After a couple more details, Mr. Morrison departed the Tropics Panamá, leaving me with many things to consider.

The following day I was on a mission. Gone was Moping Gen. Now I was filled with a nervous but excited energy, as I strategized possibilities in my mind. I needed to get to Aguimar and back tonight to go and see the family and give them some of the gifts I'd hastily put together the night before. Adri and I had a box of items to send, but once I was coming to see them, I didn't want to lose the opportunity of bringing some clothes for the kids.

At the crack of dawn, I waited for my driver while a myriad of emotions clouded my thoughts.

When Julín approached in one of LasDell's cars I sighed. I'd hoped yesterday's antagonism meant he'd reassign my account but no luck.

"Hey, Julín," I greeted as I got in the car.

"What's up," was all he said, and the same silence permeated the vehicle until we arrived in Aguimar two hours later.

I hopped out of the car, grateful not to have to deal with Julín's dry ass for hours, when Yiya cannonballed into me, robbing me of all the oxygen in my belly.

"Hey, pretty girl!" I smiled at her, feeling at home in this humble little space more than anywhere else besides when I was with Adri.

Claudia and the children all gathered around me with loud hellos, hugs, and kisses until we finally made our way to the fonda where Mario and Chichi were manning the space.

"I think Adrián is having second thoughts about marrying me," I blurted out to Claudia as we settled to have lunch together. The children all had left to go to school right after saying hello.

"Girl, that man loves you. He ain't going nowhere." She waved my worry away. That was as ineffective as wearing mosquito repellent here at night. My worries had become a stomachache that threatened never to leave.

"No, moving the wedding date…it just. I could tell how hurt he was, but you know him…"

"Yeah, I do, which is why I know he ain't going nowhere. The question is, are you going to do right by that? He is loyal.

He'll stick with you till the end." She nodded and then got up as a group of workers came to have lunch.

She left me there with my plate of fried fish, as the flies took over my lunch that I couldn't stomach finishing.

In a stark difference to when I had stayed during vacation, Claudia took advantage of my hands, putting me to work for the rest of the day. I cleaned a couple of rooms that needed to be readied for the weekend, and I hung some of the towels and linen needed for that stay. When it was time to go, I was exhausted, but the thoughts had blessedly calmed down to a buzz versus the loud chatter of yesterday.

"Claudia, I miss y'all. I know Adri misses you so bad." I hugged her, letting her scent of fried goods, laundry detergent, and that mom smell that always lingered on her comfort me. My eyes prickled with unshed tears as the babies all said bye to me, Chichi and Mario waving from the entrance of la casita.

"Call me when you get in, alright? Julín, you too! And stop glaring at Genevieve. You're so annoying." Claudia popped Julín in the head, who ducked to avoid the oncoming hit.

"Yeah, okay, chao y'all. Chao, mandona!" Julín said and ran to the passenger side when Claudia tried swatting him for calling her bossy.

Not wanting to be rude, I hadn't used my headphones on the way here, but expecting the same cold shoulder, I popped them in and got lost in my phone. After an hour of reviewing work emails, I was startled out of work mode to find Julín staring at me and then back at the road every few seconds.

I removed the earbuds and stared back. At this point I didn't have a lot of politeness left for him.

"I'm not mad at you. I never was. I'm just who I am and

can come across as an ass. Adrián is one of the few people that understands and lets me be me."

"You mean lets you be rude?"

He shrugged and nodded.

"It's a defense mechanism. Being gay…here it's not always easy. Adri and I came out around the same time. Believe it or not, I was the tough one, always fighting at school and defending us both. He tried to talk things through with people. Get them to like him to the point that everyone forgot he liked men and women. They just loved him. But they didn't realize what toll that took on him. Adrián is a giver, a people pleaser," Julín said, matter-of-fact. My stomach contracted at his words, recognizing their validity.

"When he met you…he was just coming out of the deep sadness of losing his parents. And I'm sure he's given you the workaholic speech, but Adri spent a lot of time in Colón. He basically took ten years to finish his degree because of how much he helped around in Aguimar. He focused on himself for a couple of years, and now he cannot forgive himself. Then once his parents passed, he decided to dedicate all of his time and efforts to Villa Bonita, and when I wanted to open a business, he supported that too. Do you know he gave every single cent of what he earned those successful years to people in the town that needed it? That is Adri. Few people know not to take advantage of that, so when you came…"

"I became someone that could potentially do that?"

"He loves you so much, I know that now, but I was worried at first that he was just going into the deep end to please you, then he decided to move and…" The silence was enough for me to understand. Adrián had given his life as he knew it in order for me to continue my career. I could have moved to

Panamá. We both loved it here. But we defaulted to my city, my career, putting him through a rigorous immigration process he never asked for. All for me to stay comfortable.

"I get it... I do."

"He called me about the wedding. And about the job. That job would have allowed him to come to Panamá a lot, but he's about to decline it...for the sake of your marriage and what he envisions to be the right balance between you two. The balance you won't get with your career," Julín said, and I expected the words to sting, but he said it with no malice. I sat there seeing things from Julín's perspective. He was still an ass, but I understood him better now. He was just hella protective of his friend.

"Do you love him?" I asked quietly.

"Not like people think I do. I have my phobias to conquer, and bisexuality is not something I always understood in him. I thought that was his people-pleasing side rearing its head. Being with women...made his family at ease, even if they knew about his occasional relationships with men. But when I see him with you... I get it. I've never been in love with Adri. I just wanted him to live his truth without having to please anyone." Julín shrugged, and I sat there with all this knowledge and all these questions swirling in my head.

Night settled as Julín rode into the driveway at Tropics, watching me expectantly.

"Thanks so much, Julín. I thought you were an asshole..."

"Damn." He reared back.

"And you are, but you had a reason for it." I grinned. "I'ma need your help, though. I need to call someone about a job and go home and marry my husband."

Twenty-Eight

Adrián

For a second, I'd imagined what it would be to be an architect again—consulting on worthwhile projects, traveling to Panamá, and affording to see my family often, setting the proper boundaries to allow my marriage to flourish with Genevieve.

For a second, I imagined all of that; then, I let it go.

Every single part of the dream was important but not as essential as my life with Gen.

I knew she was disappointed. I understood she had an image of us—the power couple taking over and revitalizing our communities with our corporate overlords, but that had never been my dream. What I wanted for both of us was a good life, where we could prioritize our time together. I thought she'd understood that; I could see her making strides, but when worked called, she answered. I got it, I really did.

She'd worked too hard to get to where she was. The thing was I'd worked equally as hard on myself as well, and I wasn't going to compromise my marriage for a job.

It would always be just a job.

Exciting? Yes. Fulfilling? Yes. However, it still was just a job.

But a marriage? I planned to have one of those only. I planned to love Gen hard and deeply and prioritizing that was the easiest thing I ever did.

"Hello, Adrián, how are you? Hoping you are coming to give me good news?" Ricard approached me in the reception area, looking poised in a two-piece suit that made my chest ache for Genevieve. She was probably on her way to her meeting, going to pitch the Tropics Colón to someone that hopefully would be the right fit. I couldn't lie; the fact that she had prioritized the trip over our ceremony, no matter how simple, stung. I'd planned to surprise her with flower arrangements, had bought her a dress with Anita's assistance, and had planned a little party in a restaurant Gino had recommended, with Gino's and Lissette's help, but had called the whole thing off this morning.

I stood up and shook hands with Ricard, attempting to leave my hurt feelings behind. She and I would marry…eventually, but I wondered if I would ever be a priority?

"So, are you going to leave me in suspense? I have your contract drawn and ready for your signature, cocky I know, but—"

The scent of cinnamon and honey insinuated itself in the room, tricking me to believe Genevieve stood beside me. I closed my eyes briefly, and my fingers tingled in awareness.

Ricard stopped talking as she stared past me, and before I turned, I knew.

"Hola, Adri." Gen stood there, dressed in jeans and a blouse. No makeup, a gorgeous apparition.

"What—"

"What are you doing here, Genevieve? Wasn't the meeting with Morrison today?" Ricard asked alarmed, her poise lost for a second.

"No, he was gracious enough to move it to Thursday," Gen explained but never stopped watching me. She nodded once, then grinned, making my chest expand.

"I'm here to put in my two weeks' notice, Ms. Ricard. I have found a new opportunity more suited to the life I want to lead. I did secure Morrison's interest. He is awaiting your call whenever you're ready." I gaped at Gen as she stood serene in her choice. Whatever she had decided had filled her with a peace I hadn't noticed since our best days in Aguimar.

"I'm disappointed to hear that, Genevieve, I thought you were happy with your promotion, that you were flourishing?" Ricard asked, confused, walking closer to Gen.

"I was satisfied because it was what I expected to happen, but it wasn't what my heart wanted. Once I listened to my heart—" she gazed at me with so much love, my throat closed up in emotion "—I knew I wanted a career that allowed me to spend time with my husband, with our family, without worries."

"I… I cannot pretend I understand. I'm very disappointed. You had so much potential…" Ricard shook her head in dismay.

"I *have* potential," Genevieve asserted, growing taller as she spoke. "I have the potential to love, to care for my well-being and my loved ones, to be passionate about what I do. I have the potential to evolve and want different things than I wanted before. Thank you for all you did for me. I'll always be grateful, but now is time for another chapter in my life."

I stood stunned, unable to articulate how proud I was of

Genevieve. I would support her no matter what she wanted. I would support her going to another corporate job. I would support anything she wanted as long as she was happy.

"So, I'm doing what is right for me. What will you do?" Gen turned to me with a quizzical look, her gentle nudging all the support I needed.

"Ricard, I'll be back to sign that document, but for now I need time with my future wife," I explained, and Ricard threw her hands up.

"Well, I guess I have to be glad at least you're on board… but good for you both. Progress is meant to look and feel different for each of us. All I ever wanted was to create opportunities…we're all lucky that we're expanding the view of what success looks like. The two of you look damn prosperous to me from where I'm standing. Now go. Didn't y'all have something to do?" Ricard asked.

"Come, we have a wedding to attend." Genevieve reached out her hand to me, beaming. A roar of satisfaction filled all my senses as I took Gen's hand in mine.

Holding hands, we walked out of the Tropics headquarters and to our future.

Epilogue

Genevieve

"Claudia, stop fussing," I chided while we both stood in her cabana. Three fans pointed at me, and the ceiling fan was going too. The afternoon had no regard for my comfort. Yiya and Mirna were playing jacks in the corner, looking adorable in white tops with wide shoulders and with wide skirts reminiscent of polleras. Anita sat in the opposite corner, muttering something with a glass of mimosa in her hand.

"Girl, are you alright?" I asked.

"Why didn't you tell me you invited that man?" Anita asked.

I attempted to turn my head, but Claudia disabused me of that notion real quick.

"Girl, if you don't stop!"

I scoffed but sat still when I saw Claudia's menacing gaze.

I swear, I didn't need another bossy woman in my life.

"Who, Anibal? Girl...you gotta tell me—"

"Nah, not today. Not on your wedding day." Anita winked,

then went back to her cell phone where she typed what seemed to be a very loud text and then tossed it to the side. She stood up and came to where I was sitting in a high wood chair getting ready for the ceremony.

"It's not our wedding, we're married already," I reminded them, as I had reminded everyone about a thousand times in the past few days. But clearly, they all knew me well because today was special.

It was the second wedding of my dreams.

Adrián and I got married on a Friday afternoon, him in a business suit, me wearing jeans and a blouse, with Gino and Anita as witnesses. All I ever wanted had been to be on the top of any hill in front of me, and that day I stood on top of the highest of them all as I became partners with my person. My Adrián.

Today, well, today was a celebration in the place of our hearts, where we fell in love.

Adrián received his work permit two months after we applied for his green card, and right away, he joined the Tropics team working remotely and making an immediate impact on the Colón project. Six months later, he became a permanent resident. The second he got that card, we jumped on a plane and came to visit our family.

"Shush. Did you both think we were gonna allow you to just marry without us?" Claudia screwed her face and found my gaze in the mirror; two seconds later, I was wheezing with laughter.

"How many times I gotta tell you, cuñada? I'm not the kids nor Adri. I got your number." I raised my eyebrow, and she gave me a reluctant smirk. The friendship between us flourished as we learned from each other, and I considered her a sister of my heart.

"Do you think your mom's gonna make it?" Anita asked, checking her watch. I shrugged. Mom had done her best to embrace my new life, and for the most part, things were good with her. But she was still climbing those imaginary steps that only she could see. Those had vanished from my sight, transforming to drives by the ocean, breakfast in bed, trips to different towns in the US with Adrián where I wrote my articles for my new position with *Black Travel Chronicles*. There was space for strategy too, the only way *BTC* could afford me was giving me a dual role, as business partner and senior editor. So, I was thriving in arranging partnerships with greater convention bureaus in Black cities, and Black-owned travel businesses to impact our cities the best way I knew how. And when I had to travel without Adrián, I wrote him notes of all the things we would do together once he could leave the United States again.

A video or two might have happened, and my toy chest continued to multiply.

"She's daydreaming again. God, you would think they would get tired after eight months," Claudia complained.

"Didn't I find you fixing your skirt in a dark corner this morning after being mauled by your husband?" I drawled.

"Oh please," Claudia said, then blushed. Anita cackled and went to the kitchen to get more mimosas. Every time I messed with Claudia about Mario, she got flustered, but it did not fail. But now I got it, and I got that feeling of euphoria. Of having a secret that no one knew but you and your person. I had that with Adri.

"Good afternoon." Mom waltzed in and Yiya and Mirna

ran to greet her. Yiya gave her famed introduction and caught my mom up in minutes.

"Oh, honey, you look gorgeous! Such an important day. Well, what can I do?" Mom asked after chatting with girls.

"Nothing, you can chill, because this is meant to be a chill d—" I started to say, but a chorus of protest cut me off.

"Oh, please."

"Ay ya hasta cuando. Bendito."

"Shhh I had to fly here, of course it's important."

Damn. Okay. I grinned in silent agreement.

"There, you're ready," Claudia pronounced.

I stood up from the chair and faced them. Yiya ran to me and held my hand.

"Come, Tio Adrián has been waiting for you."

"And I had been waiting for him, Yiya. I just didn't know it."

Adrián

When I first saw Gen, I'm not going to lie; I had to choke back tears. She glided on the main path to the beach, hand in hand with Mirna and Yiya, the three of them giggling, their brown skins flushed under the dying sun. Her white dress flowed in the breeze; her dark hair shined in a coiled updo with purple hibiscus Claudia had probably picked in the morning.

A dream come true, my home, Genevieve.

My chest flooded with warmth as barefoot, she beamed at me, holding my hand, and surrounded by our friends and family, we stood inside their circle and promised each other again what we promised each other every day.

"Te amo, Adrián. Te prometo amarte con ternura, quererte sin fín, buscarte siempre con pasión y nunca dejar que ninguna adversidad nos divida," Gen said in her thick-accented Spanish, and I lost the battle, tears running down my face. She reached out and swiped one of mine then dried her own tears.

"I love you, Genevieve. I promise to love with tenderness, to care with abandon, to seek you always in passion, and to never let adversity get between us," I said my own vows in English, an echo of hers.

I promised Gen to be her partner that day in the courtroom, but today... Doing this in my land with our people. It solidified everything that was good and well with the world. When we kissed, the drums started playing, and we danced our way to La Buenona, where food and tamboritos awaited us.

When the night grew darkest, I stole her away from the festivities, walking that same path of that fateful first night, and reminded her all over again, with my flesh, my hands, and my heart, that she was mine and I was hers forever.

★ ★ ★ ★ ★

Look for the next romance from A.H. Cunningham,
coming in 2025 from Afterglow Books!

Acknowledgments

Thank you. Such a simple phrase, but it holds so much weight. I tend to go long in acknowledgments, so I will have "thank you" do the heavy lifting this time.

I wouldn't have had the opportunity to write this story without the support of many people. First, thanks to my parents, who are the original inspiration for this book. Theirs is a love story transcending frontiers, time, and life's challenges.

Vanaida y Reynaldo, ahora más que nunca entiendo que las historias de amor se escriben con intencionalidad, como la de ustedes.

This book wouldn't have happened if Tasha L. Harrison didn't speak my name in spaces I seldom frequent. Thank you, friend.

To the Black indie author community, thank you for all your innovation, for the friendships, the laughs, and the quality work that comes from you! I am always in awe!

To the Latine book community, gracias por el apoyo!

To the book content creators who tirelessly shout our names

and our work to the world…thanks; because of you, this story will thrive.

To John Jacobson, thanks for loving Gen and Adrián with the same passion as I did!

Stacy and the entire Afterglow Books team! Thanks!

Last but not least, thanks to Los Cunninghams, my husband and children, who always encourage me to keep writing and keep dreaming. I love you, and I don't have enough words to tell you how much.

And to you, dear reader, thank you for picking up *Out of Office*, and thank you for the support!